I have edited Clive Gilson's books prolific and can turn his hand to mar contemporary novels, folklore and science ... common theme is that none of them ever fails to take my breath away. There's something in each story that is either memorably poignant, hauntingly unnerving or sidesplittingly funny.

Lorna Howarth, *The Write Factor*

Tales From The World's Firesides is a grand project. I've collected '000's of traditional texts as part of other projects, and while many of the original texts are available through channels like Project Gutenberg, some of the narratives can be hard to read by modern readers, & so the Fireside project was born. Put simply, I collect, collate & adapt traditional tales from around the world & publish them for free as a modern archive. *Part 1* covers a host of nations & regions across Europe. I'm not laying any claim to insight or specialist knowledge, but these collections are born out of my love of story-telling & I hope that you'll share my affection for traditional tales, myths & legends.

Image by Smim Bipi from Pixabay

ALSO BY CLIVE GILSON - *FICTION*

- Songs of Bliss
- Out of the walled Garden
- The Mechanic's Curse
- The Insomniac Booth
- A Solitude of Stars

AS EDITOR – *FIRESIDE TALES – Part 1, Europe*

- Tales from the Land of Dragons
- Tales from the Land of the Brave
- Tales from the Land of Saints and Scholars
- Tales from the Land of Hope and Glory
- Tales from Lands of Snow and Ice
- Tales from the Viking Isles
- Tales from the Forest Lands
- Tales from the Old Norse
- More Tales About Saints and Scholars
- More Tales About Hope and Glory
- More Tales About Snow and Ice
- Tales from the Land of Rabbits
- Tales Told by Bulls and Wolves
- Tales of Fire & Bronze
- Tales Told by the Samodivi
- Tales From The Land Of The Strigoi
- Tales Told By The Wind Mother
- Tales From Gallia
- Tales From Germania

EDITOR – *FIRESIDE TALES – Part 2, North America*

- Okaraxta - Tales from the Great Plains
- Tibik-kìzis – Tales from the Great Lakes & Canada

Further North American & Native American collections will be published during late 2019 & 2020

Tales From The Land Of Rabbits

Traditional tales, fables and sagas from Spain & Portugal

Compiled & Edited by Clive Gilson

'Tales from the World's Firesides'

Book 12 in Part 1 of the series: Europe

Tales From The Land Of Rabbits, edited by Clive Gilson,
Solitude, Bath, UK

www.boyonabench.com

First published as an eBook in 2019

Printed by IngramSpark

ISBN 978-1-913500-12-2

 SOLITUDE

Contents

PREFACE

WHY THE LAND OF RABBITS? JOHN A. Crow explains it perfectly in *Spain, The Root and the Flower*, University of California Press, 1985:

"Spain was first called Iberia, a name given to it by its Iberian inhabitants (from North Africa). The name was supposedly based on the Iberian word for river, Iber. They reached Spain around 6000 BCE. When the Greeks arrived on Spanish soil around 600 BCE. they referred to the peninsula as Hesperia, meaning "land of the setting sun." When the Carthaginians came around 300 BCE. they called the country Ispania (from Sphan, "rabbit"), which means "land of the rabbits." The Romans arrived a century later and adopted the Carthaginian name of the country, calling it Hispania. Later, this became the present day Spanish name for the country, España. Thus, because of the Romans and their language, the rabbits won over the sunset and over the river."

This collection contains stories either written by or collected by Rachel Harriette Busk, Charles Sellers, Gustavo Adolfo Bécquer, Andrew Lang and by José Muñoz Escámez. Translations from Bécquer are by Cornelia Francis Bates and Katherine Lee Bates.

As ever it's been a delight to work on these stories, many of which I had not read before working through some of these original collections. There is a real flavour of the peninsular in these stories, reflecting as they do Spain and Portugal's long history of thought, religion and conflict. I hope you enjoy these stories.

Clive

Bath, 2018

THE INGENIOUS STUDENT

Adapted from Charles Sellers' original, taken from Tales from the Lands of Nuts and Grapes, published in 1888 by The Leadenhall Press and others.

THERE WAS ONCE A STUDENT IN Tuy who was so very poor that, if faith in Providence was discounted, then he possessed no riches.

But Juan Rivas was endowed with a wonderfully fine gift of ingenuity, and although he was somewhat behind in the payment for the Masses sung on behalf of his predecessors, and even more so with his mundane creditors, he was still a man who meant well and would do the right thing if he only had the opportunity.

To the man of the world there is no greater pleasure than to pay his debts, for by so doing he increases his credit.

Juan Rivas would willingly have paid every creditor had his pocket been as full of the wherewithal as his heart was of gratitude for small mercies; but there is never any difficulty in showing that you want to pay your debts, - the only difficulty generally rests in being able to actually do so.

At college he had proved himself a good scholar and a true companion; but as he could no longer contribute toward the support of his college, his college could not be expected to support him.

Juan's long black cap, his flowing robes, his pantaloons, and his shoes were now altered in substance, and so was Juan Rivas.

Finally he was reduced to his last coin, and as his friends could no longer assist him, he thought it was high time he should help himself.

"Providence," he said, "has never intended me for a poor man, but Fate has almost made me one. I will believe in Providence, and become rich from this day." Saying which, he went to some of his companions, who were almost as poor as he was, and asked them if they too desired to be rich.

"Do you ask us if we want to be rich with so serious a face?" answered they. "Really, friend Juan, you are so strange that you do not seem to belong to this city!"

"No man can be rich," continued Juan, "by staying at home. We are students, and our studies should meet with some recompense. Will you do as I ask you?"

"Yes!" cried all his poor companions; "so long as you lead us not to the gallows, for we like not such playthings."

"Well, then, follow me," said Juan; "and when you see me release a prize fit the boldest among you, take it and fly with it to the market, and dispose of it at the best possible price."

"Done, and agreed to," shouted all, "if you will but seize the prize!"

"Leave that to me," said the poor student, "and I will hand you a prize fully worth twenty dollars without clothes on."

"But, surely, you are not going to hand over some man or woman to us?" inquired they.

"Ask me no questions, as the Archbishop of Compostela said to the pretty widow, and I will tell you no lies. The prize I shall hand to you will fetch money in the market, and be assured, we don't human beings in this country," urged Juan.

"That is right," they exclaimed; "and we will follow you."

The students followed Juan on to the high-road leading from the city to Ourense; and when they had walked for about two hours Juan told his companions to get behind the hedge and await results.

Soon after, the jingling of bells was heard, and a muleteer seated cross-legged on a mule leading five other mules, was seen to be approaching.

As the muleteer had sold all his wares he was indulging in a little snooze, and had it not been for the dog-flies that teased the mules they would also have slept.

Juan let the muleteer pass; but as the last mule came up he seized it, and, taking off its trappings, and disencumbering it of its ponderous albarda, or saddle, he freed the animal on the roadside, and placed the trappings and the saddle on his back.

His companions were not slow in seizing the prize mule and hurrying away with it, while Juan Rivas continued for some distance along the road, following in the train of mules.

As soon as he knew that his companions were out of sight, he started to pull backwards with all his strength, which brought the mules to a sudden halt and caused their bells to tinkle.

The muleteer looked back to see if anything was wrong, but, perceiving nothing, bestowed a hearty blow on his mule, and on he went again.

The student now began to rear and jump about so that the muleteer pulled up, and, having dismounted, proceeded to inquire into the cause of the mule so misbehaving itself; but he was utterly astonished when, instead of a mule, he saw a human being bearing the trappings and the saddle.

"What merry freak is this?" demanded the muleteer, addressing the student, "Why are you replacing my mule?"

"It is no merry freak, indeed it is not," replied Juan Rivas, "but a sad reality. You see before you, good master, a poor, miserable creature, who for his many offences against Mother Church was transformed into a mule, and sentenced to remain so for a number of years. My term of punishment has just expired, and I am restored to my natural form."

"But where is my mule that cost me one hundred crowns not many years ago?" asked the muleteer.

"You do not understand me, good master," replied the student. "I was the mule, and the mule was I; now I am I. When you used to kick your mule, you really kicked me; when you fed it, you fed me; and now, when you speak to me, you speak to all that remains of your mule. Now do you understand?"

"I am beginning to understand," said the muleteer, scratching his head and looking very sorrowful, "that for your sins you were turned into a mule, and that for mine, I had the misfortune to purchase you. I always thought there was something strange about that mule!"

"There is no doubt that we all must put up with the consequences of our evil ways, and, as you very properly say, you have been punished by the loss of your mule; but, then, you can rejoice with me, seeing that the son of the first Grandee in Spain served you in the humble capacity of a beast of burden, and now is restored to rank and wealth."

"And are you a Grandee of Spain?" inquired the poor muleteer anxiously. "Why, then, your excellency will never forgive me for the many kicks I have bestowed on your excellency's sides; and I am a ruined man, for you will have me punished."

"Not so, kind friend; not so," replied the student, in an assuring tone; "for how could you tell that your mule was not a mule?"

"Then your excellency will not be revenged on me?" continued the muleteer. "And if it will be of any consolation to your excellency, I promise never to divulge this mystery!"

"It will, indeed, be a great comfort to me to think that no one will know what became of me for so many years," replied the student. "And now I must bid you good-bye, for I am in a hurry to embrace my dear parents again if they are still living."

"Good-bye," said the muleteer, with emotion; "and may your excellency never again incur the displeasure of Mother Church."

Thus they parted good friends; the muleteer pondering over what he termed the mysteries of life, and Juan Rivas full of delight at the thought of re-joining his companions, and having a good supper with the proceeds from the sale of the real mule, which pleasure was not denied him and his friends.

In a fortnight's time there was a cattle fair in the neighbourhood of Tuy, and as the muleteer needed to replace the mule he had so mysteriously lost, he attended the fair, and was looking about for a serviceable mule, when an acquaintance called out to him asking him why he had parted with the other one.

"I have my private reasons," answered the muleteer, "and I am not here to tell you about them."

"Very true," continued his inquisitive friend; "but the proverb says that 'the mule you know is better than the mule you don't know," and if you will take my advice, you will buy your old mule back again, for there it is." With that he pointed to it.

The muleteer looked in the direction mentioned, and was horrified at seeing his late mule again; but, trying to conceal his emotion, he approached the animal and whispered in its ear, "Those who don't know what sort of a mule your excellency is may buy you, but I know what sort of charmed mule you really are;" and, turning away, he sadly exclaimed, "He has again offended. Terrible are the judgments of Providence!"

MASTER PÉREZ THE ORGANIST

Adapted from Romantic Legends of Spain. and taken from the original story written by Gustavo Adolfo Bécquer, translated by Cornelia Francis Bates and Katherine Lee Bates, 1909.

IN SEVILLE, IN THE VERY PORTICO of Santa Inés, and while, on Christmas Eve, I was waiting for the Midnight Mass to begin, I heard this tradition from a lay-sister of the convent.

As was natural, after hearing it, I waited impatiently for the ceremony to commence, eager to be present at a miracle.

Nothing could be less miraculous, however, than the organ of Santa Inés, and nothing more vulgar than the insipid motets with which that night the organist regaled us.

On walking out from the mass, I could not resist asking the lay-sister mischievously, "How does it happen that the organ of Master Pérez is so unmusical at present?"

"Why!" replied the old woman. "Because it isn't his."

"Not his? What has become of it?"

"It fell to pieces from sheer old age, a number of years ago."

"And the soul of the organist?"

"It has not appeared again since the new organ was set up in place of his own."

If anyone of my readers, after perusing this history, should be moved to ask the same question, now he knows why the notable miracle has not continued into our own time.

Chapter I

"Do you see that man with the scarlet cloak and the white plume in his hat, - the one who seems to wear all the gold of the galleons of the Indies on his waistcoat, - that man, I mean, just stepping down from his litter to give his hand to the lady there, who, now that she is out of hers, is coming our way, preceded by four pages with torches? Well, that is the Marquis of Moscoso, suitor to the widowed Countess of Villapineda. They say that before setting his eyes upon this lady, he had asked in marriage the daughter of a man of large fortune, but the girl's father, of whom the rumour goes that he is a bit of a miser, - but hush!

Speaking of the devil - do you see that man coming on foot under the arch of San Felipe, all muffled up in a dark cloak and attended by a single servant carrying a lantern? Now he is in front of the outer shrine.

"Do you notice the embroidered cross that sparkles on his breast as his cloak falls back while he salutes the saviour?

"If it were not for this noble decoration, one would take him for a shop-keeper from Culebras street. Well, that is the father in question. See how the people make way for him and lift their hats.

"Everybody in Seville knows him on account of his immense fortune. That one man has more golden ducats in his chests than our lord King Philip maintains soldiers, and with his merchantmen he could form a squadron equal to that of the Grand Turk.

"Look, look at that group of stately cavaliers! Those are the four and twenty knights. Aha! There goes that precious Fleming, too, whom, they say, the gentlemen of the green cross have not challenged for heresy yet, thanks to his influence with the magnates of Madrid. All he comes to church for is to hear the music. But if Master Pérez does not draw from him with his organ tears as big as fists, then sure it is that his soul isn't under his doublet, but sizzles in the Devil's frying-pan.

Alas, neighbour! Trouble, trouble! I fear there is going to be a fight. I shall take refuge in the church; for, from what I see, there will be more blows than Pater Nosters hereabouts. Look, look! The Duke of Alcalá's people are coming round the corner of San Pedro's square, and I think I spy the Duke of Medina-Sidonia's men in Dueñas alley. Didn't I tell you?

"Now they have caught sight of each other, and now the two parties stop short, without breaking their order. The groups of bystanders dissolve. The police, who on these occasions get pounded by both sides, slip away, and even the prefect, staff of office and all, seeks the shelter of the portico, and yet they say that there is law to be had.

"For the poor...

"There, there! already shields are shining through the dark. Our Lord Jesus of All Power deliver us! Now the blows are beginning. Neighbour, neighbour! this way - before they close the doors. But hush! What is this? Hardly have they begun when they leave off.

9

What light is that? Blazing torches! A litter! It's His Reverence the Bishop.

"The most holy Virgin of Protection, on whom this very instant I was calling in my heart, brings him to my aid. Ah! But nobody knows what I owe to that Blessed Lady - how richly she pays me back for the little candles that I burn to her every Saturday.

See him! How beautiful the Bishop is with his purple vestments and his red cardinal's cap! God preserve him in his sacred chair as many centuries as I wish to live myself! If it were not for him, half Seville would have been burned up by this time with these quarrels of the dukes.

See them, see them, the great hypocrites, how they both press close to the litter of the prelate to kiss his ring! How they drop behind and, mingling with his household attendants, follow in his train! Who would dream that those two who appear on such good terms, if within the half hour they should meet in a dark street - that is, the dukes themselves - God deliver me from thinking them cowards; good proof have they given of valour, warring more than once against the enemies of Our Lord; but the truth remains, that if they should seek each other - and seek with the wish to find - they would find each other, putting an end once and for all to these continuous scuffles, in which those who really do the fighting are their kinsmen, their friends and their servants.

"But come, neighbour, come into the church, before it is packed full. Some nights like this it is so crowded that there is not room left for a grain of wheat. The nuns have a prize in their organist. When has the convent ever been in such high favour as now?

I can tell you that the other sisterhoods have made Master Pérez magnificent offers, but there is nothing strange about that, for the

Lord Archbishop himself has offered him mountains of gold to entice him to the cathedral, but he will not have a bit of it! He would sooner give up his life than his beloved organ.

You don't know Master Pérez? True enough, you are a newcomer in this neighbourhood. Well, he is a saint; poor, but the most charitable man alive. With no other relative than his daughter and no other friend than his organ, he devotes all his life to watching over the innocence of the one and patching up the registers of the other. Mind that the organ is old. But that counts for nothing, because he is so handy in mending it and caring for it that its sound is a marvel. He knows it so perfectly but only by touch, for I am not sure that I have told you that the poor gentleman has been blind from his birth. And how patiently he bears his misfortune!

When people ask him how much he would give to see, he replies: 'Much, but not as much as you think, for I have hopes.' 'Hopes of seeing?' 'Yes, and very soon," he adds, smiling like an angel. 'Already I number seventy-six years; however long my life may be, soon I shall see God.'

"Poor dear! And he will see Him, for he is humble as the stones of the street, which let all the world trample on them. He always says that he is only a poor convent organist, when the fact is he could give lessons in harmony to the very chapel master of the Cathedral, for he was, as it were, born to the art. His father held the same position before him; I did not know the father, but my mother, God rest her soul, says that he always had the boy at the organ with him to blow the bellows. Then the lad developed such talent that, as was natural, he succeeded to the position on the death of his father.

And what a touch is in his hands, God bless them! They deserve to be taken to Chicarreros street and there enchased in gold. He always plays well, always, but on a night like this he is a wonder. He has the greatest devotion for this ceremony of the Midnight Mass, and when the Host is elevated, precisely at twelve o'clock, which is the moment Our Lord Jesus Christ came into the world, the tones of his organ are like the voices of angels.

"But, after all, why should I praise what you will hear tonight? It is enough to see that all the most distinguished people of Seville, even the Lord Archbishop himself, come to a humble convent to listen to him. And don't suppose that it is only the learned people and those who are versed in music that appreciate his genius, but the very rabble of the streets. All these groups that you see arriving with pine-torches ablaze, chorusing popular songs, broken by rude outcries, to the accompaniment of timbrels, tambourines and rustic drums, these, contrary to their custom, which is to make disturbance in the churches, are still as the dead when Master Pérez lays his hands upon the organ. When the Host is elevated, you can't hear a fly. Great tears roll down from the eyes of all, and at the end you'll hear a sound like an immense sigh, which is nothing other than the expulsion of the breath of the multitude, held in while the music lasts. But come, come! The bells have stopped ringing, and the mass is going to begin. Come inside.

"This night is Christmas Eve for all the world, but for nobody more than for us."

So saying, the good woman who had been acting as cicerone for her neighbour pressed through the portico of the Convent of Santa Inés, and by dint of elbowing and pushing succeeded in getting inside the church and disappeared amid the multitude which thronged the inner spaces near the doors.

Chapter II

The church was illuminated with astonishing brilliancy. The flood of light which spread from the altars through all its compass sparkled on the rich jewels of the ladies who, kneeling on the velvet cushions placed before them by their pages, and taking their prayer-books from the hands of their duennas, formed a brilliant circle around the choir-screen.

Grouped just behind them, on foot, wrapped in bright-lined cloaks garnished with gold-lace, stood the four and twenty knights, who, with studied carelessness let glimpses of their red and green crosses be seen. In one hand they held their hats, whose plumes kissed the carpet, the other hand resting upon the polished hilt of a rapier or caressing the handle of an ornate dagger. With them stood a large proportion of the highest nobility of Seville, all of whom seemed to form a wall for the purpose of protecting their daughters and their wives from contact with the populace. This group, swaying back and forth at the rear of the nave, with a murmur like that of a surging sea, broke out into joyous acclaim, accompanied by the discordant sounds of the timbrels and tambourines, at the appearance of the archbishop, who, after seating himself, surrounded by his attendants near the High Altar under a scarlet canopy, thrice blessed the assembled people.

It was time for the mass to begin.

There passed, nevertheless, several minutes without the appearance of the celebrant. The throng started to stir impatiently; the knights exchanged low-toned words with one another, and the archbishop sent one of his attendants to the sacristy to inquire about the cause of the delay.

"Master Pérez has been taken ill, very ill, and it will be impossible for him to come to the Midnight Mass."

This was the word brought back by the attendant.

The news spread instantly through the multitude. It would be impossible to depict the dismay which it caused; suffice it to say that such a clamour began to arise in the church that the prefect sprang to his feet, and the police came in to enforce silence, mingling with the close-pressed, surging crowd.

At that moment, a man with unpleasant features, thin, bony, and cross-eyed, too, hurriedly made his way to the place where the prelate was sitting.

"Master Pérez is sick," he said. "The ceremony cannot begin. If it is your pleasure, I will play the organ in his absence; for neither is Master Pérez the first organist of the world, nor at his death need this instrument be left unused for lack of skill."

The archbishop gave a nod of assent, and already some of the faithful, who recognized in that strange personage an envious rival of the organist of Santa Inés, were breaking out in exclamations of displeasure, when suddenly a startling uproar was heard in the portico.

"Master Pérez is here! Master Pérez is here!"

At these cries from the press in the doorway, everyone looked around.

Master Pérez, his face pallid and drawn, was entering the church, brought in a chair about which all were contending for the honour of carrying it upon their shoulders.

The commands of the physicians and the tears of his daughter had not been able to keep him in bed.

"No," he had said. "This is the end, I know it, I know it, and I would not die without visiting my organ, and this night above all, is Christmas Eve. Come, I wish it, I command it; let us go to the church."

His desire had been fulfilled. The people carried him in their arms to the organ-loft, and the mass began.

At that instant the cathedral clock struck twelve.

The introit passed, and the Gospel, and the offertory, and then came the solemn moment in which the priest, after having blessed the Sacred Wafer, took it in the tips of his fingers and began to elevate it.

A cloud of incense, rolling forth in azure waves, filled the length and breadth of the church; the little bells rang out with silvery vibrations, and Master Pérez placed his quivering hands upon the keys of the organ.

The hundred voices of its metal tubes resounded in a prolonged, majestic chord, which died away little by little, as if a gentle breeze had stolen its last echoes.

To this opening chord, that seemed a voice lifted from earth to heaven, responded a sweet and distant note, which went on swelling and swelling in volume until it became a torrent of pealing harmony.

It was the song of the angels, which, traversing the ethereal spaces, had reached the world.

Then there began to be heard a sound as of far-off hymns entoned by the hierarchies of seraphim, a thousand hymns at once, melting into one, which, nevertheless, was no more than accompaniment to a strange melody, a melody that seemed to float above that ocean of mysterious echoes as a strip of fog above the billows of the sea.

One anthem after another died away; the movement grew simpler; now there were but two voices, whose echoes blended; then one alone remained, sustaining a note as brilliant as a thread of light. The priest bowed his face, and above his grey head, across an azure mist made by the smoke of the incense, appeared to the eyes of the faithful the uplifted Host. At that instant the thrilling note which Master Pérez was holding began to swell and swell until an outburst of colossal harmony shook the church, in whose corners the straitened air vibrated and whose stained glass shivered in its narrow Moorish embrasures.

From each of the notes forming that magnificent chord a theme developed, some near, some far, these keen, those muffled, until one would have said that the waters and the birds, the winds and the woods, men and angels, earth and heaven, were chanting, each in its own tongue, an anthem of praise for the Redeemer's birth.

The multitude listened in amazement and suspense. In all eyes were tears, in all spirits a profound realization of the divine.

The officiating priest felt his hands trembling, for the Holy One whom they upheld, the Holy One to whom men and archangels did reverence, was God, was very God, and it seemed to the priest that he had beheld the heavens open and the Host become transfigured.

The organ still sounded, but its music was gradually sinking away, like a tone dropping from echo to echo, ever more remote, ever fainter, when suddenly a cry rang out in the organ-loft, a shrill, piercing cry of a woman.

The organ gave forth a strange, discordant sound, like a sob, and then was still.

The multitude surged toward the stair leading up to the organ-loft, in whose direction all the faithful, startled out of their religious ecstasy, were turning anxious looks.

"What has happened?" "What is the matter?" they asked one of another, and none knew what to reply, and all tried to understand, and the confusion increased, and the excitement began to rise to a height which threatened to disturb the order and decorum fitting within a church.

"What was it?" asked the great ladies of the prefect who, attended by his officers, had been one of the first to mount to the loft, and now, pale and showing signs of deep grief, was making his way to the archbishop, who was waiting in anxiety, like all the rest, to know the cause of that disturbance.

"What has occurred?"

"Master Pérez has just died."

In fact, when the foremost of the faithful, after pressing up the stairway, had reached the organ-loft, they saw the poor organist fallen face down upon the keys of his old instrument, which was still faintly murmuring, while his daughter, kneeling at his feet, was vainly calling to him amid sighs and sobs.

Chapter III

"Good evening, my dear Doña Baltasara. Are you, too, going tonight to the Christmas Eve Mass? For my part, I was intending to go to the parish church to hear it, but after what has happened but the truth, if I must tell it, is that since Master Pérez died, a marble slab seems to fall on my heart whenever I enter Santa Inés. Poor dear man! He was a saint.

I assure you that I keep a piece of his doublet as a relic, and he deserves it, for by God and my soul it is certain that if our Lord Archbishop would stir in the matter, our grandchildren would see the image of Master Pérez upon an altar. But what hope of it? 'The dead and the gone are let alone.'

We're all for the latest thing now-a-days; you understand me. No? You haven't an inkling of what has happened? It's true we are alike in this, from house to church, and from church to house, without concerning ourselves about what is said or isn't said, except that I, as it were, on the wing, a word here, another there, without the least curiosity whatever, usually run across any news that may be going.

Well, then! It seems to be settled that the organist of San Román, that squint-eye, who is always throwing out slurs against the other organists, that great sloven, who looks more like a butcher from the slaughter-house than a professor of music, is going to play this Christmas Eve in place of Master Pérez.

Now you must know, for all the world knows and it is a public matter in Seville, that nobody was willing to attempt it. Not even his daughter, though she is herself an expert. After her father's death she entered the convent as a novice. And naturally enough; accustomed as we all are o hear those marvellous performances, so anyone else playing seems poor to us, however much we would like to avoid comparisons.

But no sooner had the sisterhood decided that, in honour of the dead and as a token of respect to his memory, the organ should be silent tonight, than here comes along our modest squinty friend, saying that he is ready to play it. Nothing is bolder than ignorance.

It is true the fault is not so much his as theirs who have consented to this profanation, but so goes the world.

I say, it's no trifling crowd that is coming. One would think nothing had changed since last year. The same great people, the same magnificence, the same pushing in the doorway, the same excitement in the portico, the same throng in the church. Ah, if the dead should rise, he would die again rather than hear his organ played by hands like those.

The fact is, if what the people of the neighbourhood have told me is true, they are preparing a fine reception for the intruder. When the moment comes for placing the hand upon the keys, there is going to break out such a racket of timbrels, tambourines and rustic drums that nothing else will be heard.

But hush! there's the hero of the occasion just going into the church. Jesus! what a showy jacket, what a fluted ruff, what a high and mighty air! Come, come, the archbishop arrived a minute ago, and the mass is going to begin. Come; it looks as though this night would give us something to talk about for many a day."

With these words the woman, whom our readers recognize by her disconnected loquacity, entered Santa Inés, opening a way through the press, as usual, by dint of shoving and elbowing.

Already the ceremony had begun.

The church was as brilliant as the year before.

The new organist, after passing through the midst of the faithful who thronged the nave, on his way to kiss the ring of the prelate, had mounted to the organ-loft, where he was trying one stop of the organ after another with a solicitous gravity as affected as it was ridiculous.

Among the common people clustered at the rear of the church was heard a murmur, muffled and confused, sure augury of the coming storm which would not be long in breaking.

"He's a clown, who doesn't know how to do anything, not even to look straight," said some.

"He's an ignoramus, who after having made the organ in his own parish church worse than a rattle comes here to profane Master Pérez's," said others.

And while one was throwing off his coat so as to beat his drum to better advantage, and another was trying his timbrels, and the clatter was increasing more and more, only here and there could one be found to defend in lukewarm fashion that alien personage, whose pompous and pedantic bearing formed so strong a contrast to the modest manner and kindly courtesy of the dead Master Pérez.

At last the looked-for moment came, the solemn moment when the priest, after bowing low and murmuring the sacred words, took the Host in his hands. The little bells rang out, their chime like a rain of crystal notes; the translucent waves of incense rose, and the organ sounded.

At that instant a horrible din filled the compass of the church, drowning the first chord.

Bagpipes, horns, timbrels, drums, all the instruments of the populace raised their discordant voices at once, but the confusion and the clang lasted but a few seconds. All at once as the tumult had begun, so all at once it ceased.

The second chord, full, bold, magnificent, sustained itself, still pouring from the organ's metal tubes like a cascade of inexhaustible, sonorous harmony.

Celestial songs like those that caress the ear in moments of ecstasy, songs which the spirit perceives but the lip cannot repeat; fugitive notes of a far-off melody, which reach us at intervals, sounding in the bugles of the wind; the rustle of leaves kissing one another on the trees with a murmur like rain; trills of larks which rise warbling from among the flowers like a flight of arrows to the clouds; nameless crashes, overwhelming as the thunders of a tempest; a chorus of seraphim without rhythm or cadence, unknown harmony of heaven which only the imagination understands; soaring hymns, that seem to mount to the throne of God like a fountain of light and sound - all this was expressed by the organ's hundred voices, with more vigour, more mystic poetry, more weird colouring than had ever been known before.

*

When the organist came down from the loft, the crowd which pressed up to the stairway was so great, and their eagerness to see and praise him so intense, that the prefect, fearing, and not without reason, that he would be suffocated among them all, commanded some of the police to open, by their staves, a path for him that he might reach the High Altar where the prelate waited his arrival.

"You perceive," said the archbishop, when the musician was brought into his presence, "that I have come all the way from my palace here only to hear you. Will you be as cruel as Master Pérez, who would never save me the journey by playing the Midnight Mass in the cathedral?"

"Next year," responded the organist, "I promise to give you that pleasure, for not all the gold of the earth would induce me to play this organ again."

"And why not?" interrupted the prelate.

"Because," replied the organist, striving to repress the agitation revealed in the pallor of his face, "because it is old and poor, and one cannot express on it all that one would."

The archbishop retired, followed by his attendants. One by one, the litters of the great folk went filing away, lost to sight in the windings of the neighbouring streets. The groups of the portico melted, as the faithful dispersed in different directions, and already the lay-sister who acted as gate-keeper was about to lock the vestibule doors, when there appeared two women, who, after crossing themselves and muttering a prayer before the arched shrine of Saint Philip, went their way, turning into Dueñas alley.

"What would you have, my dear Doña Baltasara?" one of them was saying. "That's the way I'm made. Every fool has his fancy. The barefooted Capuchins might assure me that it was so and I wouldn't believe it in the least. That man cannot have played what we have just been hearing. A thousand times have I heard him in San Bartolomé, his parish church, from which the priest had to send him away for his bad playing. It was bad enough to make you fill your ears with cotton. Besides, all you need is to look at his face, which, they say, is the mirror of the soul. I remember, poor dear man, as if I were seeing him now, I remember Master Pérez's look when, on a night like this, he would come down from the organ loft, after having entranced the audience with his marvels. What a gracious smile, what a happy glow on his face! Old as he was, he seemed like an angel. But this fellow came plunging down the stairs as if a dog were barking at him on the landing, his face the colour of the dead, and. Come now, my dear Doña Baltasara, believe me, believe me with all your soul. I suspect a mystery in this."

With these last words, the two women turned the corner of the street and disappeared.

We count it needless to inform our readers who one of them was.

Chapter IV

Another year had gone by. The abbess of the convent of Santa Inés and the daughter of Master Pérez, half hidden in the shadows of the church choir, were talking in low tones. The peremptory voice of the bell was calling from its tower to the faithful, and occasionally an individual would cross the portico, silent and deserted now, and after taking the holy water at the door, would choose a place in a corner of the nave, where a few residents of the neighbourhood were quietly waiting for the Midnight Mass to begin.

"There, you see," the mother superior was saying, "your fear is excessively childish. There is nobody in the church. All Seville is trooping to the cathedral tonight. Play the organ and play it without the least uneasiness. We are only the sisterhood here. Well? Still you are silent, still your breaths are like sighs. What is it? What is the matter?"

"I am afraid," exclaimed the girl, in a tone of the deepest agitation.

"Afraid? Of what?"

"I don't know...of something supernatural. Last night, see, I had heard you say that you earnestly wished me to play the organ for the mass and, pleased with this honour, I thought I would look to the stops and tune it, so as to give you a surprise today. I went into the choir, alone. I opened the door which leads to the organ-loft. At that moment the clock of the cathedral struck the hour, although what hour, I do not know. The peals were exceedingly mournful, and so many. They kept on sounding all the time that I stood there by the organ and I felt as if I was nailed to the threshold, and that time seemed to me a century.

"The church was empty and dark. Far away, in the hollow depth, there gleamed, like a single star lost in the sky of night, a feeble light, the light of the lamp which burns on the High Altar. By its faint rays, which only served to make more visible all the deep horror of the darkness, I saw…I saw…mother, do not disbelieve it…I saw a man who, in silence and with his back turned toward the place where I stood, was running over the organ-keys with one hand, while he tried the stops with the other. And the organ sounded, but it sounded in a manner indescribable. It seemed as if each of its notes were a sob smothered within the metal tube which vibrated with its burden of compressed air, and gave forth a muffled tone, almost inaudible, yet exact and true.

"And the cathedral clock kept on striking, and that man kept on running over the keys. I heard his very breathing.

"The horror of it had frozen the blood in my veins. In my body I felt an icy chill and in my temples fire. Then I longed to cry out, but could not. That man had turned his face and looked at me, but no, not looked at me, for he was blind. It was my father."

"Bah, sister! Put away these fancies with which the wicked enemy tries to trouble weak imaginations. Pray a Pater Noster and an Ave Maria to the archangel Saint Michael, Captain of the celestial hosts, that he may aid you to resist the evil spirits. Wear on your neck a scapulary which has been touched to the relics of Saint Pacomio, our advocate against temptations, and go, go in power to the organ-loft. The mass is about to begin, and the faithful are growing impatient. Your father is in heaven, and thence, instead of giving you a fright, he will descend to inspire his daughter in this solemn service which he so especially loved."

The prioress went to occupy her seat in the choir in the centre of the sisterhood. The daughter of Master Pérez opened the door of the loft with trembling hand, sat down at the organ, and the mass began.

The mass began, and continued without any unusual occurrence until the consecration. Then the organ sounded, and at the same time came a scream from the daughter of Master Pérez.

The mother superior, the nuns, and some of the faithful rushed up to the organ-loft.

"Look at him! look at him!" cried the girl, fixing her eyes, starting from their sockets, upon the organ-bench, from which she had risen in terror, clinging with convulsed hands to the railing of the organ-loft.

All eyes were fixed upon the spot to which her gaze was turned. No one was at the organ, yet it went on sounding, sounding as the archangels sing in their raptures of mystic ecstasy.

*

"Didn't I tell you so a thousand times, my dear Doña Baltasara, didn't I tell you so? There is a mystery here. What? You were not at the Christmas Eve Mass last night? But, for all that, you must know what happened. Nothing else is talked about in all Seville. The archbishop is furious, and with good reason. To have missed going to Santa Inés, to have missed being present at the miracle!

25

And for what? To hear a charivari, a rattle-go-bang, for people who heard it tell me that what the inspired organist of San Bartolomé did in the cathedral was just that. I told you so. The squint-eye could never have played that divine music of last year, never. There is mystery about all this, a mystery that is, in truth, the soul of Master Pérez."

CARLO MAGNO AND THE GIANT

Adapted from Patranas; or Spanish Stories by Rachel Harriette Busk, published by Newbery and Harris, 1870.

ONE OF THE MOORISH KINGS, WHO sought his alliance in the internecine turmoils in which the chiefs of their race were at the time engaged, had an only and beautiful daughter, the apple of his eye, who was guarded with jealous care. She was indulged in every wish, waited on by the most beautiful maidens in a fairy-like palace, and suffered to know nothing of her father's wars and dangers. Life seemed all smoothness and pleasure to her; and every one, who at any time met her eye, made it their delight to obey her faintest sign.

But life passed even amid continual sunshine, flowers, and harmony may become monotonous. When the Moorish princess was fifteen years old, she began to seek some newer and more exciting pleasures. Her fond father, only glad to hear her express a wish, that he might have the satisfaction of gratifying it, promised to give her a fresh diversion such as she had never before seen.

For this purpose he ordered a great fête, and selected all the mightiest men of his forces, to perform feats of arms and mock combats before her.

The princess, who had never witnessed any combat more serious than that of her pet doves, was delighted beyond measure with the new sensation, and thought she could never tire of seeing the brave horsemen contend; dealing each other such heavy blows, and all the while seeming so indifferent to danger. Nevertheless the time came when the sameness of these shows struck her too, and she began to crave for something newer yet.

The king then ordered that valiant men from other countries should be invited to come and fight before her, each after the fashion of their own country. Many warriors of renown were happy to come and display their prowess; the Moslem in the hope of winning the bright smile of the king's daughter; Christians, to have the opportunity of displaying their might before the infidel horde.

Among the strangers, but belonging to neither of these categories, came one day a powerful giant, five cubits high, who rode on a horse as tall as a house. All the mighty men of the king's army turned pale when they saw him; and the king regretted that his invitations to all comers had been so unlimited that he could find no courteous excuse for excluding him. To offer an unfair excuse would have been dangerous, as the giant's ire would have been terrible if provoked. So the King received him as smilingly as his trepidation would permit; and the giant seemed a very good-natured person, too full of his own consequence to think of picking a quarrel with anyone.

The giant challenged everyone to fight with him, but no one would venture to do so; and this testimony to his might put him in still better humour. Then he showed off all his feats of strength, to the great delight of the court, and of none more than the princess, who was so astonished at the prodigies he performed, that she leant out from her balcony, and let the veil blow away from her face.

The giant happened to be looking towards her at that precise moment, and that moment sufficed to make him fall in love with her. For the rest of the day he exhibited his surprising strength with renewed energy; but the evening was no sooner come, than he stole up to her window, which, though it was in a very high tower of the alcázar1, was just at a convenient height for his head to reach as he stood upon the ground. Putting his face against the lattice, he whispered very softly that he must speak to her. The poor little princess was dreadfully frightened, and could not guess what he wanted, but thought it would not be dignified to show any fear; so she went near enough to the window to be heard by him, and asked him his pleasure.

The giant told her that he loved her, and she must marry him. The princess was dreadfully terrified when she heard this, for she knew she had no possible means of resisting him if he chose to carry her off by force; and she reflected, too, that her father himself would have very little chance if he attempted to fight him: and what a dreadful thing it would be if he should kill her father - her dear father, who was so fond of her! Yet in the fright she was in, she could think of no better stratagem than to stammer forth that he must give her time to think about it.

The giant was pleased with this reply, and promised he would leave her quite to herself till the next day. All that night, and all the next day, the little princess thought and thought of what excuse she could make; but she could think of nothing but to ask him to give her another day; and then again she sat and thought, and no invention would come: and she dared not tell, her father, lest he should, in his indignation, challenge the giant to fight, and be killed by him. But when the giant came the third time, and she could still think of no stratagem for getting rid of him, she was obliged to tell him plainly that she could not make up her mind to marry him.

At first the giant tried all sorts of clumsy persuasions and entreaties; but the maiden held firm; and at last, finding she would not yield, he grew fiercely angry, seized the alcázar by the roof, and made it rock backwards and forwards. He tore up the trees, and threw them on the ground, and stamped upon the soil with a noise like peals of thunder. The poor little princess was so terrified she hardly knew what was happening. Then she heard him swear that he would come back and take her in a way that meant she could not escape him; and after repeating that threat several times he eventually disappeared.

It was a long time before the princess came to her senses again, for she had fainted with the dire terror, and when she did, she began to wonder what the terrible trouble was which had so shattered her. By degrees the memory of the stormy scenes lately passed came back to her, but all was now so calm and still, she could hardly believe the truth of what she had gone through. It was a great relief to find the giant was quite gone and far away, and she learnt that he lived a long, long way off, in a valley as far below the level of the plain as the cliff on which her father's alcázar stood rose above it. She remembered, indeed, his threat that he would come back, but it seemed that it would have been so easy for him to have taken her then and there had he been so minded, that she could not think he was serious in the intention to carry her off at all. Why should he come back to do what he might just as well have done at once?

Time passed, and she heard no more of the giant. People stopped talking of his feats of strength, and she began to forget all about him. A matter happened, too, which gave another direction to her thoughts. A neighbouring king made war upon her father, and with such overwhelming force, that this time her father could not conceal the fact from her. Everyone was full of apprehensions, and the king, distracted with the fear of losing his kingdom, had no time even to think of the fancies of his beloved daughter. The princess heard from one and another of the attendants that things were going very wrong, that the enemy were getting the upper hand, and advancing nearer and nearer; but she learnt more from their anxious looks than from their lips, for everyone was afraid to distress her by giving her details of the truth.

*

We must now go back to the giant, whom we left marching off in no good humour. The truth about him was, that with all his strength he was not very courageous. He was more of a bully than a warrior. He had heard a great deal of the bravery and more particularly of the excellent arms of the Moors, and as he knew they would rise as one man to defend their princess if he carried her off, he did not like the idea of their making pincushions of his legs with their fine sharp swords, even if they could not reach to do him further damage. So he resolved to carry out his plan in a way which would be less fraught with danger to himself.

Coming down from the alcázar, he went to see the neighbouring sovereign, and treacherously gave him a description of all he had seen at the court where he had just been staying. He told him the number and situation of the army, and the condition of the defences, and pointed out the least protected points of the country by which an incursion could be made. Having received a rich

31

reward for this information, he continued his way homewards, and then set all his people to work to cut a long cave, which he made them extend further and further in a sloping direction till it should come out opposite the alcázar where the Moorish princess dwelt, He made this cave so that he could reach her unseen, and carry her off without danger to his own skin, while the city was in the midst of the tumult which he thought would be brought about by the invasion of the inimical power he had perfidiously invoked.

Various underground rumblings had been observed for some time by the country people, but as they held little communication with each other it did not strike them that the sounds continually advanced in the direction of the capital. Indeed, all minds were too much filled with the fear of the destruction the advancing foe above ground was likely to wreak upon their property. The common people had no time to give way to fears of a chimerical foe in the regions below the soil.

Thus the giant worked on steadily and without hindrance, while the poor little princess thought nothing more of her recent tormentor other than that he was as at a safe distance, much less did she dream of his continually nearing approach! She had enough to excite her anxiety without this. And she sat crying over her father's danger till her face became quite pale and her eyes worn with tears.

At last a day came when everyone seemed bright with fresh hope; and they ran hastily enough to tell her the good news. The youthful conqueror, Carlo Magno, had been appealed to by the king to help him. His arrival had entirely turned the tide of affairs. The enemy had been completely repulsed, and the victorious army was returning in triumph to the city.

The news spread like wildfire. Everyone hastened to deck their houses festively, and put on their best attire, to do honour to the conquerors; and when they appeared, shouted their thanks in loud acclamations. The little princess was longed to see the young hero who had saved her father's life; and, though it is not the custom for Moorish women to appear in public, she contrived to see him as he passed by, and thought in the silence of her heart how nice it would have been if it had been the handsome Christian who had wanted to marry her instead of the monstrous giant. Having once seen him, she was so desirous to see him again that she sent to ask him to come, that she might thank him for having saved her father's kingdom, but it was not entirely for her father's sake that she contrived the interview.

When he came, however, though he was very courteous towards her, he was also very reserved, and stayed a very short time. He assured her that what he had done was nothing at all; that his sword was ever ready to defend the right, whoever it might be who invoked his aid; and with that took his leave without paying her any compliments. The Moorish princess was sad when she saw him go out so; and sadder still when she learnt that no Christian prince cared to know a Moorish maid. Carlo Magno himself, however, was sorry for the poor child, as he had seen that she wanted to be better acquainted with him; but he could hold no intimacy with the unbeliever.

The giant, meantime, had gone on boring away; and, though he had now got quite under the alcázar, everyone was so full of festivity and rejoicing that nobody heeded the sound of his pickaxe. On his part, he had not been altogether unmindful to listen for the sounds which might keep him informed of what was going on in the upper world. He had been very well satisfied with what he heard. There had been unmistakable clashings of battle, and he never doubted that the princess's father must be getting the worst of it; and now, when he heard the sounds of busy running to and fro in the festive palace, he was sure it was his allies pillaging the place.

At last the tunnel was complete. The giant crept out in the first fall of the darkness of night, threaded the familiar way up to the princess's window, rested his foot on the cornice of the first story for a stepping-stone, and with one grasp of his hand had swept her off her couch before she had time to open her eyes. Then closing her mouth, so that she might not cry and raise an alarm, he walked quietly back with her to his subterranean passage, down the sloping path of which he carried her in exultation.

As quickly and silently as the feat had been performed, the keen bright eyes of a little African slave had followed the whole affair as she lay at the foot of her mistress's couch. She had seen the huge hand spread over the room, the nail of its little finger had sadly grazed her forehead. She recognized it at once as belonging to the giant, her mistress's dread of whom she had so often shared. And no sooner was her helplessness to rescue her mistress apparent, than she rushed madly into the banqueting-hall, tearing her clothes and plucking out her hair, and crying out in wailing accents what had befallen.

It was not easy for the people there to believe so strange a story; but at last her earnestness induced belief in her sincerity. The princess's room had to be searched to afford the necessary proof that she was gone. When this was found to be indeed too true, the wail was taken up by all the people. The banquet was broken up, and everyone went here and there, not knowing what to do, for, withal that the giant was so big, none had seen him pass to tell which way he had gone.

But Carlo Magno, brave and self-possessed in the midst of all, saw an occasion to be of service to the poor Moorish princess, and make up for the disappointment he had caused her in the morning. It was plain to him that if the giant had stood under the window, as the little African slave had said, he must have left his foot-prints there. That being so, he could thence be tracked wherever he had gone. So he raised a loud voice, and bid all the people be still: and that if they would all remain without stirring, he would deliver their princess, for he wanted them not to stir up the soil any more, lest they should destroy the track.

The voice of Carlo Magno, after what he had already done for them, possessed great authority with the people; and so all stood quite still, while he bade the little African slave guide him to the window; and there, under it, sure enough he found the giant's footprints, two great holes in the sand, like dry tanks for water. Allowing due space for his prodigious stride, the prince readily found another and another, till they brought him to the mouth of the tunnel, where he had indeed passed. When all the people saw the great gaping hole which had never appeared there before that night, and gazed down its descending gullet, no wonder they thought it was the mouth of hell opened to vomit forth its monster.

But Carlo Magno said he would deliver the princess though his enterprise should indeed lead him into the realms of Hades. And all the people applauded his courage, but he went down the black path alone.

Though he travelled at all speed, the giant had a good start, and the length of his step was equal to several of the Christian prince's charger; but Carlo Magno made such good haste that he had not got above a hundred miles before he heard the giant's laugh, exulting over his prize, resounding through the gloomy passage, though still at some considerable distance. This roused the Christian prince's indignation, and made him urge his steed yet faster, till at last he came within sight of the giant. And then, when he saw his monstrous arms bearing the little helpless princess, his compassion made him use yet greater speed, till at length just as he reached the mouth of the cave, Carlo Magno managed to overstep him by one bound of his horse, and then wheeling round confronted him with fearless eye.

The giant, as I have already said, was more of a bully than a warrior. When he saw the Christian knight so brave and firm, and withal encased in such strong armour, and brandishing his trenchant sword, he felt his best defence lay in hectoring and boasting, and thereby frightening the Christian hero from attempting to fight him.

With a terrible voice, therefore, which made the rocks resound, he asked his opponent, on whom he lavished every startling epithet, what he meant by venturing to appear before him; following up the question by such a volley of imprecations and threats as he fancied would suffice to make him wish to escape with a whole skin.

Carlo Magno, however, who knew that the dogs who bark most bite least, waited unmoved until the giant had exhausted his whole repertory of violent language, and then quite undismayed summoned him to surrender the maiden.

Another loud and angry volley followed upon this demand, with further threats of the terrible vengeance the giant intended to take on the intruder.

"Then," said Carlo Magno, "if you will not give her up quietly, I must rescue her from you by force." And with that he dismounted and drew his sword. The giant saw now that he must defend his life, or he would lose it; and so, forced to fight, he drew his clumsy sword and began laying about him in right-determined fashion; but all his blows landed far and wide of the Christian prince. Furious at finding his awkward efforts ineffectual, while the highly trained agility of the prince saved him from all of the giant's strokes, he began laying about him with such untempered violence that at last his weapon dropped from his hand. Fully expecting that Carlo Magno would try to it for himself, the giant hastily bent down to regain it. But Carlo Magno had other thoughts. Waiting calmly till the monster had bent sufficiently low, he swung his fine sharp blade and buried it deep in the giant's heart with the unerring dexterity with which the matador lays low his bull – with one single thrust.

Of course he severed the giant's head afterwards to bear away as his trophy; and raising the princess in his arms, who had swooned away at sight of the horrid combat, Carlo Magno bore her swiftly upwards through the subterranean path and delivered her, yet unconscious, to her father.

THE CITY OF FORTUNE

Adapted from Fairy Tales from Spain by José Muñoz Escámez, published by J. M. Dent & Sons Ltd, 1913.

ONCE UPON A TIME THERE WAS a boy named Rupert, the sharpest and most prudent lad in his village, and indeed in any of those to be found for twenty leagues around.

One night he was with a group of boys of his own age, who, gathered round the fire, were listening with amazement to a veteran soldier, covered with scars, which had gained him the modest stripes of a sergeant pensioner, and who was telling the story of his adventures. The narrator was at the most interesting point of his tale.

"The great City of Fortune," he said, "is situated on the summit of a very high mountain, so steep that only very few have succeeded in reaching the top. There gold circulates in such abundance that the inhabitants do not know what to do with the precious metal. Houses are built of it, the walls of the fortress are of solid silver, and the cannons which defend it are enormous pierced diamonds. The streets are paved with coins, always new, because as soon as they begin to lose their brilliance they are replaced by others just minted.

"You ought to see the cleanliness of it! What dirt lies there is pure gold dust, which the dust carts collect in order to throw in large baskets into the drains.

"The pebbles against which we stumble continually are brilliants as large as nuts, despised on account of the extraordinary abundance with which the soil supplies them. In a word, he who lives there may consider the most powerful of the earth as beggars.

"The worst of it is that the path which leads there is rough and difficult, and most people succumb without having been able to arrive at the city of gold."

Rupert did not let the words of the soldier go in at one ear and out at the other; and so it was that as soon as he was alone with the old soldier he inquired, "Do you know the way to this enchanted city?"

"I should rather think so, my son; but I do not advise you to try the journey."

"Why?"

"The way is long and rocky. I came back the first day, startled at the difficulties which must be overcome. But anyhow, if you are resolved to go, I must give you the following warning. In order to get to Fortune there are two paths. The first is a very broad one, full of stones and crags. If you go that way the sharp points of the pebbles will tear your feet to pieces and you will be crushed by fatigue. A thousand terrible difficulties will arise to meet you. You will have to struggle with cruel enemies, and if, at last, you succeed in vanquishing all, you will arrive at Fortune already old and worn, when riches will be of no use to you. The other path is level and short, but..."

"Enough! Do not say any more. Show me the path now, and I will look after the rest."

"All right, all right! I will show it to you, and God grant that you not having wished to hear me to the end will not bring you suffering."

And the little rogue, without saying good-bye to his parents or his brother, began to walk in the direction the old soldier had shown him He went on and on, happier than a sand-boy, thinking of the riches which awaited him, and which he already believed to have within reach of his hand.

At the end of two days he arrived at the bank of a large river. On it was a boat, and in the boat a man of colossal stature.

Our lad approached the boatmen and asked him, "Good man, is this the way to Fortune?"

"Yes, little boy, but it is necessary to cross the river."

"Good, then take me across."

"Do you know how much it costs?"

"No."

"Fifty coins."

"But do I look as if I had them, or had even seen that much money in my life? Be kind and take me over for nothing."

"This river, my little friend, is never crossed gratis. It is the first step towards Fortune and it must be paid for somehow. If you have no money, never mind; let me cut off a little piece of your heart.

Perhaps it will hurt you a bit at first, but later you will feel as if you were whole."

Rupert allowed the man to open his chest and to take out a piece of his heart. When he crossed to the other side he gave a sigh of satisfaction. The first step was taken, and he already saw the beautiful City of Fortune, whose resplendent walls sent out lovely reflections. But he noticed that he was much less anxious to arrive at the city of gold and had a strange emptiness in his chest.

However, he continued his walk, but he had not taken a hundred steps when a new difficulty arose to obstruct the way. This stretched between two inaccessible mountains and the entrance to the defile was kept by another guardian as huge as the one on the boat.

"Where are you going, boy?" he asked our lad.

"To the City of Fortune."

"Quite so, this is the way; but you have to pay for the passage. The payment is a little piece of heart."

Without hesitating, Rupert opened his chest and left a handful of fibres of that organ of life in the hands of the terrible gate-keeper.

And he went on and on towards the city, which each time showed itself nearer and more beautiful to his eyes. But each time he felt less anxious to get there.

Still he had not finished with the difficulties. The path soon shortened, forming a terrible ravine, To think of crossing it was more than he could dream of. Rupert believed his hopes were dashed, and he sat down disheartened on a stone.

At that moment a vulture of great size came down from the top of a mountain and, drawing near him, said, "Do you wish to go across? Well, give me a piece of your heart."

"Take it, and carry me over," said Rupert, desperate.

The vulture thrust its beak into Rupert's chest and took out a good piece of heart. At once it seized our lad with its claws and carried him to the other side of the abyss.

Now he was at the very gates of Fortune. He could already count the number of towers which raised themselves above the high walls, and Rupert took his future happiness for granted if that happiness consists in money. At the gate the guards stopped him. In that place a heart was contraband, and therefore they took out what remained of it and put a pretty one inside of him made of steel but hard as a diamond. Only one little fibre escaped their search, which sat unnoticed behind the metal heart.

"At last I am inside," said Rupert to himself; but, strangely enough, the city of gold produced neither surprise nor joy.

"What do I want riches for?" he exclaimed, "if I have lost my heart and with it my illusions?" And he walked through the city, looking with great disdain at those riches which were within reach of his hand and which had so much tempted his ambition before.

That dazzling brilliance began to disturb him.

"Here it seems," he said to himself, "there is nothing else but gold. Cursed metal, which has cost me my heart. Goodness me! Who will give me back my little heart?"

He looked for friends, but did not succeed in finding them, because those people had hearts of steel, and all the while Rupert felt the little fibre that remained of his own heart make him suffer atrociously.

Without friends or affection, in that city of gold, Rupert remembered his parents and his brother and bitterly lamented his fate.

And then he resolved to return to the little white house in his own village and to live in it as God had ordered. On his going out of the city he felt a strange joy. But that accursed steel heart made him suffer horribly and only the little fibre which remained of his own beat for joy in his breast. He took the first path he found, and then encountered no difficulties. It seemed that wings had grown on his feet. He went downhill, and so walked very quickly. When he arrived at his village he was as poor as before, and moreover that cold, hard heart did not let him breathe. It beat with the regularity of a clock, tick-tock, tick-tock!

His brother was the first to come out and meet him, full of joy. He embraced him, kissed him, and accompanied him home, transported with gladness.

But the steel heart did not allow Rupert to rejoice. Tears did not run from his eyes, and his chest felt as if a hand was pressing on it.

His old father strained him to his bosom, but not even he succeeded in moving that hard heart. Rupert felt an extraordinary anguish.

But his mother arrived running, out of breath, towards her son, and embraced him weeping, and her tears fell on Rupert's heart. Then, oh, the power of a mother's love! That steel heart quickened its beats and, unable to resist any longer, jumped out, just as a broken spring of a watch jumps out. The little fibre was already a new heart and Rupert was a happy man.

And when they spoke to him of riches he said, "God will give them if he deem it right, but don't seek them by short cuts at the expense of your heart and illusions."

THE BIRD OF TRUTH

Adapted by Andrew Lang in The Orange Fairy Book, 1906, the original taken from Cuentos, Oraciones y Adivinas by Fernan Caballero, published in 1878.

ONCE UPON A TIME THERE LIVED a poor fisherman who built a hut on the banks of a stream which, shunning the glare of the sun and the noise of the towns, flowed quietly past trees and under bushes, listening to the songs of the birds overhead.

One day, when the fisherman had gone out as usual to cast his nets, he saw borne towards him on the current a cradle of crystal. Slipping his net quickly beneath it he drew it out and lifted the silk coverlet. Inside, lying on a soft bed of cotton, were two babies, a boy and a girl, who opened their eyes and smiled at him. The man was filled with pity at the sight, and throwing down his lines he took the cradle and the babies home to his wife.

The good woman flung up her hands in despair when she beheld the contents of the cradle.

"Are not eight children enough," she cried, "without bringing us two more? How do you think we can feed them?"

"You would not have had me leave them to die of hunger," answered he, "or be swallowed up by the waves of the sea? What is enough for eight is also enough for ten."

His wife said no more; and in truth her heart yearned over the little creatures. Somehow or other food was never lacking in the hut, and the children grew up and were so good and gentle that, in time, their foster-parents loved them as well or better than their own, who were quarrelsome and envious.

It did not take the orphans long to notice that the boys did not like them, and were always playing tricks on them, so they used to go away by themselves and spend whole hours by the banks of the river. Here they would take out the bits of bread they had saved from their breakfasts and crumble them for the birds. In return, the birds taught them many things - how to get up early in the morning, how to sing, and how to talk their language, which very few people know.

But though the little orphans did their best to avoid quarrelling with their foster-brothers, it was very difficult always to keep the peace. Matters got worse and worse until, one morning, the eldest boy said to the twins:

"It is all very well for you to pretend that you have such good manners, and are so much better than we, but we have a father and mother, while you have only got the river, like the toads and the frogs."

The poor children did not answer the insult; but it made them very unhappy. And they told each other in whispers that they could not stay there any longer, but must go into the world and seek their fortunes.

So next day they arose as early as the birds and stole downstairs without anybody hearing them. One window was open, and they crept softly out and ran to the side of the river. Then, feeling as if they had found a friend, they walked along its banks, hoping that by-and-by they should meet someone to take care of them.

The whole of that day they went steadily on without seeing a living creature, till, in the evening, weary and footsore, they saw before them a small hut. This raised their spirits for a moment; but the door was shut, and the hut seemed empty, and so great was their disappointment that they almost cried. However, the boy fought down his tears, and said cheerfully, "Well, at any rate here is a bench where we can sit down, and when we are rested we will think what is best to do next."

Then they sat down, and for some time they were too tired to notice anything; but by-and-by they saw that under the tiles of the roof a number of swallows were sitting, chattering merrily to each other. Of course the swallows had no idea that the children understood their language, or they would not have talked so freely; but, as it was, they said whatever came into their heads.

"Good evening, my fine city madam," remarked a swallow, whose manners were rather rough and countryfied to another who looked particularly distinguished. "Happy, indeed, are the eyes that behold you! Only think of your having returned to your long-forgotten country friends, after you have lived for years in a palace!"

"I have inherited this nest from my parents," replied the other, "and as they left it to me I certainly shall make it my home. But," she added politely, "I hope that you and all your family are well?"

"Very well indeed, I am glad to say. But my poor daughter had, a short time ago, such bad inflammation in her eyes that she would have gone blind had I not been able to find the magic herb, which cured her at once."

"And how is the nightingale singing? Does the lark soar as high as ever? And does the linnet dress herself as smartly?"

But here the country swallow drew herself up. "I never talk gossip," she said severely. "Our people, who were once so innocent and well-behaved, have been corrupted by the bad examples of men. It is a thousand pities."

"What! innocence and good behaviour are not to be met with among birds, nor in the country! My dear friend, what are you saying?"

"The truth and nothing more. Imagine, when we returned here, we met some linnets who, just as the spring and the flowers and the long days had come, were setting out for the north and the cold? Out of pure compassion we tried to persuade them to give up this folly; but they only replied with the utmost insolence."

"How shocking!" exclaimed the city swallow.

"Yes, it was. And worse than that, the crested lark, that was formerly so timid and shy, is now no better than a thief, and steals maize and corn whenever she can find them."

"I am astonished at what you say."

"You will be more astonished when I tell you that on my arrival here for the summer I found my nest occupied by a shameless sparrow! "This is my nest," I said. "Yours?" he answered, with a rude laugh. "Yes, mine; my ancestors were born here, and my sons will be born here also." And at that my husband set upon him and threw him out of the nest. I am sure nothing of this sort ever happens in a town."

"Not exactly, perhaps. But I have seen a great deal - if you only knew!"

"Oh! do tell us! do tell us!" cried they all. And when they had settled themselves comfortably, the city swallow began. "You must know, then that our king fell in love with the youngest daughter of a tailor, who was as good and gentle as she was beautiful. His nobles hoped that he would have chosen a queen from one of their daughters, and tried to prevent the marriage; but the king would not listen to them, and it took place. Not many months later a war broke out, and the king rode away at the head of his army, while the queen remained behind, very unhappy at the separation. When peace was made, and the king returned, he was told that his wife had had two babies in his absence, but that both were dead; that she herself had gone out of her mind and was obliged to be shut up in a tower in the mountains, where, in time, the fresh air might cure her."

"And was this not true?" asked the swallows eagerly.

"Of course not," answered the city lady, with some contempt for their stupidity. "The children were alive at that very moment in the gardener's cottage; but at night the chamberlain came down and put them in a cradle of crystal, which he carried to the river.

"For a whole day they floated safely, for though the stream was deep it was very still, and the children took no harm. In the morning, so I am told by my friend the kingfisher, they were rescued by a fisherman who lived near the river bank."

The children had been lying on the bench, listening lazily to the chatter up to this point; but when they heard the story of the crystal cradle which their foster-mother had always been fond of telling them, they sat upright and looked at each other.

"Oh, how glad I am I learnt the birds" language!" said the eyes of one to the eyes of the other.

Meanwhile the swallows had spoken again.

"That was indeed good fortune!" cried they.

"And when the children are grown up they can return to their father and set their mother free."

"It will not be so easy as you think," answered the city swallow, shaking her head; "for they will have to prove that they are the king's children, and also that their mother never went mad at all. In fact, it is so difficult that there is only one way of proving it to the king."

"And what is that?" cried all the swallows at once. "And how do you know it?"

"I know it," answered the city swallow, "because, one day, when I was passing through the palace garden, I met a cuckoo, who, as I need not tell you, always pretends to be able to see into the future. We began to talk about certain things which were happening in the palace, and of the events of past years.

"Ah," said he, "the only person who can expose the wickedness of the ministers and show the king how wrong he has been, is the Bird of Truth, who can speak the language of men."

"And where can this bird be found?" I asked.

"It is shut up in a castle guarded by a fierce giant, who only sleeps one quarter of an hour out of the whole twenty-four," replied the cuckoo.

"And where is this castle?" inquired the country swallow, who, like all the rest, and the children most of all, had been listening with deep attention.

"That is just what I don't know," answered her friend. "All I can tell you is that not far from here is a tower, where dwells an old witch, and it is she who knows the way, and she will only teach it to the person who promises to bring her the water from the fountain of many colours, which she uses for her enchantments. But never will she betray the place where the Bird of Truth is hidden, for she hates him, and would kill him if she could. She knows well, however, that this bird cannot die, as he is immortal, so she keeps him closely shut up, and guarded night and day by the Birds of Bad Faith, who seek to gag him so that his voice should not be heard."

"And is there no one else who can tell the poor boy where to find the bird, if he should ever manage to reach the tower?" asked the country swallow.

"No one," replied the city swallow, "except an owl, who lives a hermit's life in that desert, and he knows only one word of man's speech, and that is 'cross'. So, even if the prince did succeed in getting there, he could never understand what the owl said. But, look, the sun is sinking to his nest in the depths of the sea, and I must go to mine. Good-night, friends, good-night!"

Then the swallow flew away, and the children, who had forgotten both hunger and weariness in the joy of this strange news, rose up and followed in the direction of her flight. After two hours walking, they arrived at a large city, which they felt sure must be the capital of their father's kingdom. Seeing a good-natured looking woman standing at the door of a house, they asked her if she would give them a night's lodging, and she was so pleased with their pretty faces and nice manners that she welcomed them warmly.

It was scarcely light the next morning before the girl was sweeping out the rooms, and the boy watering the garden, so that by the time the good woman came downstairs there was nothing left for her to do. This so delighted her that she begged the children to stay with her altogether, and the boy answered that he would leave his sisters with her gladly, but that he himself had serious business on hand and must not linger in pursuit of it. So he bade them farewell and set out.

For three days he wandered by the most out-of-the-way paths, but no signs of a tower were to be seen anywhere. On the fourth morning it was just the same, and, filled with despair, he flung himself on the ground under a tree and hid his face in his hands. In a little while he heard a rustling over his head, and looking up, he saw a turtle dove watching him with her bright eyes.

"Oh dove!" cried the boy, addressing the bird in her own language, "Oh dove! tell me, I pray you, where is the castle of Come-and-never-go?"

"Poor child," answered the dove, "who has sent you on such a useless quest?"

"My good or evil fortune," replied the boy, "I know not which."

"To get there," said the dove, "you must follow the wind, which today is blowing towards the castle."

The boy thanked her, and followed the wind, fearing all the time that it might change its direction and lead him astray. But the wind seemed to feel pity for him and blew steadily on.

With each step the country became more and more dreary, but at nightfall the child could see behind the dark and bare rocks something darker still. This was the tower in which dwelt the witch; and seizing the knocker he gave three loud knocks, which were echoed in the hollows of the rocks around.

The door opened slowly, and there appeared on the threshold an old woman holding up a candle to her face, which was so hideous that the boy involuntarily stepped backwards, almost as frightened by the troop of lizards, beetles and such creatures that surrounded her, as by the woman herself.

"Who are you who dare to knock at my door and wake me?" cried she. "Be quick and tell me what you want, or it will be the worse for you."

"Madam," answered the child, "I believe that you alone know the way to the castle of Come-and-never-go, and I pray you to show it to me."

"Very good," replied the witch, with something that she meant for a smile, "but today it is late. Tomorrow you shall go. Now enter, and you shall sleep with my lizards."

"I cannot stay," said he. "I must go back at once, so as to reach the road from which I started before day dawns."

"If I tell you, will you promise me that you will bring me this jar full of the many-coloured water from the spring in the court-yard of the castle?" asked she. "If you fail to keep your word I will change you into a lizard for ever."

"I promise," answered the boy.

Then the old woman called to a very thin dog, and said to him, "Conduct this pig of a child to the castle of Come-and-never-go, and take care that you warn my friend of his arrival." And the dog arose and shook itself, and set out.

At the end of two hours they stopped in front of a large castle, big and black and gloomy, whose doors stood wide open, although neither sound nor light gave sign of any presence within. The dog, however, seemed to know what to expect, and, after a wild howl, went on; but the boy, who was uncertain whether this was the quarter of an hour when the giant was asleep, hesitated to follow him, and paused for a moment under a wild olive that grew nearby, the only tree which he had beheld since he had parted from the dove. "Oh, heaven, help me!" cried he.

"Cross! cross!" answered a voice.

The boy leapt for joy as he recognised the note of the owl of which the swallow had spoken, and he said softly in the bird's language, "Oh, wise owl, I pray you to protect and guide me, for I have come in search of the Bird of Truth. And first I must fill this jar with the many-coloured water in the courtyard of the castle."

"Do not do that," answered the owl, "but fill the jar from the spring which bubbles close by the fountain with the many-coloured water. Afterwards, go into the aviary opposite the great door, but be careful not to touch any of the bright-plumaged birds contained in it, which will cry to you, each one, that he is the Bird of Truth. Choose only a small white bird that is hidden in a corner, which the others try incessantly to kill, not knowing that it cannot die. And, be quick, for at this very moment the giant has fallen asleep, and you have only a quarter of an hour to do everything."

The boy ran as fast as he could and entered the courtyard, where he saw the two springs close together. He passed by the many-coloured water without casting a glance at it, and filled the jar from the fountain whose water was clear and pure. He next hastened to the aviary, and was almost deafened by the clamour that rose as he shut the door behind him. Voices of peacocks, voices of ravens, voices of magpies, each claiming to be the Bird of Truth. With steadfast face the boy walked by them all, to the corner, where, hemmed in by a hand of fierce crows, was the small white bird he sought. Putting her safely in his breast, he passed out, followed by the screams of the birds of Bad Faith which he left behind him.

Once outside, he ran without stopping to the witch's tower, and handed to the old woman the jar she had given him.

"Become a parrot!" cried she, flinging the water over him. But instead of losing his shape, as so many had done before, he only grew ten times handsomer; for the water was enchanted for good and not ill. Then the creeping multitude around the witch hastened to roll themselves in the water, and stood up, human beings again.

When the witch saw what was happening, she took a broomstick and flew away.

Who can guess the delight of the sister at the sight of her brother, bearing the Bird of Truth? But although the boy had accomplished much, something very difficult yet remained, and that was how to carry the Bird of Truth to the king without her being seized by the wicked courtiers, who would be ruined by the discovery of their plot.

Soon - no one knew how - the news spread abroad that the Bird of Truth was hovering round the palace, and the courtiers made all sorts of preparations to hinder her reaching the king.

They got weapons ready that were sharpened, and weapons that were poisoned. They sent for eagles and falcons to hunt her down, and constructed cages and boxes in which to shut her up if they were not able to kill her. They declared that her white plumage was really put on to hide her black feathers - in fact there was nothing they did not do in order to prevent the king from seeing the bird or from paying attention to her words if he did.

As often happens in these cases, the courtiers brought about that which they feared. They talked so much about the Bird of Truth that at last the king heard of it, and expressed a wish to see her. The more difficulties that were put in his way the stronger grew his desire, and in the end the king published a proclamation that whoever found the Bird of Truth should bring her to him without delay.

As soon as he saw this proclamation the boy called his sister, and they hastened to the palace. The bird was buttoned inside his tunic, but, as might have been expected, the courtiers barred the way, and told the child that he could not enter. It was in vain that the boy declared that he was only obeying the king's commands. The courtiers only replied that his majesty was not yet out of bed, and it was forbidden to wake him.

They were still talking, when, suddenly, the bird settled the question by flying upwards through an open window into the king's own room. Alighting on the pillow, close to the king's head, she bowed respectfully, and said, "My lord, I am the Bird of Truth whom you wished to see, and I have been obliged to approach you in this manner because the boy who brought me is kept out of the palace by your courtiers."

"They shall pay for their insolence," said the king. And he instantly ordered one of his attendants to conduct the boy at once to his apartments; and in a moment more the prince entered, holding his sister by the hand.

"Who are you?" asked the king; "and what has the Bird of Truth to do with you?"

"If it please your majesty, the Bird of Truth will explain that herself," answered the boy.

And the bird did explain; and the king heard for the first time of the wicked plot that had been successful for so many years. He took his children in his arms, with tears in his eyes, and hurried off with them to the tower in the mountains where the queen was shut up. The poor woman was as white as marble, for she had been living almost in darkness; but when she saw her husband and children, the colour came back to her face, and she was as beautiful as ever.

They all returned in state to the city, where great rejoicings were held. The wicked courtiers had their heads cut off, and all their property was taken away. As for the good old couple, they were given riches and honour, and were loved and cherished to the end of their lives.

Tales From The Land Of Rabbits

TURIAN AND FLORETA

Adapted from Patranas; or Spanish Stories by Rachel Harriette Busk, published by Newbery and Harris, 1870.

THERE LIVED ONCE IN VERY ANCIENT times in Spain a young prince, the Infante Turian. He was a very beautiful youth, and the only child of his parents, King Canamor and his consort Leonela: they were thus tempted to indulge him very much, and, as we should say, to spoil him; in fact, he was allowed to have everything he asked for, and when any present or novel article of merchandise was brought to the palace, if it happened to take his fancy, he got into a way of expecting to have it for his own, and no one thought of thwarting him.

One day there came a foreign merchant to the court, who, instead of having a train of mules heavily laden with varieties of his wares to suit all tastes and fancies, was quite alone and unattended, and himself bore his whole stock. It consisted, indeed, of but one little parcel easily stowed away in the folds of his cloak. The servants were scandalized at such a mean apparatus, and would have driven him away without letting him have a chance of addressing himself to their masters, telling him if he had nothing more to show than the contents of one little case, it was not worthwhile to trouble them. It was in vain the merchant urged that what he had to show was of priceless value, and in itself alone was worth all the mule-loads of other merchants put together: they held it for idle raving, and bid him begone.

It happened, however, that the Infante Turian was coming home at the moment, and hearing the altercation, his curiosity was piqued to know what it could be that could be counted so precious. He had horses, and arms, and trappings, and gay clothes, and games, and baubles of every sort, and he had wearied of them all. He had acquired them without labour, and he consequently held them without esteem. Now there appeared a chance of some quite fresh sensation; moreover, the merchant himself had a strange air which fascinated him; again, his accent was different from any he had heard before, and suggested that he brought the productions of some climate which had not yet laid its stores at his feet. Proud, too, to show his power in setting the man free from the importunate scorn of the servants, he ordered them to stand back, and then gave the strange merchant permission to open his store.

Assuming an air of mystery, which excited the young prince still more, the merchant, however, now told him he must take him to some private recess apart, as what he had to show must be seen only by royal eyes. The prince accepted all conditions in his eagerness, and was indeed rather flattered by this one. As soon as they were quite alone, the strange merchant placed before him a portrait. Yes, nothing but a portrait in a very simple frame! But it was such a portrait that it quite turned poor Turian's head. He had never before dreamt of anything so beautiful; he went into ecstasies at first sight, kissed it, gazed at it, paced up and down the hall with it, raved about it, and grew almost frantic, when the strange merchant at last went up to him and said it was time for him to go home, and he must have the portrait to pack up again.

"Pack up again!" cried the prince: "why, I buy it of you at triple, tenfold, an hundredfold its weight in gold."

The merchant assured him it could not be sold; he required, indeed, a considerable price for suffering it to be seen, but part with it he could not, on any conditions whatever.

The prince threw his purse to him, and ordered him in no measured terms to depart while the way was clear, otherwise he would set on him the myrmidons from whom he had but now released him.

The strange merchant quietly picked up the purse, counted out conscientiously the sum he had named as the price for the sight of the picture, and laid down the rest; deliberately stowed away his fee in his belt, and at the same time took from it, unperceived by the prince, a little box of powder; then suddenly turning round, he scattered its contents over his face, producing instant insensibility. Prepared for the effect, the merchant caught him in his arms, and laid him gently on a bench, and then, possessing himself of his picture, he stealthily left the castle, unperceived by all.

When the Infante Turian came to himself, some hours afterwards, of course pursuit was vain; nor could any trace be learnt of the way the stranger had taken.

The prince was furious that, at least, he had not learnt some clue as to the original of the portrait, but there had not been time for a word of inquiry. And when he set himself to recall every detail, all that would come back to his mind was, that on the blue embroidery of the white drapery which veiled the matchless form, he had made out in curious characters the name Floreta. Armed with only this guide, he determined to roam the world till he discovered the real beauty whose ideal had so absorbed him.

King Canamor and Queen Leonela were inconsolable at the idea of their only son leaving them on so wild an errand; but they had never taught him obedience and self-control, and they could not move him now. All their persuasions could obtain was his consent to be accompanied by the Conde Dirlos, an ancient counsellor of great wisdom and authority in the kingdom, who would know how to procure him assistance by land and sea, in whatever enterprise he might be minded to take in hand. But it was stipulated that he was to control him in nothing: simply watch over him, and further his designs, so as to save him from fatigue and danger.

On they wandered for a year and a day, meeting many adventures and incurring many perils; but no one knew the name of Floreta. Wherever they went it was still a foreign name. At last, a year to the day that the strange merchant had brought the portrait to the castle, their travels brought them to a steep mountain-path, which led down to the sea. At a turn of the winding road, just below them, a tall figure appeared, wrapped in a long cloak, and wearing a high-peaked cap. The prince gave a bound of joy, and shouted to the figure to halt. It paid no heed, however.

"Stop! or you are dead!" shouted the prince, at the same time pointing an arrow with unerring aim at a spot a little in advance of the moving figure. As if conscious of what was going on, though he never moved his head, the strange merchant, for it was he, and the prince had instantly recognized him, stood still for an instant, as the bolt rattled in the ground on which he would have stood had he pursued his way three steps further. Then he passed on unheeding. The prince shouted more madly than before; but to no purpose; and in another moment the winding of the road had taken him out of sight.

Madly the prince spurred his horse in pursuit, and reached the turn; but no living form was to be seen. The rocks now resounded with the cries and imprecations with which he adjured the magician, for such he now rightly deemed him, to stand forth. At last, when he was silent from sheer exhaustion, a low but commanding voice from the depths of a neighbouring cave bade him listen, but, as he valued his life, advance not.

"Speak!" cried the prince, "nor torture me with longer suspense. What must I do to find Floreta? I am prepared to go to the end of the world, to undergo any hardship, any torture, to find her; but find her I am determined. If you refuse your help, then by help of some other; so you see it is idle to turn a deaf ear."

"By none other help but mine," answered the magician, "can you find Floreta; so your threats are vain. But if I had not meant you to see her, I should not have shown you the portrait at first, for I knew its influence could not be other than that it has exercised. I am going to instruct you how to reach her; but first you must give me my guerdon."

"Name it. Ask what you will," interposed the impetuous prince. "Ask my kingdom if you like, but keep me not in suspense."

"I only ask what is reasonable," answered the magician; "the real is worth a thousand times the representation;" and he named a price equivalent to a thousand times the sum he had originally received.

Without so much as waiting to reply, Turian turned to Conde Dirlos and told him now was the time to fulfil his father's behest by accomplishing this requirement, and begged him to raise the money without an instant's loss of time.

The count remonstrated in vain, and in vain represented the miseries he would be inflicting on the people by requiring, in so sudden a manner, the levy of so large a sum. Turian, blinded by his passion, bid him save his words, as nothing could change his purpose. The king's orders to obey him having been unconditional, Conde Dirlos set out with a heavy heart to comply.

Ten days of anxious suspense during his absence were spent by the prince in wandering over the rugged declivities of the coast. The ardour of his excitement demanded to be fed with deeds of daring and danger. When he was not so occupied, he was seated panting on the topmost crags, scouring the whole country with his eager glance to descry the first impression of the return of the count, with the means of pursuing his desperate resolve.

The day came at last. And afar off, first only like so many black specks, but gradually revealing themselves as Conde Dirlos on his faithful steed, and a long file of heavily-laden mules, came the anxiously expected train. The prince cursed the sluggish hours, as he watched the team now steering over the sandy plain, which seemed interminable in expanse, unmeasured by landmarks. He watched the train toil backwards and forwards up the zig-zagged steep. It seemed they were further off one hour than the last, as at each wind they turned upon their steps, now detached-liked spectres against the sky, as they crossed from one reach of the lofty sierra to the next.

All things have an end, even Turian's anxious suspense, and as the count at last neared the magician's cave, Turian descended at break-neck pace to meet him.

"There is the price," said the count, in sad and solemn accents, "but before rendering it out of your hands, stop and consider it;" and as he spoke he removed from the treasure the brilliant red and yellow cloths, the royal colours of Spain, with which it was covered. "Here, from each province of your father's dominions, is the due proportion of the tribute you have demanded. See, will you spend it so?"

The prince darted forward to glance at the goodly sight of so much gold, but drew back with horror.

What could he have seen to turn his flushed cheeks so deadly pale?

"Count!" he cried, choking with fury, "what have you brought to mock me? This is not coin. You have brought me tears, burning tears, instead of gold."

"It is all the same," replied the count; "I saw you were infatuated, and I brought the money in this form, that the sight might warn you of what you are doing, and by its sad horror arrest you. There is time to return it back into the bosom of those from whom it has been wrung, and no harm will have been done. But if you persist, you will find the magician will take them for current coin."

"Quite so!" chimed in the voice from the cave; "it is the money I like best. But I cannot stand dallying thus. If the treasure be not handed over at once, the bargain is at an end, and you never hear of me again."

It only wanted this to quench any little spark of pity and misgiving which the old count's judicious stratagem might have awakened. So without further loss of time the prince called to the magician to come forth and take the spoil.

He was not slow to comply, and taking a handful of the weird currency out of each mule-load, rang it on the rock, where it sounded like the clanking of a captive's chains.

"That is good," he said in a satisfied tone, when he had concluded his scrutiny. "Now for my part of the bargain. I am not of those who fail because I am paid beforehand. You will find me as good as my word, and even better, for I will supply an item of the bargain which you, impetuous youth, never thought to stipulate for, though the most important of all. I will not only instruct you how to see Floreta, I will give you, moreover, the means whereby, if she pleases you, you can take her captive and bear her away."

"Nay, interrupt me not," he continued, as Turian, nettled at the exposure of his want of diplomacy, was about to declare that he had never thought of any other means to captivate her being required but his own smile and his own strong arm. "I must begin, and have but time to complete my directions. You see yon castle on a rock out at sea;" and as his long bony finger pointed westward, there seemed to be traced against the sky the form of a royal castle at about three days' journey, which Turian, who had for ten days been beating about the coast, could have sworn was not to be seen there before. Nevertheless, fascinated by the magician's commanding manner, he dare say nothing but a murmur of assent.

"Then that is your haven. Take ship and steer for it. When you reach the land throw down this token," and he gave into his hand a fine coil of silken chains. "Follow its leadings till it take you to Floreta, and if she please you, cast it round her, and she is yours."

As he spoke he disappeared from sight, with the mules and their burden.

Turian now once more reminded Conde Dirlos of his father's command, and bid him provide him with the swiftest galley on all the coasts of the kingdom, manned with the stoutest rowers, and that with the utmost speed.

If the wise old count shrunk from the former mission, his horror was but the greater at this one. He reminded the prince that when the king had given his consent to the adventure, he had not contemplated any other than a loyal undertaking as such as a noble prince might entertain. He would never have trusted him on one of this nature.

Turian felt the force of the reproach, but lacked the strength of character to command himself. Hurried on by his uncontrolled desire, he bid the old man remember that the command to fulfil his orders was quite unconditional, and there was no limit whatever named.

The count owned that this was unfortunately true, and as he could prevail nothing by argument, set himself to remedy the Infante's headstrong wilfulness by making the journey as safe as possible. He not only insisted on having the galley examined as to its seaworthiness by the most experienced shipwrights, and selected the steadiest oarsmen to man the banks, but appointed a consultation of all the astronomers of the kingdom to name the day when they might be sure of safe passage, free from winds. It was pronounced that a storm was just then impending which would last ten days, and after that there would be ten days of fair weather, so that if they allowed ten days for their preparations, they would have time to make the journey and return in all security.

The delay seemed another age to the Infante. Nevertheless he was now so near the accomplishment of his object that it passed swiftly enough in the enjoyment of the pleasure of anticipation. The count, too, found some relief to his anxieties in the fact that the storm came on at the predicted moment, giving him great confidence that the halcyon days predicted to succeed might be surely counted on.

They came duly, and a shout of admiration rose from the people on the shore as the gallant vessel moved out over the face of the blue, sunlit waters, which glittered as if showered over with every precious stone at each stroke of the countless oars. And those on board were equally entranced with the gorgeous sight as they seemed to soar along over the soft bosom of the crystal deep. The noble outline of their native mountains, peak above peak, from the verdant slopes where the cattle browsed lazily, to the wild steeps where even the mountain goats ceased to find a footing, receded with ever-varying forms of beauty from their sight.

It was not on these that Turian's eye rested. His glance was bent on the castle for which they were making, and his thoughts were bound up in the beauteous treasure within. Such confidence had he in the magician's word, that he had laid his arms aside and held only the silken chain that was to be his guiding line to happiness. He toyed with it, thinking how he would throw it round the prized form of the portrait's original, and how he would gaze on her when she was his.

While he was still wrapped up in these thoughts they drew near to the mysterious shore, and everyone was occupied in admiring the strength and noble proportions of the castle. But Turian had no thought but for the treasure it contained. Springing lightly on to the land, he lost no time in fulfilling the magician's injunctions; and sure enough the chain uncoiled itself, and, wriggling with a serpent's motion, went straight before him to a gate in the castle wall. It was unlocked, and Turian, pushing it aside, gained entrance to a sumptuous garden, at one end of which was a shady arbour, and in a bank of perfumed roses Floreta herself lay asleep. How his heart beat at the sight! She was just as she had seemed in the portrait. She was just as he had pictured her in his sleeping and waking dreams. Riveted to the spot, he stood contemplating her, as well he might, for her complexion was white as snow, or rather as pure crystal, and tinted as the fresh rose yet on the rose-tree.

The cautious count, fearful of some ambush, had marshalled the crew of the galley into a guard to track his steps noiselessly and be ready in case of sudden attack. The play of light upon their arms passing in sudden reflection over the scene woke the Infante from his reverie, and roused him to action. The coiling silken links readily embraced Floreta's limbs, and such was their hidden power that, though she woke at the Infante's approach, she was powerless to resist or cry.

Thus he bore her to the galley, and the men having resumed their places on the rowers' banks, in silent order they pushed off unperceived by any one on the island, for it was the hour of the noontide rest.

But soon Floreta's maidens, coming to attend her rising, discovered her loss. The king her father and all the people quickly gathered their arms and ran wildly in every direction, till at last they saw the strange vessel making fast away, and they doubted not it was carrying off their princess, but they could only stand on the shore throwing up their arms and crying in powerless despair.

Turian had, in the meantime, removed the chain from his prize,; and thus freed from the spell, Floreta, too, held out her arms towards her parents and countrymen, and cried unavailingly on them for help. Turian, incapable of contradicting her, yet incapable also of giving her up, contented himself with admiring her at a distance, and let her spend herself in lamentations at first, but when the good galleon had put sufficient distance between itself and the castle to destroy the freshness of the impression of parting, the

Infante commanded his people to cast anchor that he might try his power of consoling her. And indeed, it was not long before his sweet words of admiration and his protestations of affection and devotion seemed to succeed in reconciling her to her situation. Before long they were very good friends and very happy, and the sun shone and the sea sparkled, and nature smiled, and all seemed fair and bright.

Nevertheless the prudent old count had his misgivings. True, there were yet several more days of the promised calm before them, but he felt he should never be easy till he had his charge safe at home again; so he urged the Infante to give orders to put under way once more, and right glad was he to feel the bark moving towards the port and in good time to reach home before the next storm.

Nevertheless...

Quando Dios quiere

En sereno lluve*,

...says the proverb, and while they were singing and making merry, and dancing to amuse Floreta, suddenly the sky became overcast and the wind sprang up, and the waves dashed against the bulwarks, and instead of being able to row the vessel into port the oarsmen could hardly keep their seats. Then in the midst of their fright and horror and piteous cries for help, an ancient seaman stood up, and having commanded silence, harangued the crew, and told them that they might be sure the tempest was sent them because they had the strange damsel on board. If they wanted to save their lives they must bid defiance to the Infante's wishes, and take her from him and cast her into the sea. The danger to all was manifest and terrible. Any way out of it was preferable to succumbing, so the old man found a willing audience. The dismayed count had but time to rush in to the Infante and tell him of the mutiny before the angry mariners had already burst into his presence. If they were for a moment staggered by pity at sight of the exceeding beauty of Floreta, and by Turian's agonized assurances that the fearful sacrifice would have no effect upon the storm, the old mariner's voice overruled their hesitation and rendered them pitiless as the blast.

Then at his command they tore the Infante from off Floreta, to whom he clung declaring that they should not destroy her without him, but that he would go down into the deep with her, and they bound him fast hand and foot and took Floreta, too full of terror to resist or cry, to throw her into the raging sea. But before they had completed the sacrifice, the cries of the prince, seconded as he was by the prudent old count, ever ready to second a middle course, prevailed, and instead of committing her to the deep, they set her on an island past which the bark was drifting, Turian thinking in his own mind that as soon as the fury of the storm was spent he should be able to induce them to put back and fetch her off.

The old seaman knew what was in his mind, and he knew that the work was but half done. He inveighed that the half-measure was useless. He predicted that the storm would not thereby be quenched. But it was too late to listen to him now:. They were carried past the land where Floreta was; and it was beyond their efforts to go back to fulfil his purpose now. Meanwhile, as he had predicted, the tempest raged higher and higher. The oarsmen were powerless, and the bark drifted nearer and nearer home, and at last, just as a great wave dashed against it and broke it up, they were brought just so near to land that they could swim to shore. One young and vigorous oarsman took charge of the old count, who was rendered more unfit for the feat by dismay at the ill-success of his mission even than by the weakness of his age. But none looked after the Infante, for he was known to be the best swimmer of all the country round about.

It was not till the hull had heeled over and gone down that they remembered they had bound him hand and foot, and he could not escape. And so he, who was the cause of all, alone was lost.

Mirandola está mirando

Que bien era de mirar;

Blanca es como la nieve

Y como lo claro cristal,

Colorada como la rosa

Y como rosa de rosal.

* If God so will, it may rain with a clear sky.

CLEVER MARIA

A story from the Portuguese, adapted from The Crimson Fairy Book by Andrew Lang, 1903.

THERE WAS ONCE A MERCHANT WHO lived close to the royal palace, and had three daughters. They were all pretty, but Maria, the youngest, was the prettiest of the three. One day the king sent for the merchant, who was a widower, to give him directions about a journey he wished the good man to take. The merchant would rather not have gone, as he did not like leaving his daughters at home, but he could not refuse to obey the king's commands, and with a heavy heart he returned home to say farewell to them. Before he left, he took three pots of basil, and gave one to each girl, saying, "I am going a journey, but I leave these pots. You must let nobody into the house. When I come back, they will tell me what has happened." "Nothing will have happened," said the girls.

The father went away, and the following day the king, accompanied by two friends, paid a visit to the three girls, who were sitting at supper. When they saw who was there, Maria said,

"Let us go and get a bottle of wine from the cellar. I will carry the key, my eldest sister can take the light, while the other brings the bottle."

But the king replied, "Oh, do not trouble; we are not thirsty."

"Very well, we will not go," answered the two elder girls; but Maria merely said, "I shall go, anyhow." She left the room, and went to the hall where she put out the light, and putting down the key and the bottle, ran to the house of a neighbour, and knocked at the door. "Who is there so late?" asked the old woman, thrusting her head out of the window.

"Oh, let me in," answered Maria. "I have quarrelled with my eldest sister, and as I do not want to fight any more, I have come to beg you to allow me to sleep with you."

So the old woman opened the door and Maria slept in her house. The king was very angry at her for playing truant, but when she returned home the next day, she found the plants of her sisters withered away, because they had disobeyed their father.

Now the window in the room of the eldest overlooked the gardens of the king, and when she saw how fine and ripe the medlars were on the trees, she longed to eat some, and begged Maria to scramble down by a rope and pick her a few, and she would draw her up again. Maria, who was good-natured, swung herself into the garden by the rope, and got the medlars, and was just making the rope fast under her arms so as to be hauled up, when her sister cried: "Oh, there are such delicious lemons a little farther on. You might bring me one or two." Maria turned round to pluck them, and found herself face to face with the gardener, who caught hold of her, exclaiming, "What are you doing here, you little thief?"

"Don"t call me names," she said, "or you will get the worst of it," giving him as she spoke such a violent push that he fell panting into the lemon bushes. Then she seized the cord and clambered up to the window.

The next day the second sister had a fancy for bananas and begged so hard, that, though Maria had declared she would never do such a thing again, at last she consented, and went down the rope into the king's garden. This time she met the king, who said to her, "Ah, here you are again, cunning one! Now you shall pay for your misdeeds."

And he began to cross-question her about what she had done. Maria denied nothing, and when she had finished, the king said again, "Follow me to the house, and there you shall pay the penalty." As he spoke, he started for the house, looking back from time to time to make sure that Maria had not run away. All of a sudden, when he glanced round, he found she had vanished completely, without leaving a trace of where she had gone. Search was made all through the town, and there was not a hole or corner which was not ransacked, but there was no sign of her anywhere. This so enraged the king that he became quite ill, and for many months his life was despaired of.

Meanwhile the two elder sisters had married the two friends of the king, and were the mothers of little daughters. Now one day Maria stole secretly to the house where her elder sister lived, and snatching up the children put them into a beautiful basket she had with her, covered with flowers inside and out, so that no one would ever guess it held two babies. Then she dressed herself as a boy, and placing the basket on her head, she walked slowly past the palace, crying as she went, "Who will carry these flowers to the king, who lies sick of love?"

And the king in his bed heard what she said, and ordered one of his attendants to go out and buy the basket. It was brought to his bedside, and as he raised the lid cries were heard, and peeping in he saw two little children. He was furious at this new trick which he felt had been played on him by Maria, and was still looking at them, wondering how he should pay her out, when he was told that the merchant, Maria's father, had finished the business on which he had been sent and returned home.

Then the king remembered how Maria had refused to receive his visit, and how she had stolen his fruit, and he determined to be revenged on her. So he sent a message by one of his pages that the merchant was to come to see him the next day, and bring with him a coat made of stone, or else he would be punished. Now the poor man had been very sad since he got home the evening before, for though his daughters had promised that nothing should happen while he was away, he had found the two elder ones married without asking his leave. And now there was this fresh misfortune, for how was he to make a coat of stone?

He wrung his hands and declared that the king would be the ruin of him, when Maria suddenly entered. "Do not grieve about the coat of stone, dear father; but take this bit of chalk, and go to the palace and say you have come to measure the king." The old man did not see the use of this, but Maria had so often helped him before that he had confidence in her, so he put the chalk in his pocket and went to the palace.

"That is no good," said the king, when the merchant had told him what he had come for.

"Well, I can't make the coat you want," replied he.

78

"Then if you would save your head, hand over to me your daughter Maria."

The merchant did not reply, but went sorrowfully back to his house, where Maria sat waiting for him.

"Oh, my dear child, why was I born? The king says that, instead of the coat, I must deliver you up to him."

"Do not be unhappy, dear father, but get a doll made, exactly like me, with a string attached to its head, which I can pull for "Yes" and "No.""

So the old man went out at once to see about it.

The king remained patiently in his palace, feeling sure that this time Maria could not escape him; and he said to his pages, "If a gentleman should come here with his daughter and ask to be allowed to speak with me, put the young lady in my room and see she does not leave it."

When the door was shut on Maria, who had concealed the doll under her cloak, she hid herself under the couch, keeping fast hold of the string which was fastened to its head.

"Senhora Maria, I hope you are well," said the king when he entered the room. The doll nodded. "Now we will reckon up accounts," continued he, and he began at the beginning, and ended up with the flower-basket, and at each fresh misdeed Maria pulled the string, so that the doll's head nodded assent.

"Who-so mocks at me merits death," declared the king when he had ended, and drawing his sword, cut off the doll's head. It fell towards him, and as he felt the touch of a kiss, he exclaimed, "Ah, Maria, Maria, so sweet in death, so hard to me in life! The man who could kill you deserves to die!" And he was about to turn his sword on himself, when the true Maria sprung out from under the bed, and flung herself into his arms. And the next day they were married and lived happily for many years.

WITHERED LEAVES

Adapted from Romantic Legends of Spain. and taken from the original story written by Gustavo Adolfo Bécquer, translated by Cornelia Francis Bates and Katherine Lee Bates, 1909.

THE SUN HAD SET. THE WHEELING masses of cloud were hastening to heap themselves one above another in the distant horizon. The cold wind of autumn evenings was whirling the withered leaves about my feet.

I was sitting by the side of a road [the road to the cemetery] where ever there return fewer than those who go.

I do not know of what I was thinking, if, indeed, I was just then thinking of anything at all. My soul was trembling on the point of soaring into space, as the bird trembles and flutters its wings before taking flight.

There are moments in which, thanks to a series of abstractions, the spirit withdraws from its environment and, self-absorbed, analyses and comprehends the mysterious phenomena of the inner life of man.

There are other moments in which the soul slips free from the flesh, loses its personality, mingles with the elements of nature, relates itself to their mode of being and translates their incomprehensible language.

In one of these latter moments was I, when, alone and in the midst of a clear tract of level ground, I heard talking near me.

The speakers were two withered leaves, and this, a little more or less exact, was their strange dialogue:

"Whence comest thou, sister?"

"I come from riding on the whirlwind, enveloped in the cloud of dust and of withered leaves, our companions, all the length of the interminable plain. And you?"

"I drifted for a time with the current of the river, until the strong south wind snatched me up from the mud and reeds of the bank."

"And where are you bound?"

"I don't know. Does, perhaps, the wind that drives me know?"

"Woe is me! Who would have said that we should end like this, faded and withered, dragging ourselves along the ground, we who lived clothed in colour and light, dancing in the air?"

Do you remember the beautiful days of our budding, that peaceful morning when, at the breaking of the swollen sheath which had served us for a cradle, we unfolded to the gentle kiss of the sun, like a fan of emeralds?"

"Oh, how sweet it was to be swayed at that height by the breeze, drinking in through every pore the air and the light!"

"Oh, how beautiful it was to watch the flowing water of the river that lapped the twisted roots of the ancient tree which sustained us, that limpid, transparent water, reflecting like a mirror the azure of the sky, so that we seemed to live suspended between two blue abysses!"

"With what delight we used to peep over the green foliage to see ourselves pictured in the tremulous stream!"

"How we would sing together, imitating the murmur of the breeze and following the rhythm of the waves!"

"Brilliant insects would flit about us, spreading their gauzy wings."

"And the white butterflies and blue dragon-flies, gyrating in strange circles through the air, would alight for a moment on our dentate edges to tell each other the secrets of that mysterious love lasting but an instant and burning up their lives."

"Each of us was a note in the concert of the groves."

"Each of us was a tone in their harmony of colour."

"In the silver nights when the moonbeams glided over the mountain tops, do you remember how we would chat in low voices amid the translucent shadows?"

"And we would relate in soft whispers stories of the sylphs who swing in the golden threads that the spiders hang from tree to tree."

"Until we hushed our murmurous speech to listen enraptured to the plaints of the nightingale, who had chosen our tree for her throne of song."

"And so sad and so tender were her lamenting strains that, though filled with joy to hear her, the dawn found us weeping."

"Oh, how sweet were those tears which the dew of night would shed upon us, and which would sparkle with all the colours of the rainbow in the first gleam of dawn!"

"Then came the jocund flock of linnets to pour into the grove life and sound with the gleeful, gay confusion of their songs."

"And one enamoured pair hung close to us their round nest of straws and feathers."

"We served to shelter the little ones from the troublesome rain-drops in the summer tempests."

"We served as a canopy to shield them from the fierce rays of the sun."

"Our life passed like a golden dream from which we had no thought there could be an awakening."

"One beautiful afternoon, when everything around us seemed to smile, when the setting sun was kindling the west and crimsoning the clouds, and from the earth, touched by the evening damp, were rising exhalations of life and the perfumes of flowers, two lovers stayed their steps on the river bank at the foot of our parent tree."

"Never will that memory fade! She was young, scarcely more than a child, beautiful and pallid. He asked her tenderly, 'Why do you weep?' 'Forgive this involuntary selfishness,' she replied, brushing away a tear; 'I weep for myself. I weep for the life which is slipping from me. When the sky is crowned with sunshine and the earth is clothed with verdure and flowers, and the wind is laden with perfumes, with the songs of birds and with far-off harmonies, and when one loves and feels herself beloved, life is good.' 'And why will you not live?' he insisted, deeply moved, clasping her hands close in his. 'Because I cannot. When these leaves, which whisper in unison above our heads, fall withered, I, too, shall die, and the wind will someday bear away their dust, and mine, to who knows where?'"

"I heard, and you heard, and we shuddered and were silent. We must wither! We must die, and be whirled about by the rushing wind! Mute and full of terror we remained even till nightfall. Oh, how terrible was that night!"

"For the first time the lovelorn nightingale failed at the tryst which she had enchanted with her mournful lays."

"Soon the birds flew away, and with them their little ones now clothed with plumage, and only the nest remained, rocking slowly and sadly, like the empty cradle of a dead child."

"And the white butterflies and the blue dragonflies fled, leaving their place to obscure insects which came to eat away our fibre and to deposit in our bosoms their nauseous larvae."

"Oh, and how we shivered, shrinking from the icy touch of the night frosts!"

We lost our colour and freshness."

"We lost our pliancy and grace, and what before had been to us like the soft sound of kisses, like the murmur of love words, now became a harsh, dry call, unwelcome, dismal."

"And at last, dislodged, we flew away."

"Trodden under foot by the careless passers-by, whirled incessantly from one point to another in the dust and the mire, I accounted myself happy when I could rest for an instant in the deep rut of a road."

"I have revolved unceasingly in the grip of the turbid stream, and in the course of my long travels I saw, alone, in mourning garb and with clouded brow, gazing absently upon the running waters and the withered leaves which shared and marked their movement, one of those two lovers whose words gave us our first presentment of death."

"She, too, has lost her hold on life, and perchance will sleep in an open, new-made grave over which I paused a moment."

"Ah, she sleeps and rests at last, but we, when shall we come to the end of our long journey?"

"Never! Even now the wind, which has given us a brief repose, blows once more, and I feel myself constrained to rise from the ground and follow. Adieu, sister!"

"Adieu!"

*

The wind, quiet for a moment, whistled again, and the leaves rose in a whirling confusion, to be lost afar in the darkness of the night.

And then there came to me a thought that I cannot remember and that, even if I were to remember it, I could find no words to say it.

THE GARDEN OF HEALTH

Adapted from Fairy Tales from Spain by José Muñoz Escámez, published by J. M. Dent & Sons Ltd, 1913.

A BOY OF TWELVE YEARS, NAMED Enrique, was taking a walk one day in the outskirts of his village. He was very sad because his little sister was ill and the doctors said she would soon die.

"Poor Luisa!" exclaimed the boy, sobbing. "So pretty and to have to leave this world so soon!"

Enrique sat down on some stones to weep over his sorrow, and there prayed to heaven for his sister's life. A goat, which was grazing near the spot, heard the sound of his lamentations and drawing near the disconsolate boy said, "Calm yourself and I will try and save Luisa."

"How?" asked Enrique, startled at hearing the goat speak.

"You have the remedy within reach of your hand. Look there, to the right in that spring, and you will see a ring which was left there and forgotten by the magician Agrajes. Put it on and ask to go to the Garden of Health, and immediately it will take you there. Ask there for the Blue Ivy whose juice will cure your sister, and if they deny it to you, use the ring and you will see."

"Ay, little goat, anything to please you. Will you tell me who you are?"

"Well, you can see: a goat with its horns and all."

"But goats don't speak, and you do."

"That is because I am a well-bred and compassionate goat. Anyway, I cannot tell you who I am. If you are grateful you will know. Meanwhile, don't lose time, and do what I tell you."

Enrique saw, indeed, a gold ring which was on the edge of the spring. He seized it and on it saw certain mysterious signs engraved.

He put it on the ring finger of his left hand and said in a loud voice: "To the Garden of Health."

Scarcely had he finished saying these words than a cloud descended and carried him through the air at lightning speed.

In a few minutes he found himself at the gates of a beautiful garden surrounded by a silver fence with golden ornaments. At the gate there were two maidens, one in white and the other in black. The one in white had a fresh and smiling face; the other was sad and taciturn. The former carried an apple in her hand, the latter bore a scythe.

"Who are you?" asked Enrique.

"I am Life," said the first.

"I am Death," replied the second in dismal tones.

"What have you come here for?" they asked the boy.

"I have come for a branch of Blue Ivy to cure my sister with."

"I cannot give it to you without the permission of this maiden," said Life, motioning towards Death.

"I will not permit it, because Luisa belongs to me. She is a prize which I will not give up," growled Death angrily.

Life smiled sadly and turning to Enrique said, "I cannot give you what you wish, but bear in mind that you can take it without my giving it to you."

"Well, then, I will enter, cost what it may," exclaimed the boy.

"You shall not enter alive," shouted Death, brandishing her scythe.

"Oh, yes, he will, if he is quick," said Life provoked. "Do not meddle with this boy who is mine for many years."

"We shall see now."

Enrique jumped over the threshold of the garden gate and Death dealt him a terrible blow with her scythe, which would have deprived him of existence if at that moment Life had not made him smell the apple which she held in her hand and which quite cured him.

So Enrique passed between Life and Death into the Garden of Health and once inside commenced his quest in order to see if he could find the famous ivy which was to cure his little sister. It was difficult to find it among so many and such different plants as filled that beautiful garden where there was a medicine for every illness; but Enrique was resolved to find it, and passed through, one after another, the avenues of trees which crossed the park of health in all directions.

"I am the Red Celery, that cures all chest diseases," said a highly coloured celery plant bowing to Enrique.

"And I am the Spanish Onion, that cures the kidneys."

"And I am the Valerian, that cures the nerves."

"And I this, and I the other," cried the other plants and trees.

"That's enough!" shouted Enrique, "otherwise you will drive me mad."

"I cure madness," cried a shrub from the bottom of the garden.

"What I want is the Blue Ivy," exclaimed the boy.

"Here I am," cried the plant alluded to, "but I am kept closely guarded."

Enrique searched everywhere, without ascertaining where the precious plant was, but he always seemed to hear the noise in different places.

The trees laughed at Enrique's despair.

"And who keeps you so hidden?" said Enrique, stopping still for a moment.

"Death hides me in order that you may not find me. You have passed near and have not seen me. Your sister will die if you cannot find me."

Enrique now did not know what to do, until he presently remembered his ring.

"Ring of Agrajes, I want to see the Blue Ivy," he exclaimed.

Instantly he saw, within reach of his hand, a lovely ivy that, clinging to an oak, displayed beautiful leaves to the winds.

"Do not cut me now," cried the Ivy, "because your sister is going to die, and you will not arrive in time. Death is now close to her bedside."

"Ring of Agrajes," exclaimed Enrique at once, "bring Death to me tied up."

Hardly had he finished saying it than Death appeared quite dishevelled, without her scythe, her elbows tied together like a criminal. All the health-giving plants began to applaud.

"Bravo, bravo!" they cried.

"Don't spare her; she is our enemy!" shouted some.

"Don't let her go, and the world will be grateful to you!" said others.

"What have you done to my sister?" said Enrique, angrily.

"Nothing yet, but as soon as you let me go you will see," answered Death.

"Well, if you wait until you are free before killing her, my little sister will die of old age. Ring, give this shameful woman a thrashing."

Immediately a number of sticks came through the air and commenced to bestow a fine thrashing upon Death.

The latter screamed like a mouse whose tail has been trodden on, and heaped insults on the boy, threatening to kill him as soon as she was free.

"Do not spare her!" said Enrique at each insult.

And the blows again descended on Death like rain. One knocked an eye out, another knocked all her teeth out, although it must be

91

admitted they were false, and another took her hair out by the roots, leaving her head quite bald.

Then Enrique cut a sprig of the Ivy and said to the ring, "Take me to my sister's side."

Immediately he found himself at the bedside, where all the family were weeping over the approaching death of the girl.

"Here is something which will cure my little sister," said the boy.

And drawing near her, he squeezed into her mouth the juice of the fresh ivy he had plucked in the Garden of Health.

The girl at once opened her eyes and called her mother, and, amidst the general surprise, asked to be dressed.

The family would not do so until the doctor said that indeed she was well and sound. They all complimented Enrique enthusiastically, until at length the boy said, "All this is due to a goat, and I must go and thank her."

He went to the same place where he had met the goat, but did not see her. In vain he ran about in all directions. But he had not got the ring of Agrajes for nothing.

"Ring," he said, "bring me the goat that was here a short time ago."

And the goat appeared.

"What do you want of me, Enrique?" asked the animal.

"To thank you, and to ask how I may serve you," answered Enrique.

"I see that you are grateful, and I wish you to know who I am. I am called Atala, and am the daughter of Agrajes, the magician. I put my father's ring beside you with the object that you might be able to save your sister."

"I should like to know you in your real form and not in that of a goat."

"Well, here I am," exclaimed Atala.

And thereupon she transformed herself into a lovely girl of more or less Enrique's age.

How pretty you are!" exclaimed the boy. "Come home and play with my little sister, who is now quite well, thanks to you."

"I can deny you nothing while you wear this ring," answered the girl.

"No, take it, I beg of you."

Atala disappeared at once, and when Enrique thought she had gone never to return, she reappeared smiling, and said, "I have been for a moment to ask my father's permission to accompany you."

They went to Enrique's house together, and he introduced her to his parents as Luisa's saviour. They fêted her with cakes and sweets, and on saying good-bye she promised to come back every afternoon to play with her little friends.

One day Agrajes himself visited Enrique's home, to make the acquaintance of the family of which his daughter spoke so much, and as he was about to leave he touched in a special way an old chest. "Open it, presently," he said on saying farewell.

On opening it the family found it full to the brim of gold coins. On it there was a paper which said, "A present from Agrajes to two very nice children."

With that money Enrique followed his career and Luisa had a splendid dowry, and with that and the love of their parents and friends they were two very happy beings.

JUANITA THE BALD, OR, A DAUGHTER'S LOVE

Adapted from Patranas; or Spanish Stories by Rachel Harriette Busk, published by Newbery and Harris, 1870.

THERE LIVED ONCE UPON A TIME on the banks of the Tagus a poor shepherd named Juan, and he was as honest as he was poor, and as contented as he was honest. He had just enough wages to buy the coarse meal which supported him and his hard-working wife, Consolacion. A zamarra, or suit of rough sheepskin, which served to keep out the cold for several years together, was afforded him from the flock, and with weaving and knitting Consolacion provided the rest of their scanty wardrobe.

Now Juan had a large flock confided to his care, and his master reposed entire trust in him, but if he never had the provocation of being looked after, neither had he ever the satisfaction of being praised. Yet, notwithstanding this lack of all earthly stimulus, Juan was always faithful to his trust. No sheep ever strayed that he did not seek out over the barren waste and the steep mountain-side. No little lamb was ever left by any sad accident without its dam, but he brought it home to Consolacion, and the honest pair reared it as tenderly as if it had been their own infant.

But if Juan's master neglected to commend his integrity, there was One who did not forget him, but kept a just account of all his actions. Thus it chanced one day, when after a long drought the herbage was dried up, and he had had endless trouble in keeping his flock together, as the poor things would wander here and there while seeking pasture, that eventually he got led away far from home, along a wild path he had never trodden before. The country all around him looked strange, and yet there was the track of his runaway sheep before him, so on and on he went. The way was sandy, and the sun was fierce, and at last his strength failed him. Footsore and dispirited he sank down at the foot of a tree, whose shelter he vainly sought, as its foliage had long been burnt up by the parching sun, and only the bleached trunk and thirsty branches remained. Half maddened with thirst and heat, he fell into a sort of trance, and he thought he saw an ancient hermit of severe aspect standing before him, who scolded him for lying there taking his rest while his master's sheep were astray, calling him only a zagal (or shepherd's helper).

Juan did not lose his temper at the reprimand, but meekly begged forgiveness, and endeavoured to rise that he might get upon his way again. His strength failed him, however, and he sank once more upon the ground. Then, in the place of the hermit, he saw before him a beautiful child with a shepherd's crook in his hand, and carrying a lamb in his bosom, who told him to be comforted, for he had found his sheep, and fed them, and led them safely home to the fold. He commended too his faithful service, and told him that he was come to offer him a reward, and gave him the choice of three. The first was a large sum of money, with which he could go down to one of the rich seaports of Spain and trade. The second was a grand castle in the mountains, where he would have ease and luxury and plenty of retainers to do his bidding. The third was to retain his present humble condition, while to his hearth was added the presence of a gentle daughter.

Then honest Juan did not hesitate which to choose. "Give me not money," said he, "for money begets covetousness. Give me not power, for I was not born to it, and the proverb of our forefathers says, A fallen rich man may make a good master, but not an enriched poor man. But give me, oh, give me a child to love me in my old age! I am but a poor, worthless servant to ask this thing. Nevertheless, it is the bounty of God."

When Juan woke to consciousness, the great heat of the day had passed away, and his shaggy dog was licking his face, as if to warn him that he had but little time to get home before dark. Trusting to the animal's sagacity for guidance, he soon found his way home, where the sheep were safely folded, as the beautiful shepherd-child had promised, and Consolacion was waiting on the threshold of the hut, to welcome him home to supper.

To his other virtues Juan added humility, and, indeed, without it they would have been of little value, and it seemed so much like vanity to talk of his vision that he never mentioned a word of it, till it slipped off his tongue unawares years after. Nevertheless, before the year was done, a dear little baby was found in Consolacion's arms, completing their simple happiness.

Juanita was beautiful, as a child of promise should be, but her chief glory was the rich profusion of waving hair which covered her like a veil, and rested gracefully on the ground as she knelt in prayer. She grew up the joy of her parents, and being very docile soon learnt all the domestic arts of her mother, and was never so happy as when she was relieving her of her household cares. If they had anything to complain of with her it was that she had quite a passion for admiring her beautiful hair, and when she was sent to the fountain she would sometimes waste hours looking at herself, and arranging it according to various fancies. But when her mother looked grave on her return, it was quite sufficient to keep her from offending so again for many days.

Thus many years of tranquil, homely joy passed away. Peace and gladness is not of long continuance in this world for the good, and Juan's time of trouble was at hand. First, it pleased Providence to take Consolacion to Himself. Then, as a result of much weeping over her, and his great privations and long exposure to sun and weather, his eyes grew dim, and then his sight failed him entirely. Then the old dog, by whose help he still managed to keep the sheep together, in spite of his blindness, died too. Juan was of no use any longer as a shepherd, and he had nothing left to him but Juanita. Juanita, it is true, fulfilled all a daughter's part, and by her industry supported him above actual want.

But her little head was always running on how his sight could be regained, and one day she revealed the result of her cogitations. "Father dear, do not all the wise people live in great cities? Let us now get us down to prosperous Segovia, or noble Toledo, or beautiful Sevilla, and let us find some of the cunning healers of whom we have heard, and get you back your sight."

But Juan lacked the courage to undertake so great a journey and expose his little daughter to all the attendant risks by the way, and he was a man of great patience to endure what the Lord sent. So they remained in the mountain-hut for five years more. By that time Juanita was fifteen, and quite a little woman, and her advice began to have the weight of a woman's authority with her father, and at last she got him to consent to her often-urged prayer that they should journey to seek a doctor.

Juanita's ears had been ever open to learn every story of healing from every traveller who chanced to pass their cottage, and in this way she had learnt of the fame of a certain accomplished mediciner, who dwelt at Toledo, and to Toledo therefore she was bent on directing their steps.

A beautiful sight it was to see the venerable old man leaning his hand, withered with honest labour, on the silken tresses of his courageous child. The way was long, but there was no lack of hospitality. The admiration of the peasants they passed was everywhere kindled by Juan's patience and Juanita's devotion, and a bite and a sup never failed them. At last they came to Toledo, and in a great city it was not so easy to find shelter, but God warmed to them the heart of an old woman who had herself suffered and learnt compassion by suffering. She gave them a bed, and Juanita's busy fingers, before long, provided means of subsistence.

Her next care was to make out the doctor, which was not of the easiest, as those of his ilk were scarcely tolerated, and did not care to make themselves known too publicly. However, a daughter's love overcomes all obstacles, and at last she found the means to bring her father before the wise man. Imagine her joy, when after all her labours, he pronounced with confidence that he could restore her father's sight! Her a moment of joy turned into a year's worth of anxiety, however. In another minute she learned that he would demand 500 maravedis for the cure!

"Abate something for charity? What! Charity to a dog of a peasant! Why, it is enough that I soil my fingers with healing him, but to forego my pitiful fee too? Never! By the Holy City, never!"

Juanita could speak no word more for tears. In silence she placed her father's hand on her glittering hair, and in sadness guided his weak footsteps back to their poor shelter.

Hard work it had been to provide subsistence for them both, and to make a little extra to have something to offer to the lone widow, who had taken them in, but how could she ever hope to make up 500 maravedis? If in the first days of their arrival she had wasted some precious hours over her old favourite pastime of arranging her luxuriant tresses, and had taken pleasure when people called out in admiration, well, all that was gone by now. She sat at her little loom and worked, worked, worked! She never took her hands off, never lifted her eyes, never even saw that the barber who lived opposite was constantly gazing upon her. The only thing to cheer her was the placid voice of Juan, who would continually bid her be of good comfort and put her trust in God.

One day, in the midst of her toil, there came a messenger from the Corregidor of the city. His aunt had died that day, and as she died unmarried, a procession of girls equal in number to the years of her life must follow her to the grave, draped in white. She numbered eighty years, and Juanita was required to make up the eightieth attendant. Juanita could not say "Nay," even though it cost her such precious hours.

When she came into the hall where the mourners were assembled she found to her no slight disgust that the dress she had to wear consisted in part of a great white hood. It was hard, on the only day she suffered herself to part from her work, to have to cover up her glorious hair! At all events, till the procession began to move she would throw it back. She did so, and it made her look the picture of an angel, as it fell in rich curls over the white dress. At the same moment the Corregidor's wife passed through the hall. Though younger than her defunct sister-in-law she had arrived at that age when nature sometimes thinks it right to withdraw her gift of hair, and sorely did she lament the loss. For a long time past she had left an order with a clever barber of the city to manufacture her a wig which should make good the defect, and he was to swear it was no dead person's hair. She had a superstition that in wearing the hair of a dead person, you assumed the responsibility of all their sins, and, the good lady being sufficiently satisfied with her own position in the scale of grace, had no desire to run the risk of getting a worse one, even for the sake of the coveted wig. But a wig made of the hair of a living person was not an order easy to execute. The moment her eyes fell on Juanita's magnificent cabellera (head of hair) she determined that it should not be long before it should decorate her own head.

Accordingly, she hastened to call the Corregidor aside and assure him he must procure it for her. The Corregidor knowing the attachment a maiden was likely to have for such an adornment, endeavoured to convince her of the impossibility of the task. All was of no use, save to render her more resolute. The Corregidor knew that in disputes with his wife he always had to give in at last, and so, to pacify her, promised he would do his best, and to satisfy her that he did so the interview was arranged to take place in her presence.

The funeral was no sooner over than the Corregidor beckoned Juanita to follow him into his wife's room.

Poor little Juanita never thought of resisting an order from so great a functionary, but tripped along lightly behind him.

What was her surprise to find herself severely scolded for wasting the time she might spend in working for her father in the vanity of decking out her hair! Juanita did not grow angry, or deny her fault, but could not forbear asking, with great simplicity, "Was it her fault if God had given her a great mass of hair to comb out?"

"Not your fault at all, my dear child," said the Corregidor, much relieved to find she took his admonitions so meekly. "Not your fault at all, so long as you keep it on your head; but you might cut it all off."

"Cut it off!" repeated poor Juanita, mechanically; "what would be the use of that?"

"Why, you might sell it, child. I myself would give you fifty maravedis for it."

"Give me fifty maravedis for it!" exclaimed the child, wondering what he could possibly want it for.

The Corregidor, fancying her surprise was dictated by indignation at the smallness of his offer, and incited by a gesture from his wife, impatient lest she should lose the prize, hastened to reply, "Well, if that does not content you, I'll give you 100 maravedis."

But Juanita's astonishment only increased, so she stared at him instead of answering.

"I'd even say 150," continued the Corregidor.

But Juanita only looked the more surprised. And so they went on, his anxiety bidding against her bewilderment, till at last he got up to 500 maravedis!

"500 maravedis!" echoed the child, as if waking from a trance at the words which brought back to memory the fee required to restore her father's sight. "Oh, yes! give me 500 maravedis, it is all yours at that!" And then the thought of her great loss made her burst into a flood of tears. It was a thought which for a moment almost overpowered her strong sense of filial piety, and in the depth of her little heart she half wished the Corregidor would repent of his bargain. But no such luck. At her first sign of yielding the lady had run off to fetch her largest scissors, and in a trice she had begun shearing at the glittering spoil. Down the bright silken masses fell on the snowy drapery, and beside them fell the child's pearly tears over her lost treasure. At last the sacrifice was complete; and poor Juanita stood in the midst of the ruin more dead than alive.

Then the Corregidor counted into her lap the promised sum, and the reckoning once more woke a sensation of joy. Wrapping her hood close round her, Juanita lost not a moment in flying to conduct her father to the house of the doctor.

Her thoughts were now entirely fixed on the moment of his restoration, but even this thought was embittered by the reflection that his one reason for desiring to have his sight back was to look on her, and she was no longer what she had been!

The strange alteration in her appearance soon got whispered about among the neighbours, and she got so much stared at that she never ventured into the street but when forced by sheer necessity, and then she ran along, looking neither to the right hand nor the left, and not even perceiving how considerately her opposite neighbour the barber followed her steps, and defended her from the rudeness of the street boys.

At last her father's tedious cure was completed, and she was admitted to see him. Someone had, unperceived by her, followed her respectfully all the way, ready to protect her at all hazards. In the zaguan (sort of vestibule) of the Doctor's house this faithful follower confronted her, and she recognized the gallant barber at once. Gently pushing back her hood he substituted another covering for her head. Juanita put up her hand, and, to her surprise, found it tangled in the masses of her own rich hair! She stroked it with both hands, and found it all there, just as if by enchantment. Finding her dumb with astonishment, the barber hastened to explain that the wife of the Corregidor having sent the hair to him to make up, he had resolved no one should wear it but herself, and for the Corregidora he had put together the best match he could from the store he kept by him for such purposes.

They were now interrupted by a summons from the doctor, who was ready to remove Juan's bandages. They no sooner reached the room where he was, than he ran and clasped Juanita in his arms, exclaiming, "God be praised that I can see you, my child. A few years' blindness are well repaid when it is reserved to one to see such a daughter as you!" Then, perceiving the barber, he embraced him too, and said, "God be praised for my sight, since I can now work for my living again, and repay you, my benefactor, for well I know, though I would never tell Juanita to increase her burden, that it is you who have paid the rent of our lodging all this time! My son, my dear son, what can I do for you?"

"There is one thing, father, you can do for me. One only thing, but it is too great to ask!"

"Nothing is too great today. Ask away, boy, never fear!"

The barber looked towards Juanita to gain courage, and, seeing her approving smile, fell on his knees and begged Juan to let him marry her.

"With all my heart, if the wench so will," replied the old man. "I cannot see her wedded to a more honest fellow!"

Juan was not slow to read in her eyes what her sentiments were, and so, without more ado, he took the hand of each to place them in one another. But both drew back. The barber, with all his charity and delicacy and taste, was very ugly, and he could not believe in his good fortune; and Juanita had one condition to lay down first. "How now! what's this?" said the father. "Come, friend barber, explain yourself."

"Well, sir, I think it is but fair to give Juanita time to consider it all. I know I'm not so good-looking as her husband ought to be. Long ago should I have told her how I loved her but for this, but I dared not! I longed to offer the 500 maravedis over and over again, but I dared not speak to her; and now the joy is all so strange I feel I must not hurry her."

"Well spoken, young man! but, Juanita, what do you hang back for?"

"I…I have one little condition to make;" and she turned to the barber. "I have been thinking that we have not acted quite honestly with the Corregidora. She has a superstition against wearing dead people's hair, and she has paid honourably for that of a living person. So, what she has bought must be taken back to her. Moreover, I recognize that all my life this hair has been a snare to me, and whenever I have been led from the path of duty it has been by its means, so I am resolved never to wear it again, and to be known in future by no other name but that of Juanita the Bald! What say you, are you content to marry me now?"

The honest barber, perhaps on the whole not very sorry for a stipulation which put them somewhat nearer on a condition of equality in regard to personal appearance, only answered by clasping her in his embrace.

"What! What is all this," fell in the old man, "about hair and the Corregidora, and Juanita the...the Bald eh?" Then the barber was obliged to explain to him the sacrifice Juanita had made, first to obtain his cure, and again to her sense of honour, and her delicacy of conscience. The old man was quite unnerved by the recital. At first he was determined to resist her resolution, but his own mind was too well regulated not to acknowledge on reflection that she had chosen the good part.

Then, after blessing solemnly, both her and her betrothed, he exclaimed, "Did I not choose rightly from among the three gifts?" (in his humility he would not say rewards). "If I had chosen riches, they would have burst the bag and run away. And if I had chosen power, my retainers would have mocked my want of knowledge, and forsaken me. But a daughter's love? What can compare with it?"

THE UGLY PRINCESS

Adapted from Charles Sellers' original, taken from Tales from the Lands of Nuts and Grapes, published in 1888 by The Leadenhall Press and others.

THERE WAS ONCE A KING WHO had an only daughter, and she was so very ugly and deformed that, when she rode through the streets of Alcantara, the children ran away, thinking she was a witch.

Her father, however, thought her the most lovely creature in his kingdom; and as all the courtiers agreed with him, and the Court poet was always singing her praises, the princess believed what most princesses like to believe. As she was expecting a prince from a distant country, who was coming expressly to marry her, she had ordered many rich dresses which only made her look uglier.

The city of Alcantara was ready to receive Prince Alanbam, who was going to marry the Princess Altamira.

Crowds thronged the streets, martial music was heard everywhere, and in the public square a splendid throne had been erected for the king, Princess Altamira, and Prince Alanbam.

Around the throne were formed large bodies of well-equipped cavalry, dark visaged warriors clad in white and gold, and mounted on superb Arab steeds.

Behind the king, on his left side, stood the royal barber with his retinue of apprentices; and on his right side was seen Nabó the headsman, a man of gigantic stature, with his implement of office, an axe, slung over his shoulder.

Seated on the steps of the throne were a number of musicians, and below these a guard of honour, composed of foot soldiers dressed in short vests, called "aljubas," and wide lower garments, and with their aljavas, or quivers, full of bright arrows.

From the throne the king could see the splendid bridge on six pillars, built by Trajan, along which a brilliant cavalcade was proceeding, namely, the procession formed by Prince Alanbam and his retainers.

As soon as the prince, after saluting the king, beheld the princess, he turned pale, for he had never seen anyone so ugly; and however much he might have desired to keep up an appearance of courtesy to the princess before her father's subjects, he could not kiss her as she expected him to do, nor could he be persuaded to occupy the chair reserved for him beside the princess.

"Your mercy," said he, addressing the king, "must excuse my insuperable bashfulness; but the fact is that the Princess Altamira is so transcendently beautiful, and so dazzling to behold, that I can never expect to look upon her face again and live."

The king and the princess were highly flattered; but as Prince Alanbam continued to be obdurate in his professions of bashfulness, they started to feel somewhat vexed, and at last the king said in a loud voice, "Prince Alanbam, we fully appreciate the motive that prompts your conduct, but the fact is the Princess Altamira is present to be wedded to you; and, as a Christian king, the first of my line, I desire to lead to the altar my only daughter, Princess Altamira, and her affianced husband, Prince Alanbam."

"It cannot be," said the prince. "I would rather marry someone less beautiful. Sir king, forgive me if I annoy you, but I will not be wedded to so much beauty."

The king was now incensed beyond measure, and the princess his daughter, thinking to spite Prince Alanbam, said, "With your permission, royal father, since I am too beautiful for a prince, I will be married to the most learned man in your kingdom - Bernardo, the royal barber."

"And that you shall," said the king; but, on turning round to speak to the barber, he found that this the most learned man in his kingdom was all of a tremble, as if dancing to the music of St. Vitus.

"What has possessed you, caitiff?" asked the king. "Do you. Not understand the honour that is to be conferred on you?"

"My royal master," muttered the poor frightened man of learning and lather, "I can no more avail myself of the honour which you would confer on me than the Archbishop of Villafranca could. His grace is bound to celibacy, and I am already married."

Now, the barber had on many occasions rendered himself obnoxious to Sanchez, the royal cobbler, who, seeing the king's perplexity, and a chance of avenging past insults, exclaimed,

"Royal master, it would be most acceptable to your subjects that so much beauty should be wedded to so much learning. Our good friend, Bernardo, was, it is true, married; but since he has been in attendance at the palace, he has so fallen in love with Princess Altamira that he no longer notices his wife. Therefore, may it please your mercy to dissolve the first marriage, and announce this new one with her highness, your daughter?"

The barber became so infuriated that he rushed blindly at the cobbler, and with his razor would have severed his head from the rest of his body, but he was prevented by the guard, who held him down.

"Executioner, do your work!" cried the baffled king; and at one blow the head of the unfortunate barber rolled on the ground.

Prince Alanbam seeing this, and fearing that more mischief might ensue, proposed to the king that one hundred knights should be chosen, and that these should fight for the hand of the lovely Princess Altamira. "I myself will enter the lists," said the prince; "and the survivor will be rewarded by marrying your daughter."

"That is a good idea," said the king; and calling together ninety-nine of his best knights, he bade them fight valiantly, for their reward was very precious.

Fifty knights, mounted on beautiful chargers, placed themselves on one side, and were opposed by forty-nine equally well-mounted knights and Prince Alanbam. At the word of command, given by the king, they advanced at headlong speed against each other; but, much to the astonishment of the spectators, not a single knight was unhorsed. It seemed that each knight did his utmost to get run through by his opponent.

They went at it all again and again, but with the same result, for no man was hurt, although seeming to court death.

"We will alter the order of things," exclaimed the king. "The knight who is first wounded shall be the one to marry the princess."

This was no sooner said than the knights seemed to be possessed of a blind fury, and at the first charge nearly every knight was unhorsed and every one wounded, while the confusion and noise were awful. They all accused each other of being the first wounded. In utter despair, the king declared his daughter should be married to the Church, enter a convent, and thus hide her transcendent beauty.

"No, father," exclaimed the ugly princess; "I will get a husband; and if in all the states of Spain no one be found worthy enough to be my husband, I will leave Spain for ever. There is a country where the day never dawns, and night is eternal. There will I go; for in the dark, as all cats are grey, so are all degrees of beauty brought to one common level. I now know that it is just as unfortunate to be too beautiful as it is to be very ugly."

Having delivered herself of this speech, Princess Altamira bade the king, her father, good-bye, and was on the point of leaving the royal presence, when the handsome figure of Felisberto, the blind fiddler, was seen to approach.

"Princess," exclaimed blind Felisberto, "to Spain nothing is denied. You speak of proceeding to the North, where the day never dawns, in search of a husband. You need but look at me to behold one to whom night and day, extreme ugliness and transcendent beauty, are alike; and since all are so bashful that they will not marry you, allow me, fair princess, to offer you my services as a husband. In my world 'handsome is that handsome does.'"

111

The king was so pleased with the blind fiddler's speech that he immediately made him a Grandee of Spain, and acknowledged him as his son-in-law elect.

STARVING JOHN THE DOCTOR

Adapted from Patranas; or Spanish Stories by Rachel Harriette Busk, published by Newbery and Harris, 1870.

NO ONE WAS EVER MORE APPROPRIATELY named than 'Starving John.' He had nothing to live upon, yet he had a wife and a whole tribe of children to support. How to feed them all he knew not, and as for himself it was seldom enough he got a morsel to eat.

One day the cat caught a hare, and John's wife managed to take it from him, and having made a savoury mess of it, she put it into a wallet and said to John, "Here, take this hato, it's a lucky taste of something nice, such as you don't often get, and go out into the fields with it before those sharks of children snatch it out of your mouth."

John, who was ready to die of hunger, didn't wait to be told twice, but set off running as fast as his legs would carry him. At last he came to an olive-grove and there, making an easy-chair of a hollow olive-tree, he sat down to eat his hare, as happy as a king.

Somehow however - he could never tell how - there suddenly stood before him a dreadful old woman, all dressed in black. She had sunken eyes as dull as a blown-out candle, or a lamp-wick when the oil fails. Her skin was as withered and yellow as a Simancas parchment and her mouth was as dry as a clothes-basket. Her nose I don't know how to describe, for she had no nose at all to speak of.

"A pretty figure this to fall from heaven, like God's rain, on a poor fellow!" said John to himself, but as he was polite and hospitable, as a Spanish peasant always is, he nevertheless asked if she would share his meal.

This was just what the old creature wanted. Down she sat, and at once attacked the hare heto. But it was not like ordinary eating. This was a regular devouring, and, before you could say Jack Robinson, she had stowed away the whole mess between her heart and her shoulders!

John was too polite to grumble out aloud, but he said to himself, "Why, the children had better have had the hare than this old hag! but then nothing really goes right with the unlucky ones.

When his visitor had finished her meal, not leaving so much as the tail of the hare in, she exclaimed, "Do you know, John, your hare was very good!"

"So I see," said John, who could not repress a little bitterness. And he added, ironically, in honour of her decrepit appearance, "May your honour live a thousand years!"

"So I shall," answered the hag; "I have lived many thousands already, for I have to tell you I am no less a person than Death!"

John gave a start, and was like one struck dumb at this announcement.

"Don't be afraid, John," she continued, "I don't want to hurt you; and what is more, as you have treated me so well, I'll give you a good counsel in return. Make yourself a doctor. There's nothing like it for making money!"

"I am much obliged to you, Mistress Death," answered John, very respectfully, "but it will be quite return enough, if you'll promise to leave me alone for a good number of years. As to being a doctor, I've no notion how to set about it. I know neither Latin nor Greek. I can't write because my hand is palsied, and I can't read because I hate poring over those little black figures!"

"Go along with you, you silly fellow!" answered Mrs. Death; "you don't suppose any of this is necessary? It's I who lead the doctors, not they me. You are not such a goose as to think I go and come because they hiss me or call me, are you? When I get tired of any one, I take him by the ear and drag him off, doctor or no doctor. When the world began there were no doctors, and men lived to a good old age. But since they invented doctors there have been no more Methuselahs! You make yourself a doctor, as I advise you. If you are perverse and obstinate, I'll carry you off with me, more surely than the clock! Don't prate!" she added, as she saw he was going to urge some objection. "This is all you have to do; when they call you into a bed-room look out for me. If you see me standing at the head of the bed, you'll know it's all up. You have only to say so, and they'll find you're a wise prophet. If, on the other hand, you don't see me, you have only to prescribe a dose of clean water, with anything harmless you like in it, and the sick person will recover."

115

With that the ugly old lady took herself off, curtseying like a French dancing-mistress.

"I hope your worship won't forget, Mistress Death, what I asked you!" John cried after her. "Your worship won't visit me again for a long time to come, eh?"

"Don't be afraid, John," she answered, as she disappeared, "until your house crumbles to pieces you won't have a visit from me."

John returned home to his wife, and told her all that had happened, and his wife, being sharper than he, determined to make use of Mrs. Death's advice, and in spite of his remonstrances spread about everywhere the news that her husband was a famous doctor. She told everyone that he had only to look at a patient to tell whether he would live or die.

All the neighbours, however, only laughed at the idea of Starving John turning doctor in his old age, and called him "Don John" in ridicule.

One Sunday they went so far as to arrange a practical joke to show off his ignorance. A number of girls were to sit round a basket of figs, as they often did of a holiday afternoon in the fruit season, when, all of a sudden, one of them was to give a terrible cry as if taken ill, and some of the others were to carry her off to bed, while the rest ran for Starving John the Doctor.

John had no great faith in Mrs. Death's promises, and was loath to expose himself to the ridicule of the girls, but at his wife's urging he went along with them. Lo and behold, he no sooner entered the room of the pretended patient, than he saw Mrs. Death herself standing at the head of the bed! "The girl is very ill indeed. Too ill for me to save. She'll die before night!" pronounced John, in a knowing tone. And he went home amid the laughter of the assembled neighbours, who knew what the girls were playing at. But it so happened that the unfortunate girl had been eating the fruit too freely and she was taken ill and died that very night!

As you will readily guess, this made Starving John's fortune.

Far or near, there was no patient slightly or dangerously ill to whom he was not called and fees flowed in like rain. No longer was he dressed in rags. His clothes were properly made by a tailor. Instead of his pinched, woebegone look, his face grew as ruddy as the sun, and his withered hands, as smooth as pork-sausages. His shaking legs became as firm as marble columns; and his empty stomach assumed dimensions to vie with the dome of a church. For his children he bought honourable employments, and badges of office to sew on in front, and keys of office to hang out behind.

But what he spared least of all was the money required to keep his house in good repair. He even salaried a bricklayer, whose business it was to see there was never so much as a tile loose, remembering that Mrs. Death had said she would never come to visit him till his house crumbled to pieces.

Years rolled by as John's fortune increased, but prosperous years always roll away fast; and there came less fortunate years. First his hair fell off, and then he lost his teeth. Then his spine got curved like a reaping-hook, and then he grew halt in one of his legs.

One day, when he was ill, Mrs. Death sent him a bat, with her compliments, to inquire after him, but John didn't like the look of the creature, and drove it away. After that he had a cough and Mrs. Death sent an owl, to say she would come and see him very soon, and John drove him away too. After that he had a fit and Mrs. Death sent a dog, to give him to understand, by howling at his door, that she was on her way, and John drove him away also. But

117

he got ill for all that, and then he got worse, and then Mrs. Death knocked at the door, so John hobbled out of bed, and locked it and put up the bar, but Death contrived to creep in under the door.

"Mrs. Death!" said John, indignantly, "this isn't fair. You told me you wouldn't come so long as my house was not crumbling to pieces."

"Oh!" answered Death, "isn't your body your house, and hasn't that been crumbling to pieces? Didn't your strength fail first, and then your hair, and then your teeth, and then your limbs. Haven't they all been crumbling away?"

"I certainly didn't understand you so!" answered John, dolefully, "and relying on your word, then your coming now takes me by surprise."

"That is your fault, John," answered Death. "Men ought to be always prepared for my coming, and then I should never take them by surprise."

THE CAPTAIN'S EXPLOIT

Adapted from Fairy Tales from Spain by José Muñoz Escámez, published by J. M. Dent & Sons Ltd, 1913.

"WHAT RUINS ARE THOSE WHICH ARE to be seen on the top of that ridge?" asked a genteel Captain of the policeman of a village.

"The accursed ruins!" answered the first authority of the village with extreme terror. "Many years ago," he said, "there used to be a fine castle there, inhabited by a feudal lord who was more avaricious than anybody in the world before. There stands his statue amidst the rubbish, and terrible stories are told about it which frighten all the neighbours.

"In the archives of the town several curious documents are kept, and if your worship, Sir Captain, wishes to read them, I will lend them to you with great pleasure."

The soldier smiled disdainfully on hearing the policeman, and begged him to let him see those curious documents, because he had the idea of visiting the ruins and removing for ever the superstitious fear that they inspired.

That night he received a bundle of yellowed papers falling to pieces through age and dampness, and shut up in his room he read them from beginning to end.

The following morning when Captain Pero Gil, for such was his name, went out into the square, the hollows of a night of insomnia and fever were clearly seen in his face. What had happened to him?

Among the papers which formed the bundle, one above all had attracted his attention. It ran more or less as follows:

"It is said by neighbour Nuno Perez that in the castle, at the foot of the tower of Homage, there must be an immense treasure, but it is guarded by one hundred dwarfs with long beards who strike anybody who comes near.

"At twelve o'clock in the night a gap opens in the ground which gives access to enormous riches piled up in the cellar; but exactly at one o'clock the earth closes up until the following night. If, instead of one person, two or three go to the place, then the earth does not open and the treasure remains hidden.

"That is the news which, on the evidence of an eyewitness, has reached me, and which I certify. Signed by Inigo Lopez, the constable."

The Captain remained perplexed for a good while, and at last said to himself resolutely, "Tomorrow night I will go to the tower of Homage at the foot of the castle."

Indeed, at twelve o'clock in the night he went out of the house where he lodged and went towards the ruins, first making sure that his sword came out of the sheath without difficulty, and that the pistols which he wore in his belt were well loaded.

At eleven o'clock, or a little later, he arrived at the castle. A splendid moon was shining, which gave the landscape a melancholy appearance. The Captain hid himself behind some stones close to the big tower, and there waited, twisting his moustache, to see the marvel take place. The village clock struck twelve, and on the last stroke the earth opened and a crowd of dwarfs, with beards down to the ground, came out of the narrow gap. They were armed with thick sticks, and began to dance round the entrance of the vault, singing:

"Let us defend the treasure.

Let us defend our gold

Against every mortal

Not knowing the signal."

The Captain advanced quickly, and taking up his place at the side of the circle of little men, saluted the dwarfs with great courtesy.

"Good evening, friends,"

"Daring man!" said the tiny men. "Who are you? What have you come here for?"

And armed with their thick sticks they rushed towards the intruder. But the latter, without being frightened, unsheathed his sword, and said to them very calmly, "Let us be serious, comrades, and leave off making bad-natured jokes, because I will cut down any one who comes too near me. Are you willing to let me have the treasures?"

"Never!" they exclaimed. "It is necessary for you to give us the signal. If you do not know it, we shall kill you."

"That is easier said than done," said Pero Gil, with great deliberation. "You must grow a little before you can put a man like me in pickle. If your height had grown as much as your beard, it might have been different."

"Let us kill him," shouted the dwarfs. "He does not know the signal!"

And they threw themselves upon the Captain. But the latter drew out a pistol, and with one shot the most daring of them fell to the ground, which checked the rest.

"It seems that I came off best," said the Captain, laughing. "What I have done to this fellow I will do to the remainder if you come near. Therefore let me pass without hindrance."

"We would let ourselves be killed before permitting you to get to the treasure, unless you gave us the signal."

"And what signal is that?"

"We cannot tell you."

"It seems to me that I shall not require it for grinding up your ribs."

"Away! Away!" said the little men, and armed with their sticks they rushed upon Pero Gil. The latter fired off his second pistol, bowling over another, but they threw themselves upon him, until his back looked like a snake turning round amidst the crowd of those who were attacking him. At last he saw that he was surrounded and defenceless, and therefore was obliged to jump over the wall at the risk of being dashed to pieces, and so left the place, ashamed of his defeat.

"My goodness! what can the signal be?" he asked himself while on his way to the village.

The following morning he returned to the ruins, armed with a lever, and recognised the place where on the previous night he had seen the opening. There was nothing there! However much he poked about he could not find the least sign which showed the entrance to the mysterious vault, and what was still stranger, he could not distinguish the slightest trace of the past fight.

Then he resolved to try if cunning could succeed where strength had failed.

The following night he hid himself in the ruins and watched the place where the marvellous event took place. The dwarfs came out with their accustomed dance and song:

"Let us defend the treasure.

Let us defend our gold

Against every mortal

Not knowing the signal."

The dance over, one of them said, "The Captain will not return, but if he does come back we will kill him."

"It would be better to allow him to enter the vault and there let him die of hunger."

"And if he seizes the bell?"

"Then we are lost."

"But he must first give the statue of the old master of the castle a thrust with his sword."

Pero Gil did not wait to hear any more, and at one bound approached the statue, which was situated in what used to be the armoury of the fortress, and struck it a stout blow with his blade.

The statue fell down flat as if struck by lightning, and at once the dwarfs surrounded the Captain and forced him down a flight of steps.

Hardly had he entered than the gap closed up and the Captain found himself alone in a cave which was lighted by a lamp hanging from the ceiling. On the floor there were great heaps of gold and precious stones, but this was not the thing that claimed the Captain's attention. He was looking for the bell which he had heard the dwarfs speak about.

For half an hour his search was fruitless. He turned over the yellow piles of money and the sacks of gems, but the desired object was not to be found.

Weary and perspiring he threw himself down on a pile of gold bars, and there rested before again returning to his task.

The mysterious bell had to be found.

Persuaded that it was not to be come across in a visible spot, he began to strike the walls, until at last one of them sounded hollow. With his sword he made a hole and from it drew out a leaden bell of a very rare shape, which in a good sale might be worth as much as four farthings.

"And now what must I do?" thought the Captain. He carefully examined the object he had found, which bore the following inscription, "Do not ring me unless you know how." But the Captain was not a man to hesitate, and rang the bell. Immediately the walls closed together, threatening to crush him by their enormous mass. Without being daunted he gave another ring, and then a thousand points of steel came forth from the walls as if they were going to pass through him. Then he gave a third ring, and immediately the vault returned to its original form.

At the fourth the dwarfs humbly presented themselves and said to him, "What do you want of us? Command us as your slaves."

"In the first place, to dance the saraband in order to amuse me, as a compensation for the unpleasant time you have given me."

And the dwarfs danced like anything for a good while, until Pero Gil told them to stop.

"Now you will take the sacks of money and carry them to my house."

The dwarfs obeyed without making the slightest observation, loading up those precious things.

"Leave us the bell," they said, "since you take away the riches."

Pero Gil was going to leave it, when he suddenly had a presentiment and thought better of it.

"This talisman shall never leave me."

Then the dwarfs carried the riches to his house, singing on the way:

"Don't let us guard the treasure now,

For it is being taken away

By this fortunate mortal

Who knows the signal."

So Captain Pero Gil became master of immense riches, which he distributed among his soldiers, naturally keeping for himself the largest part.

And whenever he thought of that famous adventure, he rightly used to say, "After all, the true talisman to get what we want is cunning and bravery."

THE WOLF-CHILD

*A Portuguese story adapted from Charles Sellers' original, taken
from Tales from the Lands of Nuts and Grapes, published in 1888
by The Leadenhall Press and others.*

IN THE NORTH OF PORTUGAL THERE are many sequestered
spots where the enchanted wizards meet when it is full moon.
These places are generally situated among high rocks on the
precipitous sides of the hills overlooking rivers; and when the wind
is very boisterous their terrible screams and incantations can be
distinctly heard by the peasantry inhabiting the neighbouring
villages.

On such occasions the father of the family sets fire to a wisp of
straw, and with it makes the sign of the cross around his house,
which prevents these evil spirits from approaching. The other
members of the family place a few extra lights before the image of
the Virgin; and the horse-shoe nailed to the door completes the
safety of the house.

But it will so happen that sometimes an enchanted wizard, with
more cunning than honesty, will get through one of the windows on

the birth of a child, and will brand the infant with a mark on his shoulder or arm, in which case it is well known that the child, on certain nights, will be changed into a wolf.

The enchanted wizards have their castles and palaces under the ground or beneath the rivers, and they wander about the earth, seeing but not seen; for they died unbaptized, and have, therefore, no rest in the grave.

They seem to have given preference to the North of Portugal, where they are held in great fear by the peasantry; and it has been observed that all such of the natives as have left their homes to study at the universities, on their return have never been visited by the enchanted wizards, as it is well known that they have a great respect for learning. In fact, one of the kings has said that until all his subjects were educated they would never get rid of the enchanted wizards.

In a village called Darque, on the banks of the Lima, there lived a farmer whose goodness and ignorance were only equalled by those of his wife. They were both young and robust, and were sufficiently well off to afford the luxury of beef once or twice a month. Their clothes were home-spun, and their hearts were homely. Beyond their landlord's grounds they had never stepped; but as he owned nearly the whole village, it is very evident that they knew something of this world of ours. They were both born and married on the estate, as their parents had been before them, and they were contented because they had never mixed with the world.

One day, when the farmer came home to have his midday meal of broth and maize bread, he found his wife in bed with a new-born baby boy by her side, and he was so pleased that he spent his hour of rest looking at the child, so that his meal remained untasted on the table.

Kissing his wife and infant, and bidding her beware of evil eyes, he hurried out of the house back to his work; and so great was his joy at being a father that he did not feel hungry.

He was digging potatoes, and in his excitement had sent his hoe through some of them, which, however, he did not notice until he happened to strike one that was so hard that the steel of his hoe flashed.

Thinking it was a pebble, he stooped to pick it up, but was surprised to see that it was no longer there. However, he went on working, when he struck another hard potato, and his hoe again flashed.

"Ah," said he, "the evil one has been sowing this field with stones, as he did in the days of good Saint Euphemia, our patroness." Saying which, he drew out the small crucifix from under his shirt, and the flinty potato disappeared; but he noticed that one of its eyes moved.

He thought no more of this untoward event, and went on hoeing until sunset, when, with the other labourers, he shouldered his hoe and prepared to go home.

Never had the distance seemed so great; but at last he found himself by his wife's bedside. She told him that while he was absent an old woman had called, asking for something to eat, and that as she seemed to have met with some accident, because there was blood running down her face, she invited her in, and told her she might eat what her husband had left untasted.

Sitting down at the table, the old woman commenced eating without asking a blessing on the food; and when she had finished she approached the bed, and, looking at the infant, she muttered some words and left the house hurriedly.

The husband and wife were very much afraid that the old woman was a witch; but as the child went on growing and seemed well they gradually forgot their visitor.

The infant was baptized, and was named John; and when he was old enough he was sent out to work to help his parents. All the labourers noticed that John could get through more work than any man, he was so strong and active, but he was also very silent.

The remarkable strength of the boy got to be so spoken about in the village that at last the wise woman, who was always consulted, said that there was no doubt that John was a wolf-child; and this having come to the ears of his parents, his body was carefully examined, and the mark of the wolf was found under his arm.

Nothing now remained to be done but to take John to the great wise woman of Arifana, and have him disenchanted.

The day arrived for the parents to take John with them to Arifana, but when they looked for him he could nowhere be found. They searched everywhere - down the well, in the river, in the forest - and made inquiries at all the villages, but in vain. John had disappeared.

Weeks went by without any sign of him; and the winter having set in, the wolves, through hunger, had become more undaunted in their attacks on the flocks and herds. The farmer, afraid of firing at them, lest he might shoot his son, had laid a trap, and one morning, to his delight, he saw that a very large wolf had been caught, which one of his fellow-labourers was cudgelling.

Fearing it might be the lost wolf-child, he hastened to the spot, and prevented the wolf receiving more blows; but it was too late, apparently, to save the creature's life, for it lay motionless on the ground as if dead. Hurrying off for the wise woman of the village, she returned with him; and, close to the head of the wolf, she gathered some branches of the common pine-tree, and lighting them, as some were green and others dry, a volume of smoke arose like a tower, reaching to the top of a hill where lived some notorious enchanted wizards Between the wolf and the said wizards the distance was covered by a tunnel of smoke and fire. Then the wise woman intoned the following words, closing her eyes, and bidding the rest do so until she should tell them they might open them:

"Spirit of the mighty wind

That across the desert howls,

Help us here to unbind

All the spells of dreaded ghouls;

Through the path of smoke and fire

Rising to the wizards' mound,

Bid the cursèd mark retire

From this creature on the ground;

Bid him take his shape again,

Free him from the Wolf-mark's power,

May the holy Cross remain

On his temple from this hour."

She now made the sign of the Cross over the head of the wolf, and continued:

"River, winding to the west,

Stay your rippling current, stay,

Jordan's stream your tide has blest,

Help us wash this stain away;

Bear it to the ocean wide,

Back to Devil's shore.

Those who washed in you have died

But to live for evermore."

Then she sprinkled a few drops over the fire, which caused a larger amount of smoke, and exclaimed:

"Hie you, spirit, up through smoke,

Quenched by water and by fire;

Hie you far from Christian folk,

To the wizard's home retire.

Open wide your eyelids now,

All the smoke has curled away;

'Neath the peaceful olive bough

Let us go, and let us pray."

Then they all rose, and the wolf was no longer there. The fire had burned itself out, and the stream was again running. In slow procession they went to the olive grotto, headed by the wise woman; and, after praying, they returned to the house, where they found, to their delight, John fast asleep in his bed; but his arms showed signs of bruises which had been caused by the cudgelling he had received when he was caught in the trap.

There were great rejoicings that day in the village of Darque, and no one was better pleased than John at having regained his proper shape.

He was never known to join in the inhuman sport of hunting wolves for pleasure, because, as he said, although they may not be wolf-children, they do but obey an instinct which was given them, and to be kind-hearted is to obey a precept which was given us. And, owing to the introduction into Portugal of the Book in which this commandment is to be found, wolf-children have become scarcer, and the people wiser.

Tales From The Land Of Rabbits

THE BALLAD-MAKER AND THE BOOT-MAKER

Adapted from Patranas; or Spanish Stories by Rachel Harriette Busk, published by Newbery and Harris, 1870.

THERE WAS A MINSTREL WHO WENT travelling about the country from time to time singing sweet songs which people loved to hear. His music was not like the music of the Spanish people, for he came from the kingdom of Provence, and every one thronged to hear the strange sweet melody. And when he had passed on, and there was no one left to sing as he sang, people tried to remember his words and his tones, and to sing like him.

At one of the towns where he passed there was a boot-maker, who, as he sat all day alone at his last, diverted himself with singing, and as he had sung a good deal, he thought he could sing very well. He was much delighted with the minstrel's songs, caught up a good many of them, and never tired of singing them after his fashion. But from being quite ignorant both of music and of the Provençal language, he made, as we should say, a great mess of it. Yet, as the

135

people knew no more about it than himself, they were very well pleased to listen to him.

So, a long time after, when the Provençal minstrel came back that way, they would not admit him, but cried out, "We have one of our own people who sings your songs for us as well as you, and we need no Frenchman here."

Now the minstrel was one greatly devoted to his art, he did not merely sing for sordid gain; so instead of being angry because he was supplanted, he was really pleased to hear that the people in that far-off town had learned the language and melody of his dear Provence, and he said he would hear the boot-maker himself.

Imagine how great was his annoyance and mortification, when he heard the beautiful ballads lamed and spoiled by the rude, unlearned attempts of the boot-maker!

"Is it possible," he said, "that this man has been deluding all the people into the idea that what he sings is like my songs? And how can I prevent his going on keeping them under this error?" Then he bethought him what to do. He went by night to the boot-maker's workshop, and putting all the wrong pieces of leather together, he sewed them up into all sorts of foolish, useless shapes.

When daylight returned, and the boot-maker came to his work, he was in a great fury at what was done, and began shouting to the neighbours to come and avenge him, for the Frenchman had spoiled all his work. Then they all came running helter-skelter to exercise summary justice on the minstrel.

But the minstrel stood up and confronted them, and said, "Good people! First hear me. This man is a maker of boots and I am a maker of ballads. True I have spoiled his boots, I do not deny it, but he first spoiled my ballads. What I have done is but fair. If you will hear us sing one after the other, you will yourselves give judgment in my favour." So the people told the boot-maker to stand up and sing, which he did in his clumsy droning way, with plenty of false notes and mispronunciations. After him the minstrel stood up and warbled his song in tones so soft and sweet, that the people wondered how they ever could have listened to the other, and with one voice they cried out, "The minstrel is right! The minstrel is right!"

Then the minstrel, who bore no malice, and had only acted out of love for his art, repaid the boot-maker amply for all the damage to his leather, but took a promise of him that he would never sing his songs again.

Tales From The Land Of Rabbits

THE WHITE CAT OF ECIJA

Adapted from Charles Sellers' original, taken from Tales from the Lands of Nuts and Grapes, published in 1888 by The Leadenhall Press and others.

FROM THE GATES OF THE PALACE, situated on a gentle eminence in the vicinity of Ecija, down to the banks of the Genil, the ground was covered with olive-trees; and the wild aloes formed a natural and strong fence around the property of the White Cat of Ecija, whose origin, dating back to the days of Saracenic rule, was unknown to the liberated Spaniard.

There was a great mystery attaching to the palace and its occupants; and although the servants of the White Cat were to all appearances human beings, still, as they were deaf and dumb, and would not, or could not, understand signs, the neighbours had not been able to discover the secret or mystery.

The palace was a noble building, after the style of the alcazar at Toledo, but not so large; and the garden at the rear was laid out with many small lakes, round which, at short distances, stood beautifully sculptured statues of young men and women, who seemed to be looking sorrowfully into the water. Only the brain and hand of an exceptionally gifted artist could have so approached perfection as to make the statues look as if alive. At night strings of small lamps were hung round the lakes, and from the interior of the palace proceeded strains of sweet, but very sad music.

Curiosity had long ceased to trouble the neighbours as to the mysterious White Cat and her household, and, with the exception of crossing themselves when they passed by the grounds, they had given up the affair as incomprehensible.

Those, however, who had seen the White Cat, said that she was a beautiful creature; her coat was like velvet, and her eyes were like pearls.

One day a knight in armour, and mounted on a coal-black charger, arrived at the principal hostelry in Ecija, and on his shield he bore for his coat of arms a white cat rampant, and, underneath, the device, "Invincible."

Having partaken of some slight repast, he put spurs to his horse and galloped in the direction of the palace of the White Cat; but as he was not seen to return through the town, the people supposed that he had left by some other road.

The White Cat was seen next day walking about in the grounds, but she seemed more sorrowful than usual.

In another month's time there came another knight fully equipped, and mounted on a grey charger. On his shield he also displayed a white cat, with the device, "I win or die." He also galloped off to the palace, or alcazar, and was not seen to return; but next day the White Cat was still more sorrowful.

In another month a fresh knight appeared. He was a handsome youth, and his bearing was so manly that a crowd collected. He was fully equipped, but on his shield he displayed a simple red cross. He partook of some food, and then cantered out of the town with his lance at rest. He was seen to approach the palace, and as soon as he thrust open the gate with his lance, a terrific roar was heard, and then a sheet of fire flashed from the palace door, and they saw a horrid dragon, whose long tail, as it lashed the air, produced such a wind that it seemed as if a gale had suddenly sprung up.

But the gallant knight was not daunted, and eagerly scanned the dragon as if to see where he might strike him.

Suddenly it was seen that the dragon held the White Cat under its talons, so that the Knight of the Cross in charging the dragon had to take care not to strike her. Spurring his horse on, he never pulled up till he had transfixed the dragon with his lance, and, jumping off the saddle, he drew his sword and cut off the monster's head.

No sooner had he done this than he was surrounded by ten enormous serpents, who tried to coil round him; but as fast as they attacked him, he strangled them.

Then the serpents turned into twenty black vultures with fiery beaks, and they tried to pick out his eyes; but with his trusty blade he kept them off, and one by one he killed them all, and then found himself surrounded by forty dark-haired and dark-eyed lovely maidens, who would have thrown their arms around him, but that he, fearing their intentions were evil, kept them off. Finally, looking on the ground, he saw the White Cat panting, and heard her bid him "strike."

He waited no longer, but struck at the maidens and cut off their heads, and then saw that the ground was covered with burning coal,

141

which would have scorched the White Cat and killed her, had not the gallant knight raised her in his arms. He then placed her on his shield, and as soon as she touched the cross she was seen to change into a beautiful maiden, and all the statues round the lakes left their positions and approached her.

As soon as she could recover herself sufficiently to speak, she addressed the knight as follows, "Gallant sir, I am Mizpah, only daughter of Mudi Ben Raschid, who was governor of this province for many years under the Moorish king, Almandazar the Superb. My mother was daughter of Alcharan, governor of Mazagan, and she was a good wife and kind mother. But my father discovering that she had forsaken the faith of her fathers, and had embraced the religion of the Cross, so worried her to return to her childhood's faith that she died broken-hearted. Then he married again, and his second wife, my stepmother, was a very wicked woman. She knew that I was a Christian at heart, and that my lover was also a Christian; so one day, when my father was holding a banquet, she said to him, 'Mudi Ben Raschid, the crescent of the Holy Prophet is waning in your family, your daughter is a renegade!'

"Then he was very much annoyed, and exclaimed that he would his palace and his riches were made over to the enemy of mankind and I turned into a cat, than that so great a stain should fall on his family. No sooner had he finished speaking than he fell dead and his wicked wife also, and I was turned into a cat; my lover, Haroun, and all my young friends were turned into stone, and my servants were stricken deaf and dumb. Many a brave knight has been here to try and deliver me; but they all failed, because they only trusted in themselves, and were therefore defeated. But you, gallant knight, trusted more on the Cross than in yourself, and you have freed me.

I am, therefore, the prize of your good sword; deal with me as you will."

The Knight of the Cross assured her that he came from Compostela, where it was considered a duty to rescue maidens in distress, and that the highest reward coveted was that of doing their duty. He had in various parts of the world been fortunate enough in freeing others, and he had still more work before him. He trusted that the lovely Mizpah might long be spared to Haroun, and, saluting her, he galloped off.

Then was the wedding held, at which all the people from Ecija attended; and the bridegroom, rising, wished prosperity to the good knight, St. James of Compostela, who had been the means of bringing about so much happiness.

Tales From The Land Of Rabbits

DON SUERO THE PROUD

*Adapted from Fairy Tales from Spain by José Muñoz Escámez,
published by J. M. Dent & Sons Ltd, 1913.*

ONCE THERE WAS, IN VERY REMOTE times, a knight named
Don Suero de las Navas, feudal lord of a number of Spanish
villages, with a quantity of titles sufficient to fill one of the biggest
pages, so many and so long were they.

Now, this knight was so proud that he thought it was a great
dishonour to learn how to read and write things which he
considered not only useless for a man of his accomplishments, but
even shameful for a noble so rich as he was, who could indulge in
the luxury of a secretary. And so it was indeed, that a poor man,
who on account of his humble condition was obliged to learn those
trifling necessities, went, like a vagabond, behind his master, pen
and ink in satchel, ready to put into good Castilian the thousand
and one mistakes that Don Suero frequently made.

On a certain occasion the king summoned the powerful Don Suero
to go with his soldiers to the war, and as it could not be otherwise,
the poor secretary, carrying a pen instead of a sword and a horn

inkstand instead of an arrow, was obliged to place himself at the side of his lord and to march to the war.

At the beginning all went well. The orders and the letters acquainting the king with the results of the struggle were written by the hand of the unfortunate secretary, who earned each month, if my particulars are not wrong, the enormous sum of two silver threepenny pieces. Enough to have a carriage and to build good castles - in the air!

But an arrow shot at hazard in the fury of the fight against the Moors put Don Lesmes, for so the secretary was called, out of action, and Don Suero was under the necessity of seeking a new dependant who knew how to read and write, which was not an easy matter at that time.

He could not find one, to his great unhappiness, and if he had not had that quantity of pride in his body, he would surely have felt his lack of education, which might place him in an awkward situation, which happened soon afterwards.

He was engaged in a campaign against the Moors, who occupied a great part of Spain, when he received a packet from the king. And here the difficulty began. What did the King say in those pot-hooks written on an enclosed parchment? To advance? To retreat? It was difficult to guess. The messenger had confined himself to delivering the packet and, putting spurs to his horse, disappeared in a cloud of dust.

Don Suero, perplexed, found himself with the parchment in his hand, turning it round and round, without knowing what it said. He made a man of a neighbouring village come to him, a man who was an enemy of his because of a certain thrashing which he had ordered him to be given some days before, and said, "I have been told that you know how to read and write, and as nobody else here knows how to, you will read to me what this document from the king says, and if you do not tell me the truth I will have you skinned alive. Moreover, I require from you absolute secrecy. What is said here only you and I must know."

The offended peasant promised him all, but with the idea of taking complete vengeance. And indeed hardly had he cast a glance at the document than he exclaimed in accents of the greatest surprise, "The king orders you to give up the command of the troops and to go immediately to the court, where you have been accused of treason."

"I a traitor! Ah, what scoundrels are those who have said that of me! I will cut off their ears with my own hand."

No sooner said than done. He at once left the command of his troops and started on his march to the court.

The journey was long and wearisome, and our Don Suero was obliged to halt in an uninhabited place, to dismount from his horse and to sleep on the blessed ground, neither more nor less than if he had been the poorest of peasants.

So he passed the night, until dawn surprised him. On collecting himself he saw a large board close to a ditch situated at the side of the road. What might that say? It ought to be something important when it was written in such large letters. He went as near as he could to see if any sign, which was not in writing, might indicate something to him of what the board said, but, alas! On going nearer he slipped and fell headlong into the ditch.

The notice said, "Take care in approaching!"

It cost him no little work to get out of it, and still the shock left him so weak that he could hardly move.

As well as he could, he approached the nearest village and got into bed. The first person whom he met was the cunning peasant who had so badly translated his majesty's letter. He was flying from Don Suero and had come face to face with him where he least expected to.

On seeing Don Suero's friendly gestures gesture, he knew that his deceit had not been discovered, and, without trembling, he approached the noble knight.

"You can be useful to me," said the latter. "I do not feel disposed to go to the court. Write to the king what has happened to me and tell him that as soon as I am a little better I will come and confound those who have calumniated me."

But the peasant wrote what he liked and sent off the letter.

In it he heaped insults on the king, with the object of causing the latter to have the knight's head cut off.

The effect that the insulting letter produced was so great that the king rose in his anger and commanded Don Suero to be brought dead or alive, and that if he resisted he was to be tied to the tail of a horse.

The knight was imprisoned, but as he was so proud he would not give the king any explanations, and the latter commanded him to be tortured.

Not even the severest tortures could succeed in taming that will of iron. He was innocent, and would not ask grace of the king, who condemned him without any further motive. At length they were going to sentence him to death for his insults to the king, when one of the judges mentioned to the king the possibility of Don Suero having put his seal at the foot of a document he had not signed.

"Because," he said, "it is stated he does not know how to read and write."

"What!" angrily exclaimed the king. "Did I pass five long years in learning how to spell, and that silly Don Suero does not know how to do it? I do not believe it. If you cannot prove to me that the letter in which he calls me a weak and stupid king is unknown to him, I will have him killed tomorrow."

The judge did not neglect to see. He wrote out the sentence of death and took it to the prison, saying to the knight, "Sign this and you are free!"

"What is this?"

"A writing in which you say to the king that you are innocent of what you are accused."

"If that is so, bring it and I will sign it."

And he put a cross and his seal at the foot of it.

The judge bore to the king that sentence that the prisoner had signed, believing it to be his salvation, and then the king, convinced of his innocence, commanded him to be set free and returned all his honours to him.

After that the knight dedicated himself to learning reading and writing, and made such progress that, after eight years of lessons, he already knew which was the letter O, both capital and small, which indeed showed a progress not too rapid.

And the peasant? He was sought for, being a wicked man, and as soon as he was caught he was put into prison, where he finished his life.

Ignorance is bad, but the wicked are worse than the ignorant.

EL CONDE FERNAN GONZALEZ

Adapted from Patranas; or Spanish Stories by Rachel Harriette Busk, published by Newbery and Harris, 1870.

CONDE FERNAN GONZALEZ WAS A BOLD lance. He was as restless as he was brave, and when not engaged in chasing the Moors, he kept his appetite for noble exploits whetted with the dangers of the chase.

One day, the furious course of a wild boar, and his own impetuosity in the pursuit, led him far away from his companions, and the hills and leafy oaks of Lara soon hid him from sight. On went the boar, and on went the Conde after him, till, in the thickest of the forest, the brute took refuge in a hermit's cell long deserted and forgotten, and overgrown with ivy. The trees grew so close round the spot, that the horse could not go through for the low interlacing branches, so Gonzalez dismounted. He took his sword in his hand, and wrapped his cloak round his arm by way of shield. Cutting his way through to the low doorway, he found the boar lying panting at the foot of a little altar which was there.

The good Count would not hurt the animal under such circumstances, so he put up his sword into the sheath, and, before he turned to go, knelt to offer up a prayer upon the sacred spot.

Suddenly, as he knelt, there appeared before him a vision of the former inhabitant of the place. He was a venerable man, dressed in white, with bald head and a long grey beard, his feet were bare and he leant upon a crook.

"Good Conde Fernan Gonzales," he said, "Behold, the King Almanzor is even now preparing to come out to meet you. Now, go out and give him battle, and be of good heart, for though you shall be badly wounded, and the infidels shall spill much of your blood, yet shall a hundred of them fall for one of yours. God guard you, Conde, and that which you shall do this day shall resound throughout all Spain. But this sign must come to pass first; and when it is fulfilled do not lose courage, for all that are with you shall be stricken with fear and be ready to flee away. But only stand fast, and the day shall be given you. After that shall come days of peace; and a good wife shall also be given you, who shall be called Sancha. And now return to Lara, for your people are seeking you with fear and anxiety; and when these things come to pass, remember the hermit who foretold them."

Then, without answering him a word, the good Count rose from his knees, and, mounting his horse, rode back to Lara. There he found his people, all running here and there in search of him. But he, without telling them what had befallen, ranged them in order of battle, and went out to meet King Almanzor.

Thus they went their way, and sure enough they were none too soon, for even as the hermit had said, King Almanzor was on his way to meet him.

When the followers of Gonzalez saw the host that was marching towards them, they were stricken with fear, for they were but a handful. But Gonzalez, seeing their disorder, turned and said to them, "It is a shame, noble Castilian knights, to flee at sight of an infidel host, for who is there that can stand against our banner and our arms? At them! My friends, at them! Let there be not one of us wanting!"

With that he set spurs to his charger, and rode into the midst of the Moors, and he did this so valiantly, that all his followers dashed into the enemy with like impetuosity, and none could stand before them. For each one of the Spanish that was slain, a hundred of the infidels lay stretched upon the ground. But the good Conde was wounded, and his blood was poured out upon the ground, yet still they pushed their way into the Moorish camp, where they found much precious spoil.

And when they divided the treasure, Gonzalez remembered the hermit, and set aside a portion of his share, and with it he built the church of San Pedro de Arlanza.

Tales From The Land Of Rabbits

THE COBBLER OF BURGOS

Adapted from Charles Sellers' original, taken from Tales from the Lands of Nuts and Grapes, published in 1888 by The Leadenhall Press and others.

NOT FAR FROM THE GARDEN OF the Widows, in Burgos, lived a cobbler who was so poor that he had not smiled for many years. Every day he saw the widow ladies pass his small shop on the way to and from the garden; but in their bereavement it would not have been considered correct for them to have bestowed a glance on him, and they required all the money they could scrape together, after making ample provision for their comfort, which, as ladies, they did not neglect, to pay for Masses for the repose of the souls of their husbands, according to the doctrines of the faith which was pinned on to them in childhood.

The priests, however, would sometimes bestow their blessing on Sancho the cobbler; but beyond words he got nothing from the comforters of the widows and of the orphans.

Some of the great families would have their boots soled by him; but being very great and rich people, they demanded long credit, so that he was heard to say that a rich man's money was almost as scarce as virtue.

Now, one night, when he was about to close his shop, a lovely young widow lady pushed her way by him into the shop, and sitting on the only chair in the room, she bid him close the door immediately, as she had something to say to him in confidence.

Being a true Spaniard, he showed no surprise, but obeyed orders, and stood before the young widow lady, who, after looking at him carefully for a minute, implored him to go upstairs and see that the windows were secure and the shutters barred and bolted.

This done, he again stood before her, when she showed signs of fear, and requested him to ensure against the doors being burst open by piling what furniture he had against them and against the shutters; and then, assuring herself that she was safe, she exclaimed, "Ah, friend Sancho, it is good to beware of evil tongues. I come to you because I know you to be honest and silent. Tonight you must sleep on the roof; get out through the skylight, and I will rest here."

To refuse a lady's commands, however singular they may be, is not in the nature of a Spaniard, so Sancho got out through the skylight, when the young widow began screaming, "Let me out, kind people, let me out!"

The cobbler was now very much afraid of the consequences, especially as the night watchmen were banging against the street door, which they soon forced, knocking all the furniture which had been placed against it into the middle of the room.

When inside, they discovered the lovely young widow, who exclaimed, "Good men, I am Guiomar, of Torrezon, widow of the noble Pedro de Torrezon, and because my late husband was owing

Sancho for soling a pair of boots, I came here to pay the debt; but Sancho would have detained me against my will. He is concealed on the roof of the house, and if you leave me here he will murder me."

Then she naturally fainted and screamed for so long a time that the street was soon full of people who, hearing what had happened, cried out against Sancho.

The watchmen having secured him, he was led before the alcaide, and, being a poor man, he was sent to prison until such time as Donna Guiomar should feel disposed to pardon him.

At the end of a year Donna Guiomar obtained his liberty, but on the condition that he should forthwith proceed to Rome and do penance, which was to count for the benefit of her deceased husband.

This act of piety on her part was very much approved of by the priests, who required of Sancho that during the whole of his pilgrimage there he should not shave, nor have his hair nor his nails cut. He was, furthermore, to wear a suit of horse-hair cloth next to his skin, and was to subsist solely on onions, garlic, maize bread, and pure water.

But liberty is so sweet that Sancho did not mind his hard fare, and he went on his way to Rome repeating penitential prayers, while his hair and beard grew until his head and face were nearly hidden.

Arrived at Rome, the people wondered much to see such a strange-looking being; but when he opened his mouth to inquire his way to St. Peter's, so strong was the smell of onions and garlic that the people, accustomed as they were to these vegetables, could not stand against it, and as Sancho spoke in a foreign tongue they could not have understood him very easily.

At last he met a priest who was kind enough to listen to him, and he said he would be allowed audience of the Pope next morning with other pilgrims, but that meantime he had better confess what his fault had been.

Sancho recounted all about the lovely young widow, and the priest very properly admonished him for having dared to frighten a lady whose anxiety respecting her deceased husband was quite enough of sorrow without having it added to by being forcibly detained by a cobbler.

"It is a pity," said the worthy your priest, "that you were not handed over to the inquisitorial brothers, for they would have burned you before you were allowed to import the odour of all the fields of Spanish onions and garlic into the Eternal City. It is a sign of the bad times that are approaching when errant cobblers are allowed to vitiate the precincts of St. Peter's with their pestilential breath. Tomorrow you will be regaled with a view - mind, only a view - of his holiness's toe, and then you must depart this city."

Sancho recognized the truth of what the good priest said, and, having refreshed himself with some more onions and a glass of water, he lay down to sleep behind one of the large stone pillars and slept until next morning, when the large bell of the cathedral awoke him. He then hurried in to the presence of the Pope, nor had he much difficulty in so doing, for the other pilgrims were glad to get out of his way. Bowing low before the golden chair, he exclaimed, "One weary soul, though cobbler he by trade, comes here to seek a pardon for his sin. Most holy father, ere the daylight fade, oh, let me in! From sunny Spain, where runs the Arlanzon, to you, oh, father, come I now to crave that you will raise Don Pedro Torrezon from his restless grave and to his widow him restore again. This done, dismiss me to my home in peace, to be your servant as a priest in Spain, and faith increase."

To which the Pope replied, "We smelt you from afar, oh, son of Spain. We know your errand, and we grant your prayer. Where onions shed their perfume, son, remain, and your presence spare. Yes, spare us all your Spanish odours strong. Return to your country, Sancho – go! And as a blessing on your journey long, stoop now and kiss our toe."

And when Sancho got back to Burgos he was met by Don Pedro de Torrezon, who, half in anger and half in sorrow, exclaimed, "Good Sancho, I would rather spend eternity surrounded by the pains of purgatory, than be restored unto this mortal life, where purgatory is but the name for wife."

Tales From The Land Of Rabbits

HORMESINDA

Adapted from Patranas; or Spanish Stories by Rachel Harriette Busk, published by Newbery and Harris, 1870.

AT THE PERIOD OF THE MOORS' most complete dominion over Spain, Pelayo, the noble scion of her ancient kings, stood almost alone in the defence of his country. Undismayed by the misfortunes of his race and people, or by the oppressive rigours of the conquerors, he never tired of rousing his brethren to a sense of their shameful condition, and stirring them up to the desire of again restoring their religion and the throne of their native rulers.

Meantime, his sister Hormesinda, no less ardent and patriotic, but weaker and more short-sighted, had thought to benefit her people by sealing a compromise with the invaders. Forgetful of the religious laws which forbid such a union, she married Munuza, one of the Moorish chiefs who reigned at Gijon, and for a few years imagined she had effected wonders because she had induced the conqueror to mitigate his oppressions.

Pelayo, however, was almost more distressed at the contamination of his sister, married to an unbeliever, than by the bondage of his fellow-countrymen, and being on the point of leading the people he had collected to an attack on the Moorish Alcázar, he first obtained an interview with her, within the king's private apartments, with the view of inducing her to abandon her infidel lord.

Hormesinda, however, had chosen her path, and could not now escape its leadings. The interview was both stormy and touching. Pelayo, unflinching in his morality and patriotism, could find nothing to say to her but words of reproach. And Hormesinda could only urge, that though she might have been wrong in marrying the Moor, yet, now her word, and life, and love were pledged to him, she could not leave him.

Munuza despised the Christians, but Pelayo had no difficulty in gaining access to Hormesinda accompanied by the venerable Veremundo, his father, but a Jewish servant of Munuza's betrayed the information that he had no less a person than Pelayo himself in his power. Munuza ordered him to be captured and thrown into a dismal dungeon called a mazmorra.

No sooner did Munuza know that he had nothing to fear from Pelayo, than it became evident his moderation towards the Christians had been dictated less by Hormesinda's representations than by dread of Pelayo's reprisals, for he now began to add to the burdens of the conquered, without mercy. To crown it all, he issued a decree by which all who would not make themselves Mohammedans were declared to be slaves.

This measure completed the indignation of the Christians; and when it became known where Pelayo was held in durance, it needed but little urging of Leandro, his brother, to lead the outraged population to the assault of the Alcázar of Gijon.

The impetuosity of the despairing population was irresistible. Munuza, inclined to despise them at first, found himself surrounded before he was aware, and sallied out with his reserve to give life to his troops and repel the insurgents. He had no sooner left the precincts of the palace than Hormesinda took advantage of the circumstance to set free her brother, who was thus able to show himself at the head of his people like a miraculous apparition, inspiring them with courage to drive all before them.

Munuza, obliged to escape for his life, re-entered the Alcázar, where Hormesinda awaited him with feminine tenderness, desirous only to make a bulwark of her body between him and Pelayo's fury. Munuza, however, had doubtless courage, though it was the courage of an infidel; and not only refused to owe his life to the protection of a woman, but recognizing that it was her hand alone could have set his captive free, stabbed her and himself just in time to die at the entering feet of Pelayo and his victorious host.

This victory of the Christian arms was the first-fruits of many others, which, hard fought through succeeding centuries, restored at last the whole of Spain to Christendom.

Tales From The Land Of Rabbits

Tales From The Land Of Rabbits

THE SPIRITS' MOUNTAIN

Adapted from Romantic Legends of Spain. and taken from the original story written by Gustavo Adolfo Bécquer, translated by Cornelia Francis Bates and Katherine Lee Bates, 1909.

Chapter I

"LEASH THE DOGS! BLOW THE HORNS to call the hunters together, and let us return to the city. Night is at hand, the Night of All Souls, and we are on the Spirits' Mountain."

"So soon!"

"If it was any day but this, I would not give up till I had made an end of that pack of wolves which the snows of the Moncayo have driven from their dens, but today it is impossible. Very soon the Angelus will sound in the monastery of the Knights Templars, and the souls of the dead will commence to toll their bell in the chapel on the mountain."

"In that ruined chapel! Bah! Would you frighten me?"

"No, fair cousin; but you are not aware of all that happens hereabout, for it is not yet a year since you came here from a distant part of Spain. Rein in your mare. I will keep mine at the same pace and tell you this story on the way."

The pages gathered together in merry, boisterous groups. The Counts of Bórges and Alcudiel mounted their noble steeds, and the whole company followed after the son and daughter of those great houses, Alonso and Beatriz, who rode at some little distance in advance of the company.

As they went, Alonso related in these words the promised tradition, "This mountain, which is now called the Spirits' Mountain, belonged to the Knights Templars, whose monastery you see yonder on the river bank. The Templars were both monks and warriors. After Soria had been wrested from the Moors, the King summoned the Templars here from foreign lands to defend the city on the side next to the bridge, thus giving deep offense to his Castilian nobles, who, as they had won Soria alone, would alone have been able to defend it.

"Between the knights of the new and powerful Order and the nobles of the city there fermented for some years an animosity which finally developed into a deadly hatred. The Templars claimed for their own this mountain, where they reserved an abundance of game to satisfy their needs and contribute to their pleasures. The nobles determined to organize a great hunt within the bounds notwithstanding the rigorous prohibitions of the clergy with spurs, as their enemies called them.

"The news of the projected invasion spread fast, and nothing availed to check the rage for the hunt on the one side, and the determination to break it up on the other. The proposed expedition came off. The wild beasts did not remember it, but it was never to be forgotten by the many mothers mourning for their sons. That was not a hunting-trip, but a frightful battle. The mountain was strewn with corpses, and the wolves, whose extermination was the end in view, had a bloody feast. Finally the authority of the King was brought to bear. The mountain, the accursed cause of so many bereavements, was declared abandoned, and the chapel of the Templars, situated on this same wild steep, friends and enemies buried together in its cloister, began to fall into ruins.

"They say that ever since, on All Souls' Night, the chapel bell is heard tolling all alone, and the spirits of the dead, wrapped in the tatters of their shrouds, run as in a fantastic chase through the bushes and brambles. The deer trumpet in terror, wolves howl, snakes hiss horribly, and on the following morning there have been seen clearly marked in the snow the prints of the fleshless feet of the skeletons. This is why we call it in Soria the Spirits' Mountain, and this is why I wished to leave it before nightfall."

Alonso's story was finished just as the two young people arrived at the end of the bridge which admits to the city from that side. There they waited for the rest of the company to join them, and then the whole cavalcade was lost to sight in the dim and narrow streets of Soria.

Chapter II

The servants had just cleared the tables and the high Gothic fireplace of the palace of the Counts of Alcudiel was shedding a vivid glow over the groups of lords and ladies who were chatting in friendly fashion, gathered about the blaze; and the wind shook the leaded glass of the ogive windows.

Two persons only seemed to hold aloof from the general conversation, Beatriz and Alonso. Beatriz, absorbed in a vague reverie, followed with her eyes the capricious dance of the flames.

Alonso watched the reflection of the fire sparkling in the blue eyes of Beatriz. Both maintained for some time an unbroken silence.

The duennas were telling gruesome stories, appropriate to the Night of All Souls,—stories in which ghosts and spectres played the principal roles, and the church bells of Soria were tolling in the distance with a monotonous and mournful sound.

"Fair cousin," finally exclaimed Alonso, breaking the long silence between them. "Soon we are to separate, perhaps forever. I know you do not like the arid plains of Castile, its rough, soldier customs, its simple, patriarchal ways. At various times I have heard you sigh, perhaps for some lover in your far-away demesne."

Beatriz made a gesture of cold indifference. The whole character of the woman was revealed in that disdainful contraction of her delicate lips.

"Or perhaps for the grandeur and gaiety of the French capital, where you have lived hereto," the young man hastened to add. "In one way or another, I foresee that I shall lose you before long. When we part, I would like to have you carry hence a remembrance of me. Do you recollect the time when we went to church to give thanks to God for having granted you that restoration to health which was your object in coming to this region? The jewel that fastened the plume of my cap attracted your attention. How well it would look clasping a veil over your dark hair! It has already been the adornment of a bride. My father gave it to my mother, and she wore it to the altar. Would you like it?"

"I do not know how it may be in your part of the country," replied the beauty, "but in mine to accept a gift is to incur an obligation. Only on a holy day may one receive a present from a kinsman, though he may go to Rome without returning empty-handed."

The frigid tone in which Beatriz spoke these words troubled the youth for a moment, but, clearing his brow, he replied sadly, "I know it, cousin, but today is the festival of All Saints, and yours among them, a holiday on which gifts are fitting. Will you accept mine?"

Beatriz slightly bit her lip and put out her hand for the jewel, without a word.

The two again fell silent and again heard the quavering voices of the old women telling of witches and hobgoblins, the whistling wind which shook the ogive windows, and the mournful, monotonous tolling of the bells.

After the lapse of some little time, the interrupted dialogue was thus renewed, "And before All Saints' Day ends, which is holy to my saint as well as to yours, so that you can, without compromising yourself, give me a keepsake, will you not do so?" pleaded Alonso, fixing his eyes on his cousin's, which flashed like lightning, gleaming with a diabolical thought.

"Why not?" she exclaimed, raising her hand to her right shoulder as though seeking for something amid the folds of her wide velvet sleeve embroidered with gold. Then, with an innocent air of disappointment, she added, "Do you recollect the blue scarf I wore today to the hunt, the scarf which you said, because of something about the meaning of its colour, was the emblem of your soul?"

"Yes."

"Well! It is lost! It is lost, and I was thinking of letting you have it for a souvenir."

"Lost! where?" asked Alonso, rising from his seat with an indescribable expression of mingled fear and hope.

"I do not know, perhaps on the mountain."

"On the Spirits' Mountain!" he murmured, paling and sinking back into his seat. "On the Spirits' Mountain!"

Then he went on in a voice choked and broken, "You know, for you have heard it a thousand times, that I am called in the city, in all Castile, the king of the hunters. Not having yet had a chance to try, like my ancestors, my strength in battle, I have brought to bear on this pastime, the image of war, all the energy of my youth, all the hereditary ardour of my race. The rugs your feet tread on are the spoils of the chase, the hides of the wild beasts I have killed with my own hand. I know their haunts and their habits; I have fought them by day and by night, on foot and on horseback, alone and with hunting-parties, and there is not a man will say that he has ever seen me shrink from danger. On any other night I would fly for that scarf, fly as joyously as to a festival. But tonight, this one night, why disguise it? I am afraid. Do you hear? The bells are tolling, the Angelus has sounded in San Juan del Duero, the ghosts of the mountain are now beginning to lift their yellowing skulls from amid the brambles that cover their graves. The ghosts! the mere sight of them is enough to curdle with horror the blood of the bravest, turn his hair white, or sweep him away in the stormy whirl of their fantastic chase as a leaf, unwitting where, is carried by the wind."

While the young man was speaking, an almost imperceptible smile curled the lips of Beatriz, who, when he had ceased, exclaimed in an indifferent tone, while she was stirring the fire on the hearth, where the wood blazed and snapped, throwing off sparks of a thousand colours, "Oh, by no means! What folly! To go to the mountain at this hour for such a trifle! On so dark a night, too, with ghosts abroad, and the road beset by wolves!"

As she spoke this closing phrase, she emphasized it with so peculiar an intonation that Alonso could not fail to understand all her bitter irony. As moved by a spring, he leapt to his feet, passed his hand over his brow as if to dispel the fear which was in his brain, not in his breast, and with firm voice he said, addressing his beautiful cousin, who was still leaning over the hearth, amusing herself by stirring the fire, "Farewell, Beatriz, farewell. If I return, it will be soon."

"Alonso, Alonso!" she called, turning quickly, but now that she wished, or made show of wishing, to detain him, the youth had gone.

In a few moments she heard the beat of a horse's hoofs departing at a gallop. The beauty, with a radiant expression of satisfied pride flushing her cheeks, listened attentively to the sound which grew fainter and fainter until it died away.

The old dames, meanwhile, were continuing their tales of ghostly apparitions; the wind was shrilling against the balcony glass, and far away the bells of the city tolled on.

Chapter III

An hour had passed, two, three. Midnight would soon be striking, and Beatriz withdrew to her chamber. Alonso had not returned. He had not returned, though less than an hour would have sufficed for his errand.

"He must have been afraid!" exclaimed the girl, closing her prayer-book and turning toward her bed after a vain attempt to murmur some of the prayers that the church offers for the dead on the Day of All Souls.

After putting out her light and drawing the double silken curtains, she fell asleep; but her sleep was restless, light, uneasy.

The Postigo clock struck midnight. Beatriz heard through her dreams the slow, dull, melancholy strokes, and half opened her eyes. She thought she had heard, at the same time, her name spoken, but far, far away, and in a faint, suffering voice. The wind groaned outside her window.

"It must have been the wind," she said, and pressing her hand above her heart, she strove to calm herself. But her heart beat ever more wildly. The larch wood doors of the chamber grated on their hinges with a sharp creak, prolonged and strident.

First these doors, then the more distant ones, all the doors which led to her room opened, one after another, some with a heavy, groaning sound, some with a long wail that set the nerves on edge. Then silence, a silence full of strange noises, the silence of midnight, with a monotonous murmur of far-off water, the distant barking of dogs, confused voices, unintelligible words, echoes of footsteps going and coming, the rustle of trailing garments, half-suppressed sighs, laboured breathing almost felt upon the face, involuntary shudders that announce the presence of something not seen, though its approach is felt in the darkness.

Beatriz, stiffening with fear, yet trembling, thrust her head out from the bed-curtains and listened a moment. She heard a thousand diverse noises; she passed her hand across her brow and listened again. Nothing but silence.

She saw, with that dilation of the pupils common in nervous crises, dim shapes moving here and there all about the room, but when she fixed her gaze on any one point, there was nothing but darkness and impenetrable shadows.

"Bah!" she exclaimed, again resting her beautiful head upon her blue satin pillow, "am I as timid as these poor kinsfolk of mine, whose hearts thump with terror under their armour when they hear a ghost-story?"

And closing her eyes she tried to sleep, but her effort to compose herself was in vain. Soon she started up again, paler, more uneasy, more terrified. This time it was no illusion. The brocade hangings of the door had rustled as they were pushed to either side, and slow footsteps were heard upon the carpet. The sound of those footsteps was muffled, almost imperceptible, but continuous, and she heard, keeping measure with them, a creaking as of dry wood or bones. And the footfalls came nearer and nearer. The prayer-stool by the side of her bed moved. Beatriz uttered a sharp cry, and burying herself under the bedclothes, hid her head and held her breath.

The wind beat against the balcony glass. The water of the far-off fountain was falling, falling, with a monotonous, unceasing sound. The barking of the dogs was borne upon the gusts, and the church bells in the city of Soria, some near, some remote, tolled sadly for the souls of the dead.

So passed an hour, two, the night, a century, for that night seemed to Beatrix eternal. At last the day began to break. Putting fear from her, she half opened her eyes to the first silver rays. How beautiful, after a night of wakefulness and terrors, is the clear white light of dawn! She parted the silken curtains of her bed and was ready to laugh at her past alarms, when suddenly a cold sweat covered her body, her eyes seemed starting from their sockets, and a deadly pallor overspread her cheeks. On her prayer-stool she had seen, torn and blood-stained, the blue scarf she lost on the mountain, the blue scarf Alonso went to seek.

When her attendants rushed in, aghast, to tell her of the death of the heir of Alcudiel, whose body, partly devoured by wolves, had been found that morning among the brambles on the Spirits' Mountain, they discovered her motionless, convulsed, clinging with both hands to one of the ebony bedposts, her eyes staring, her mouth open, the lips white, her limbs rigid. She was dead! Dead of fright!

Chapter IV

They say that, sometime after this event, a hunter who, having lost his way, had been obliged to pass the Night of the Dead on the Spirits' Mountain, and who in the morning, before he died, was able to relate what he had seen, told a tale of horror. Among other awful sights, he avowed he beheld the skeletons of the ancient Knights Templars and of the nobles of Soria, buried in the cloister of the chapel, rise at the hour of the Angelus with a horrible rattle and, mounted on their bony steeds, chase, as a wild beast, a beautiful woman, pallid, with streaming hair, who, uttering cries of terror and anguish, had been wandering, with bare and bloody feet, about the tomb of Alonso.

ISSY-BEN-ARAN

Adapted from Patranas; or Spanish Stories by Rachel Harriette Busk, published by Newbery and Harris, 1870.

ISSY-BEN-ARAN WAS A VENERABLE MULETEER, well-known in all the towns of Granada for his worth and integrity. He was an elder and a father among his tribe.

One day, as he was journeying over a wild and sequestered track of the Sierra Nevada, he heard a cry of pain proceeding from the roadside. The good old man immediately turned back to render help to the unfortunate. He found a young man lying among the sharp points of an aloe hedge, groaning as if at the last gasp.

"What ails you? Son, speak," said Issy-ben-Aran.

"I was journeying along the road, father, an hour ago, as full of health as you may be, when I was set upon by six robbers, who knocked me off my mule, and not satisfied with carrying off all I possessed in the world, beat me till they thought I was dead, and then flung my body into this aloe hedge."

Issy-ben-Aran gave him a draught of water from his own bottle and bound his head with linen cloths steeped in fresh water, then he set him on his own beast to carry him at a gentle pace to the nearest town and further care for him, with great strain of his feeble arms lifting him tenderly into the saddle.

No sooner was the stranger well mounted, with his feet firmly set in the stirrups, than, drawing himself up with no further appearance of weakness, he dug his heels into the horse's side, and setting up a loud laugh, started off at a rapid gallop.

Issy-ben-Aran, to whom every stone of the road was known as the lines upon his right hand, immediately scrambled down the mountain-side, so as to confront the stranger at the next turning of the road.

"Hold!" he cried. And the nag, who loved his master well, stood still and refused to move for all the stranger's urging.

"Son! think not that I have come to reproach you," said the old man. "If you desire the horse, take it as a gift. You shall not burden your conscience with a theft on my account."

"Thank you!" scoffed the heartless stranger. "It is fine to make a merit of necessity, but I have nothing to do but ride to the nearest town, and sell the brute."

"Beware! Do not do it", said the old man. "The nag of Issy-ben-Aran is known at every market in the kingdom, and any man of all our tribes who frequents them, finding you with him, will reckon you have killed me, and slay you in turn. Even in this have I a gift for you. Take this scroll to show that you have the horse of me as a free gift, and so no harm shall come to you.

"Only one condition I exact. Bind yourself to me, that you tell no man of what has passed between us, lest peradventure, should it become known, a man hearing his brother cry out in distress might say, 'This man is feigning, that he may take my horse like the horse of Issy-ben-Aran," and the man who is really in danger be thus left to perish miserably."

THE WATCHFUL SERVANT

Adapted from Charles Sellers' original, taken from Tales from the Lands of Nuts and Grapes, published in 1888 by The Leadenhall Press and others.

THERE WAS ONCE A PRINCE WHO was going to visit his lady-love, the only daughter of a neighbouring king; and as he required the services of an attendant, he sent for his barber, who was known in the town for his very good behaviour, as well as for his eccentric ways.

"Pablo," said the prince, "I want you to go with me to Granada to assist me on my journey. I will reward you handsomely, and you shall lack for nothing in the way of food. But you must don my livery, salute me in the fashion of Spain, hold my stirrup when I mount, and do everything that is required of a servant. Above all, you must not let me oversleep myself, for otherwise I shall be late in arriving at Granada."

"Sir," answered the barber, "I will be as true to you as the dog was to St. Dominic. When you are sleeping I will be on guard, and when you are awake I will see that no harm approaches you. But I beg you not to be annoyed with me if, in trying to be of service to you, I do unwillingly cause you any annoyance."

"Good Pablo," continued the prince, "say no more, but return to your shop, pack up your linen, and come here as soon as you can this evening. If I am in bed when you arrive, you will know that it is because I must get up tomorrow morning by five o'clock, and see to it that you let me not sleep beyond that time."

Pablo hurried home, packed up his few articles of underclothing, and then proceeded to the principal wine tavern to tell his friends of his good fortune. They were all so pleased to hear of Pablo's good luck that they drank to his health, and he returned the compliment so often that at last the wine was beginning to tell on him, so he bid his friends good-bye and left, saying to himself, "I must wake his highness at five o'clock." This he kept repeating so often that he had arrived at the large courtyard of the palace before he was aware of it.

The prince's bedroom looked into the courtyard, and Pablo saw by the dim light that was burning in the room that the prince had retired to rest.

Afraid lest the prince should think he had forgotten all about awaking him, and that he might therefore be keeping awake, Pablo seized a long cane, with which he tapped at the window of the prince, and kept on tapping until the prince appeared, and opened the window, shouting out,   "Who's there? Who wants me?"

It is I," said Pablo. "I have not forgotten your orders. Tomorrow morning I will wake your highness at five."

"Very good, Pablo; but let me sleep awhile, or else I shall be tired tomorrow."

As soon as the prince had disappeared Pablo commenced thinking over all the princes of whom he had heard, and he had become so interested in the subject that when he heard the cock crow, imagining it was daybreak, he again seized the cane and tapped loudly at the window.

The prince again lifted up the sash, and cried out, "Who is it? What do you want? Let me sleep, or else I shall be tired tomorrow."

"Sir," exclaimed the barber, "the cock has already crowed, and it must be time to rise."

"You are mistaken," replied the prince, "for it is only half an hour ago since you woke me; but I am not annoyed with you."

Pablo was now sorely troubled in his mind because he thought he might give offence to the prince, and so he kept revolving in his mind all that his mother had told him about the anger of princes, and how much it was to be dreaded. This thought so perplexed him that he resolved on putting an end to the life of the cock that had caused the mistake. He therefore proceeded to the poultry-yard close by, and seeing the offender surrounded by the hens, he made a rush at him, which set all the fowls cackling as if a fox had broken in.

The prince, hearing the noise, hurried to the window, and in a loud voice inquired what the noise was all about.

"Sir," said Pablo, "I was but trying to punish the disturber of your rest. I have got hold of him now, and your highness may go to sleep without further care, as I will not forget to waken you."

"But," continued the prince, "if you waken me again before it is time, I will most decidedly punish you." Saying which he again retired to rest.

"Since the days when cocks crew in the Holy Land they have always brought sorrow into this world," inwardly ejaculated Pablo. "His proper place is in the pan, and that is where he should go if I had my way."

All at once Pablo commenced to feel very sleepy, so he walked up and down the yard to keep awake; but becoming drowsy he sank on the ground, and was soon so fast asleep that he dreamt a heathen prince was attacking him, which made him scream so terribly that it woke, not only the prince, but also all the dogs in the neighbourhood.

The prince again rushed to the window, and hearing Pablo scream out, "Don't murder me, I will give you all!" hurried down into the yard, and seeing how matters stood bestowed such a hearty kick on Pablo that he jumped up.

The frightened barber, beholding the prince near to him, took to his heels, and ran home as fast as he could.

When he had got into bed he began regretting that he had run away from the prince's service, so he got up again, saying to himself, "The prince shall have a sharper spur than I could ever buckle on…" and, proceeding to the principal door of the palace, he wrote the following words with chalk, "Pablo has gone before your highness to court the Princess of Granada himself."

This had the desired effect, for when the prince arose in the morning and was leaving the palace alone, he read the words, and they caused him to be so jealous that he performed the distance in half the time he would otherwise have taken.

Pablo after that used to say that "a jealous man on horseback is first cousin to a flash of lightning and to a true Spaniard."

MÓSTAFA ALVILÁ

Adapted from Patranas; or Spanish Stories by Rachel Harriette Busk, published by Newbery and Harris, 1870.

MÓSTAFA ALVILÁ WAS CALIFF OF A conquered province in Spain, where he reigned with oriental state. The tributary people were ground down with hard work to minister to his treasury, and the vast sums he amassed were spent in beautifying his Alcázar, and filling it with costly productions from all parts. Merchants from every climate under heaven were encouraged to come and offer him their choicest wares.

One day, a merchant of Persia brought a large pack of shawls and carpets, all woven in gold and pearls, and wools and silks of brilliant colours, but among them all the most beautiful was one carpet of great price, on which Móstafa Alvilá's choice was immediately set. But in all his treasury there was not found the price of it. Nothing would do. He must possess it. Then Ali Babá his vizier came forward and said, "Let ten thousand dogs of Christians be sold, and with the price of them you shall purchase the carpet."

Móstafa Alvilá answered and said, "The advice is good!" So they sent and sold ten thousand Christians, and with the price of them the carpet was bought.

Móstafa Alvilá sat contemplating the curious devices, and tracing the wonderful arabesque patterns with which the carpet was covered; and there was one pattern, all shining with gold and pearls, quite prominent in the centre, which had a likeness to the characters of an inscription. When Móstafa Alvilá saw it, he was very curious to know if it was an inscription, and what it meant, so he sent to recall the merchant; but he was gone from the Alcázar.

Then he sent his servants after him, and though they travelled three days' journey by every road, they could neither find him nor obtain any tidings of where he had passed. Then Móstafa Alvilá was more curious still, and sent and gathered all the learned men in his califate, and inquired of them what the inscription might mean. They all looked troubled, and said they could not tell, for they had never seen such letters. But one there was who concealed the difficulty he was in so ill, that Móstafa Alvilá saw he knew what the writing meant, so he looked very severely upon him and threatened him with instant death if he did not tell him exactly what the writing was.

Then the interpreter, when he found there was no other way to save his life, with great fear and trembling said, this is the meaning: "Shiroes, son of Chosroes, killed his father; and he died six months after."

Móstafa Alvilá was greatly troubled when he heard the sentence; for he had ascended the califate by killing his father, and he had reigned six months all but one day. So he sent and commanded that the interpreter and all who had heard the sentence should be put to death, that no one might know the omen.

But that night, in the middle of the dark hours, when Móstafa Alvilá was alone in his chamber, a horrible vision came to him. He thought he saw the body of his father whom he had murdered rise up to convict him. He sunk down in his bed, and covered his face in fear and horror.

In the morning, when they came to call him, they found only his lifeless corpse.

Tales From The Land Of Rabbits

THE EMIR IN SEARCH OF AN EYE

Adapted from Patranas; or Spanish Stories by Rachel Harriette Busk, published by Newbery and Harris, 1870.

THE EMIR ABU-BEKIR LOST AN EYE in battle against the Christians. "The Christians shall pay me what they have taken from me," he said, and he sent for a number of Christian captives, and had one of their eyes taken out, in the idea of replacing his own; but it was found that none of them agreed with his in size, and form, and colour. The Emir Abu-Bekir was a very comely person, and his eyes had been so mild and soft, that it was at last thought only the eye of a woman could replace the missing one. The choice fell upon a beautiful maiden named Sancha. Sancha was brought into the Emir's presence, and his physician was ordered to take out her eye, and place it in the vacant socket.

Now Sancha stood trembling and wailing, and by her very crying damaging the perfection of the coveted feature. Then there stood up a travelling doctor who was in great fame among the people, and who begged a hearing of the Emir, for albeit he was a Turk, yet he possessed pity and gratitude. He knew that the operation, while a torment to the Christian maiden, would be of no service to the Emir; and he pitied the waste of pain. It happened further, that once, when on a journey he had sunk fainting by the way-side, this very Sancha had comforted and relieved him, and now he determined to rescue her.

Accordingly, he stepped up to the Emir, and told him that he had eyes made of crystal, and coloured by cunning art, which no one could tell from living eyes, and which would be of much greater service and ornament than those of the Christian dogs, whose eyes he might have observed lost all their lustre and consistency the moment they were taken from their natural place. The Emir admitted the truth of the last statement, and being marvellously pleased with the glass eyes the travelling doctor displayed, asked him the price.

"The maiden for a slave," replied the doctor.

The Emir gladly consented to so advantageous a bargain, and suffered the glass eye to be fixed in his head. All the Court applauded the appearance.

"But I cannot see with it!" cried the Emir.

"Oh! you must give it a little time to get used to your ways," answered the doctor, readily. "You can't expect it all of a sudden to do as well as the other, that you have had in use so long."

So the Emir was content to wait. Meanwhile, the doctor made off with his fair prize, whom he conducted safely back to Spain, and restored her faithfully to her friends and her liberty.

SILVER BELLS

Adapted from Charles Sellers' original, taken from Tales from the Lands of Nuts and Grapes, published in 1888 by The Leadenhall Press and others.

IT WAS IN A LOVELY PINE-WOOD that little Mirabella wandered lonely and hungry. The sand under her feet was very cool, and the tufted pine-trees sheltered her from the fierce rays of the sun.

Through an avenue of tall but bare pine-trees she could see the big sea, which she looked upon for the first time. Faint and hungry as she was, she could not help wishing to be nearer the waves; but she recollected what her father had once told her, that little children should be careful not to go too near the sea when they are alone.

Her father, however, was dead. He was King of the Silver Isles, and for his goodness had been loved by all his subjects. Mirabella was his only child; and her mother having married again, she wanted to get rid of Mirabella, so that her little boy Gliglu might inherit the crown. So she ordered one of her servants to lead

Mirabella into the pine-wood far away and leave her there, hoping the wolves would find her and eat her.

When Mirabella was born, her aunt, who was a fairy, gave her a silver bell, which she tied around the child's neck with a fairy chain that could not be broken. In vain did her mother try to take it from her; no scissors could cut through it, and her strength could not break it, so that wherever Mirabella went the silver bell tinkled merrily.

Now, it so happened that on the second night on which she was out the silver bell tinkled so loudly, that a wolf who happened to be near, hearing it, approached her and said, "Silver bell, silver bell, do not fear. To obey you, Mirabella, I am here."

At first the little girl was very much afraid, because she had heard of the cruelty of wolves; but when he repeated the words, she said, "Dear Mr. Wolf, if you would be so kind as to bring me my mamma, I would be so obliged."

Off ran the wolf without saying another word, and Mirabella commenced jumping for joy, causing her silver bell to tinkle more than ever. A fox, hearing it, came up to her and said, "Silver bell, silver bell, do not fear. To obey you, Mirabella, I am here."

Then she said, "Oh, dear Mr. Fox, I am so hungry! I wish you would bring me something to eat."

Off went the fox, and in a short time he returned with a roast fowl, bread, a plate, knife, and fork, all nicely placed in a basket. On the top of these things was a clean white cloth, which she spread on the ground, and on which she placed her dinner. She was indeed thankful to the fox for his kindness, and patted his head, which made him wag his thick brush. She enjoyed her dinner very much; but she was very thirsty. She thought she would try tinkling her bell, and no sooner had she done so than she heard the tinkling of another bell in the distance, coming nearer and nearer to her. She stood on tiptoe, and she saw a stream of water flowing towards her, on which floated a pretty canoe. When it got up to her it stopped, and inside the canoe was a silver mug; but on the bows of the canoe was hanging a silver bell just like her own.

"Silver bell, silver bell, do not fear. When your mother comes, step in here."

So sang the canoe, but Mirabella could not understand why she should get into the canoe if her mother came, because she loved her mother, and thought her mother loved her. Anyhow she took hold of the mug, and, filling it with water, drank it up. Water, which is always the most refreshing of all drinks, was what the tired little girl most needed, and as her father had brought her up very carefully and properly, she had never tasted anything stronger; but her thirst made her enjoy the water more than she ever had.

Suddenly she heard someone screaming for help, and the screams came nearer and nearer to her. She turned round and saw the wolf bearing her mother on his back, and however much she tried to get off she could not, because the wolf threatened to bite her. Springing up to Mirabella's side, the wolf said, "Silver bell, silver bell, do not fear. To obey you, Mirabella, I am here."

The wicked mother now jumped off his back, and commenced scolding Mirabella for having sent for her. She said that as soon as she got back to the palace she would make a law that all the wolves should be killed, and that if Mirabella ever dared return she should be smothered. The poor little girl felt very miserable, and was afraid that her mother might kill her, so she stepped into the canoe, and said, "Bear me where my father dwells. Tinkle, tinkle, silver bells."

The stream continued to flow, and as the canoe moved on she saw her mother turned into a cork-tree, and she bid good-bye to the wolf and the fox. On sped the boat, and it soon neared the big sea. Mirabella felt no fear, for the stream struck out across the ocean, and the waves did not come near her. For three days and nights the silver bells tinkled and the canoe sped on; and when the morning of the fourth day came, she saw that they were approaching a beautiful island, on which were growing many palm-trees, which are called sacred palms. The grass was far greener than any she had ever seen, for the sun was more brilliant, but not so fierce, and when the canoe touched the shore - oh, joy! - she saw her dear father.

"Silver bell, silver bell, do not fear. To protect you Mirabella, I am here."

She was so pleased to see her father again and to hear him speak. It was so nice to be loved, to be cared for, to be spoken kindly to. Everything seemed to welcome her. The boughs of the sacred palms waved in the summer breeze, and the humming-birds, flitting about, seemed like precious stones set in a glorious blaze of light. Her father was not changed very much; he looked somewhat younger and stronger, and as he lifted her in his arms his face seemed handsomer and his voice more welcome. She felt no pang of sorrow, she had no fears, for she was in her father's arms, to which the fairy silver bells had led her.

Farther up in the island she saw groups of other children running to meet her, all with silver bells around their necks; and some there were among them whom she had known in the Silver Islands. These had been playmates of hers, but had left before her.

So, the days sped on, in which joy was her companion, but after a while, looking into a deep but very clear pond, she saw a gnarled cork-tree, which seemed to have been struck by lightning. Long did she stand there gazing into the pond wondering where she had seen that tree. All at once she spied a canoe passing close by the tree, in which stood a young man, whom she recognized as her step-brother Gliglu. He seemed to cast a sorrowful look at the tree, and then she recollected the fate of her mother. At this moment her silver bell fell off, and, sinking into the pond, it went down—down, until it reached the tree, and, tinkling, said, "Take your shape again, Oh queen!"

Then Mirabella saw her mother step into the canoe; and tinkling bells in a short space of time told her that others dear and near to her had arrived, and, running down to the shore, she cried out, "Silver bells, O mother, wait you here. Nought but joy with father, nought to fear."

Tales From The Land Of Rabbits

THE THREE QUESTIONS

Adapted from Fairy Tales from Spain by José Muñoz Escámez, published by J. M. Dent & Sons Ltd, 1913.

IN THE HISTORY OF SPAIN, KING Pedro I of Castile, son of Alfonso XI. the Just, is known by the surname of the Cruel.

And his fame as a heartless man was such that his subjects, on whom he satisfied his terrible thirst for blood and violence, held him in great terror.

One day while hunting, of which sport he was very fond, King Pedro lost his way in the wood, and came to rest himself, the night being well advanced, in an hospitable convent, where without being known he was offered food, bed, and shelter.

Hardly returning thanks, he passed into the refectory, and on entering was recognised by a lay brother, who knew that the king suffered from a certain illness called synovitis, the principal effect of which was that the malady produced, when he was walking, a strange sound of bones knocking together. By this noise he was recognised by the lay brother.

Instantly informing the community, due homage was hastily rendered to the monarch, but King Pedro was in a bad temper, and facing one of the reverend fathers, said to him in a disconcerting tone, "How fat you are, Father Prior! Study makes no hollows in you, from which I gather that you cannot be so wise as the people hereabout say."

The community was so taken aback, that no one dared to say a word to that monster of a king.

"Well, if you wish to please me," he continued, "I summon you to come to my palace within ten days, and to answer satisfactorily the following questions: First, what is the distance between the earth and the sun? Second, how much am I worth? And third, what do I believe which is false? If you do not answer me to my taste I will have you beheaded at once."

And saying this, he went away.

Needless to say the poor friar was frightened, for he knew only too well that King Pedro was quite capable of doing what he threatened. So he devoted himself to thinking day and night about the questions, without hitting upon any answers.

At the time when King Pedro reigned the distance between the planets had not been discovered, so there were many discussions between the brethren over the questions of the king. They were still disputing when the day arrived on which the prior was summoned to the palace. And even yet he did not know what to answer. In his distress he invoked the Holy Virgin, certain that She would not refuse to help him.

After which he was about to set out for Seville when one of the lay brothers, a sharp and daring lad, said to him, "Father Prior, your reverence and I are about the same height, and even look somewhat alike. Why not let me go in your place, father, and answer the king?"

On seeing him so resolved he did not doubt for a moment that the lay brother had been inspired by God to save him, and after hearing him, allowed him to go to Seville.

When he arrived at the palace and announced himself, the king gave orders for him to be allowed to enter.

"Have you thought out the answers to the questions that I asked you?" asked King Pedro.

"Yes, sire."

"Well, begin then. What is the distance between the earth and the sun?"

"Eight hundred and forty-seven thousand leagues. Not one more, nor one less. And if your majesty does not believe me, have it measured."

As this was impossible, the king was obliged to say that he was satisfied.

"Not bad," he said. "Now the second: How much am I worth?"

"Twenty-nine pieces of silver."

"And why twenty-nine pieces?"

"Because your majesty is not worth so much as our Saviour, Jesus Christ, and He was sold for thirty."

"And what do I think which is not true?" exclaimed King Pedro, somewhat piqued.

"Well, your majesty thinks that I am the prior, and I am not."

The king was surprised at the ingenuity of the lay brother and pardoned the substitution, and heaped both with favours.

This proves that the fiercest men are overcome and appeased by the forces of ingenuity.

THE PROMISE

Adapted from Romantic Legends of Spain. and taken from the original story written by Gustavo Adolfo Bécquer, translated by Cornelia Francis Bates and Katherine Lee Bates, 1909.

Chapter I

MARGARITA, HER FACE HIDDEN IN HER hands, was weeping. She did not sob, but the tears ran silently down her cheeks, slipping between her fingers to fall to the earth toward which her brow was bent.

Near Margarita was Pedro, who from time to time lifted his eyes to steal a glance at her and, seeing that she still wept, dropped them again, maintaining for his part utter silence.

All was hushed about them, as if respecting her grief. The murmurs of the field were stilled, the breeze of evening slept, and darkness was beginning to envelop the dense growth of the wood.

Thus some moments passed, during which the trace of light that the dying sun had left on the horizon faded quite away. The moon began to be faintly sketched against the violet background of the twilight sky, and one after another shone out the brighter stars.

Pedro broke at last that distressful silence, exclaiming in a hoarse and gasping voice and as if he were communing with himself, "Tis impossible... impossible!"

Then, coming close to the inconsolable maiden and taking one of her hands, he continued in a softer, more caressing tone, "Margarita, for you love is all, and you see nothing beyond love. Yet there is one thing as binding as our love, and that is my duty. Our lord the Count of Gômara goes forth tomorrow from his castle to join his force to the army of King Fernando, who is on his way to deliver Seville out of the power of the Infidels, and it is my duty to depart with the Count.

"An obscure orphan, without name or family, I owe to him all that I am. I have served him in the idle days of peace, I have slept beneath his roof, I have been warmed at his hearth and eaten at his board. If I forsake him now, tomorrow his men-at-arms, as they sally forth in marching array from his castle gates, will ask, wondering at my absence, 'Where is the favorite squire of the Count of Gômara?' And my lord will be silent for shame, and his pages and his fools will say in mocking tone, 'The Count's squire is only a gallant of the jousts, a warrior in the game of courtesy.'"

When he had spoken thus far, Margarita lifted her eyes full of tears to meet those of her lover and moved her lips as if to answer him; but her voice was choked in a sob.

Pedro, with still tenderer and more persuasive tone, went on, "Weep not, for God's sake, Margarita; weep not, for your tears hurt me. I must go from you, but I will return as soon as I have gained a little glory for my obscure name.

"Heaven will aid us in our holy enterprise; we shall conquer Seville, and to us conquerors the King will give fiefs along the banks of the Guadalquivir. Then I will come back for you, and we will go together to dwell in that paradise of the Arabs, where they say the sky is clearer and more blue than the sky above Castile.

"I will come back, I swear to you I will. I will return to keep the troth solemnly pledged you that day when I placed on your finger this ring, symbol of a promise."

"Pedro!" exclaimed Margarita, controlling her emotion and speaking in a firm, determined tone, "Go, go to uphold your honour," and on pronouncing these words, she threw herself for the last time into the embrace of her lover. Then she added in a tone lower and more shaken: "Go to uphold your honour, but come back! Come back to save mine."

Pedro kissed the brow of Margarita, loosed his horse, that was tied to one of the trees of the grove, and rode off at a gallop through the depths of the poplar-wood.

Margarita followed Pedro with her eyes until his dim form was swallowed up in the shades of night. When he could no longer be discerned, she went back slowly to the village where her brothers were awaiting her.

"Put on your gala dress," one of them said to her as she entered, "for in the morning we go to Gômara with all the neighbourhood to see the Count marching to Andalusia."

"For my part, it saddens rather than gladdens me to see those go forth who perchance shall not return," replied Margarita with a sigh.

201

"Yet come with us you must," insisted the other brother, "and you must come with mien composed and glad, so that the gossiping folk shall have no cause to say you have a lover in the castle, and that your lover goes to the war."

Chapter II

Hardly was the first light of dawn streaming up the sky when there began to sound throughout all the camp of Gômara the shrill trumpeting of the Count's soldiers, and the peasants who were arriving in numerous groups from the villages round about saw the seigniorial banner flung to the winds from the highest tower of the fortress.

The peasants were everywhere; seated on the edge of the moat, ensconced in the tops of trees, strolling over the plain, crowning the crests of the hills, forming a line far along the highway. They had already been waiting for nearly an hour awaiting the show, not without some signs of impatience, when the ringing bugle-call sounded again, the chains of the drawbridge creaked as it fell slowly across the moat, and the portcullis was raised, while little by little, groaning upon their hinges, the massive doors of the arched passage which led to the Court of Arms swung wide.

The multitude ran to press for places on the sloping banks beside the road in order to see their fill of the brilliant armour and sumptuous trappings of the following of the Count of Gômara, famed through all the countryside for his splendour and his lavish pomp.

The march was opened by the heralds who, halting at fixed intervals, proclaimed in loud voice, to the beat of the drum, the commands of the King, summoning his feudatories to the Moorish war and requiring the villages and free towns to give passage and aid to his armies.

After the heralds followed the kings-at-arms, proud of their silken vestments, their shields bordered with gold and bright colours, and their caps decked with graceful plumes.

Then came the chief retainer of the castle armed cap-à-pie, a knight mounted on a young black horse, bearing in his hands the pennon of a grandee with his motto and device, and at his left hand rode the executioner of the seigniory, clad in black and red.

The seneschal was preceded by fully a score of those famous trumpeters of Castile celebrated in the chronicles of our kings for the incredible power of their lungs.

When the shrill clamour of their mighty trumpeting ceased to wound the wind, a dull sound, steady and monotonous, began to reach the ear; the tramp of the foot-soldiers, armed with long pikes and provided with a leather shield apiece. Behind these soon came in view the soldiers who managed the engines of war, with their crude machines and their wooden towers, the bands of wall-scalers and the rabble of stable-boys in charge of the mules.

Then, enveloped in the cloud of dust raised by the hoofs of their horses, flashing sparks from their iron breastplates, passed the men-at-arms of the castle, formed in thick platoons, looking from a distance like a forest of spears.

Last of all, preceded by the drummers who were mounted on strong mules tricked out in housings and plumes, surrounded by pages in rich raiment of silk and gold and followed by the squires of the castle, appeared the Count.

As the multitude caught sight of him, a great shout of greeting went up and in the tumult of acclamation was stifled the cry of a woman, who at that moment, as if struck by a thunderbolt, fell fainting into the arms of those who sprang to her aid. It was Margarita, who had recognized her mysterious lover in that great and dreadful lord, the Count of Gômara, one of the most exalted and powerful feudatories of the Crown of Castile.

Chapter III

The host of Don Fernando, after going forth from Cordova, had marched to Seville, not without having to fight its way at Écija, Carmona, and Alcalá del Rio del Guadaira, whose famous castle, once taken by storm, put the army in sight of the stronghold of the Infidels.

The Count of Gômara was in his tent seated on a bench of larch wood, motionless, pale, terrible, his hands crossed upon the hilt of his broadsword, his eyes fixed on space with that vague regard which appears to behold a definite object and yet takes cognizance of naught in the encompassing scene.

Standing by his side, the squire who had been longest in the castle, the only one who in those moods of black despondency could have ventured to intrude without drawing down upon his head an explosion of wrath, was speaking to him.

"What is your ail, my lord?" he was saying. "What trouble wears and wastes you? Sad you go to battle, and sad return, even though returning victorious. When all the warriors sleep, surrendered to the weariness of the day, I hear your anguished sighs; and if I run to your bed, I see you struggling there against some invisible torment. You open your eyes, but your terror does not vanish. What is it, my lord? Tell me. If it be a secret, I will guard it in the depths of my memory as in a grave."

The Count seemed not to hear his squire, but after a long pause, as if the words had taken all that time to make slow way from his ears to his understanding, he emerged little by little from his trance and, drawing the squire affectionately toward him, said to him with grave and quiet tone, "I have suffered much in silence. Believing myself the sport of a vain fantasy, I have until now held my peace for shame, but nay, what is happening to me is no illusion.

"It must be that I am under the power of some awful curse. Heaven or hell must wish something of me, and tell me so by supernatural events. Do you recall the day of our encounter with the Moors of Nebriza in the Aljarafe de Triana? We were few, the combat was stern, and I was face to face with death. you saw, in the most critical moment of the fight, my horse, wounded and blind with rage, dash toward the main body of the Moorish host. I strove in vain to check him. The reins had escaped from my hands, and the fiery animal galloped on, bearing me to certain death.

"Already the Moors, closing up their ranks, were grounding their long pikes to receive me on the points; a cloud of arrows hissed about my ears; the horse was but a few bounds from the serried spears on which we were about to fling ourselves, when, and believe me, it was not an illusion, I saw a hand that, grasping the bridle, stopped him with an unearthly force and, turning him in the direction of my own troops, saved me by a miracle.

"In vain I asked of one and another who my deliverer was, but no one knew him, no one had seen him. 'When you were rushing to throw yourself upon the wall of pikes,' they said, 'you went alone, absolutely alone. This is why we marvelled to see you turn, knowing that the steed no longer obeyed his rider.'

"That night I entered my tent distraught; I strove in vain to extirpate from my imagination the memory of the strange adventure, but on advancing toward my bed, again I saw the same hand, a beautiful hand, white to the point of pallor, which drew the curtains, vanishing after it had drawn them. Ever since, at all hours, in all places, I see that mysterious hand which anticipates my desires and forestalls my actions. I saw it, when we were storming the castle of Triana, catch between its fingers and break in the air an arrow which was about to strike me; I have seen it at banquets where I was trying to drown my trouble in the tumultuous revelry, pour the wine into my cup. Always it flickers before my eyes, and wherever I go it follows me; in the tent, in the battle, by day, by night, even now, see it, see it here, resting gently on my shoulder!"

On speaking these last words, the Count sprang to his feet, striding back and forth as if beside himself, overwhelmed by utter terror.

The squire dashed away a tear. Believing his lord mad, he did not try to combat his ideas, but confined himself to saying in a voice of deep emotion, "Come. Let us go out from the tent a moment. Perhaps the evening air will cool your temples, calming this incomprehensible grief, for which I find no words of consolation."

Chapter IV

The camp of the Christians extended over all the plain of Guadaira, even to the left bank of the Guadalquivir. In front of the camp and clearly defined against the bright horizon, rose the walls of Seville flanked by massive, menacing towers. Above the crown of battlements showed in its rich profusion the green leafage of the thousand gardens enclosed in the Moorish stronghold, and amid the dim clusters of foliage gleamed the observation turrets, white as snow, the minarets of the mosques, and the gigantic watch-tower, over whose aerial parapet the four great balls of gold, which from the Christian camp looked like four flames, threw out, when smitten by the sun, sparks of living light.

The enterprise of Don Fernando, one of the most heroic and intrepid of that epoch, had drawn to his banners the greatest warriors of the various kingdoms in the Peninsula, with others who, called by fame, had come from foreign, far-off lands to add their forces to those of the Royal Saint. Stretching along the plain might be seen, therefore, army-tents of all forms and colours, above whose peaks waved in the wind the various ensigns with their quartered escutcheons; stars, griffins, lions, chains, bars and caldrons, with hundreds of other heraldic figures or symbols which proclaimed the name and quality of their owners. Through the streets of that improvised city were circulating in all directions a multitude of soldiers who, speaking diverse dialects, dressed each in the fashion of his own locality and armed according to his fancy, formed a scene of strange and picturesque contrasts.

Here a group of nobles were resting from the fatigues of combat, seated on benches of larch wood at the door of their tents and playing at chess, while their pages poured them wine in metal cups. There some foot-soldiers were taking advantage of a moment of leisure to clean and mend their armour, the worse for their last skirmish. Further on, the most expert archers of the army were covering the mark with arrows, amidst the applause of the crowd marvelling at their dexterity, and the beating of the drums, the shrilling of the trumpets, the cries of pedlars hawking their wares, the clang of iron striking on iron, the ballad-singing of the minstrels who entertained their hearers with the relation of prodigious exploits, and the shouts of the heralds who published the orders of the camp-masters, all these, filling the air with thousands of discordant noises, contributed to that picture of soldier life a vivacity and animation impossible to portray in words.

The Count of Gômara, attended by his faithful squire, passed among the lively groups without raising his eyes from the ground, silent, sad, as if not a sight disturbed his gaze nor the least sound reached his hearing. He moved mechanically, as a sleepwalker, whose spirit is busy in the world of dreams, steps and takes his course without consciousness of his actions, as if impelled by a will not his own.

Close by the royal tent and in the middle of a ring of soldiers, little pages and camp-servants, who were listening to him open-mouthed, making haste to buy some of the tawdry knickknacks which he was enumerating in a loud voice, with extravagant praises, was an odd personage, half pilgrim, half minstrel, who, at one moment reciting a kind of litany in barbarous Latin, and the next giving vent to some buffoonery or scurrility, was mingling in his interminable tale devout prayers with jests broad enough to make a common soldier blush. He recounted romances of illicit love along with the legends of the saints. In the huge pack that hung from his shoulders were a thousand different objects all tossed and tumbled together; ribbons touched to the sepulchre of Santiago, scrolls with words which he averred were Hebrew, the very same that King Solomon spoke when he founded the temple, and the only words able to keep you free of every contagious disease. He had marvellous balsams capable of sticking together men who were cut in two and secret charms to make all women in love with you. He could provide Gospels sewed into little silk bags, relics of the patron saints of all the towns in Spain, tinsel jewels, chains, sword-belts, medals and many other gewgaws of brass, glass and lead.

When the Count approached the group formed by the pilgrim and his admirers, the fellow began to tune a kind of mandolin or Arab guitar with which he accompanied himself in the singsong recital of his romances. When he had thoroughly tested the strings, one after another, very coolly, while his companion made the round of the circle coaxing out the last coppers from the flaccid pouches of the audience, the pilgrim began to sing in nasal voice, to a monotonous and plaintive air, a ballad whose stanzas always ended in the same refrain.

The Count drew near the group and gave attention. By an apparently strange coincidence, the title of this tale was entirely at one with the melancholy thoughts that burdened his mind. As the singer had announced before beginning, the lay was called the Ballad of the Dead Hand.

The squire, on hearing so strange an announcement, had striven to draw his lord away; but the Count, with his eyes fixed on the minstrel, remained motionless, listening to this song.

A maiden had a lover gay

Who said he was a squire,

The war-drums called him far away;

Not tears could quench his fire.

"Thou goest to return no more."

"Nay, by all oaths that bind"

But even while the lover swore,

A voice was on the wind:

Ill fares the soul that sets its trust

On faith of dust.

Forth from his castle rode the lord

With all his glittering train,

But never will his battle-sword

Inflict so keen a pain.

"His soldier-honour well he keeps;

Mine honour - blind! oh, blind!"

While the forsaken woman weeps,

A voice is on the wind.

Ill fares the soul that sets its trust

On faith of dust.

Her brother's eye her secret reads;

His fatal angers burn

"Thou hast us shamed." Her terror pleads,

"He swore he would return."

"But not to find you, if he tries,

Where he was wont to find."

Beneath her brother's blow she dies;

A voice is on the wind:

Ill fares the soul that sets its trust

On faith of dust.

In the trysting-wood, where love made mirth,

They have buried her deep, - but lo!

However high they heap the earth,

A hand as white as snow

Comes stealing up, a hand whose ring

A noble's troth doth bind.

Above her grave no maidens sing,

But a voice is on the wind:

Ill fares the soul that sets its trust

On faith of dust.

Hardly had the singer finished the last stanza, when, breaking through the wall of eager listeners who respectfully gave way on recognizing him, the Count fronted the pilgrim and, clutching his arm, demanded in a low, convulsive voice, "What part of Spain do you come from?"

"From Soria," was the unmoved response.

"And where did you learn this ballad? Who is that maiden of whom the story tells?" again exclaimed the Count, with ever more profound emotion.

"My lord," said the pilgrim, fixing his eyes upon the Count with imperturbable steadiness, "this ballad is passed from mouth to mouth among the peasants in the fief of Gômara, and it refers to an unhappy village-girl cruelly wronged by a great lord. The high justice of God has permitted that, in her burial, there shall still remain above the earth the hand on which her lover placed a ring in plighting her his troth. Perchance you know whom it is that should keep that pledge."

Chapter V

In a wretched village which may be found at one side of the highway leading to Gômara, I saw not long since the spot where the strange ceremony of the Count's marriage is said to have taken place.

After he, kneeling upon the humble grave, had pressed the hand of Margarita in his own, and a priest, authorized by the Pope, had blessed the mournful union, the story goes that the miracle ceased, and the dead hand buried itself forever.

At the foot of some great old trees there is a bit of meadow which, every spring, covers itself spontaneously with flowers. The country-folk say that this is the burial place of Margarita.

THE BLACK CHARGER OF HERNANDO

Adapted from Patranas; or Spanish Stories by Rachel Harriette Busk, published by Newbery and Harris, 1870.

HERNANDO WAS A POOR KNIGHT, WHO had spent all in the service of his country. He had nothing to call his own but his stout armour, his courageous black charger, and his bold lance, and with these he was ever in the thickest of the fray against the Moors. But at last his turn came; and in return for the losses he had caused them, the Moors contrived to surround and slay him.

Now, when his black charger knew that his master was wounded to death, like a valiant steed true to his Christian master, he turned and bore him out of the fight to a lonely dell, where a pious hermit might minister the last consolations of religion to his parting soul. But a Moor, seeing the helpless dying man thus borne along, determined to possess himself of his stout armour and his bold black charger. He followed with fruitless attempts to arrest the gallant beast until it pleased him to stop before the hermit's cell, where it waited patiently while the hermit and the Moor lifted the sacred burden down. The hermit and the Moor worked together, for the Moor desired to possess himself of the outer shell of the knight's armour, and the hermit, the inner shell, namely, his body, that the kernel, that is his soul, might go up holy and clean before God.

Then his soul had scarcely passed away, when the Moor stripped him of his armour, and packed it all safely on the back of the black charger, and prepared to lead him home, for he was afraid himself to mount him. But the black charger no sooner perceived his dear master's remains safe in the care of the hermit, to bury them, and his armour safe in his own, than he started off at his wildest speed, leaving the Moor who had ventured to lay his infidel hands on the reins, to measure his length in the dust. And on and on he went, nor stopped till he reached Hernando's hillside home.

Doña Teresa, his wife, had never ceased every day to look out for her Hernando's return. And when she saw his black charger, bearing his empty armour, she knew at once all that had come to pass, and like a noble Christian spouse, she had the strength to thank God that her Hernando had spent his life in the service of his religion and his country. Then she took his precious armour and laid it safely by, and she caressed the gallant black charger, and led him away to his fresh-littered stall.

Then every day she tried the armour on her son, the young Hernando, and made him bestride the black charger, that he might be a valiant knight like his father.

Now young Hernando was slight, and young Hernando was pale. And he shrank from the cold, hard armour, and the tall, snorting steed. But his mother Teresa was brave, brave as became a Christian spouse, and she listened not to his fears; but bade him be of good heart, and put his trust in Christ.

And at last the day came when she bade him go forth and do battle to the Moors. Young Hernando's heart beat high, for his spirit indeed was willing and he burned to add his name to the long traditions of prowess which his mother told him of his house. But his arm was all untried, and he shrank from the thought of pain, for the young tender flesh was weak. But he would not belie his mother, so he crossed the bold black charger, and the noble charger snorted, when he felt that once more he bore a Christian to the battle.

By night they travelled on, and by day they slept in the shade. In the morning, when the sun began to dawn, they rose, and set out on their way; and as they crossed a plain, young Hernando saw a tall Moor coming towards them. And his heart smote him for fear, and he would gladly have turned out of the way. But he thought it became not a Christian knight to shrink away before a Moor, so he nerved himself with what courage he might, and rode on steadily along his way.

Now, when the bold black charger scented the Moor, he snorted, and shook his mane, and darted to the encounter. So young Hernando was borne along, and found himself face to face with his foe. Then his father's shield rose to protect him, and the lance lifted up his arm; and the black charger rode at the Moor, and the lance cast him down from his seat. Then the sword leaped from its scabbard, and planting itself in young Hernando's grasp, struck off the Moor's head.

So Hernando tied the head to his saddle and bound the body upon its mule. Thus he rode on to the town of Royal Burgos. And when the people saw him bestriding the bold black charger, the grisly head hanging from his saddle, and the headless body following behind, bound fast to the African mule, they cried, "All hail to the victor! All hail to young Hernando, who conquered the pagan Moor!"

And so they brought him to the king, and his ghastly burden with him, and the headless rider behind. And the king rose and embraced him, and the queen held her fair white hand and gave it the youth to kiss. And she said, "A youth so comely and valiant should have armour rich and bright, and a steed with a shining coat." So she called a page to bring a suit of polished steel, and a horse from the royal stables, and present them to young Hernando. Then they took off his ancient armour and laid it on the old black charger, and Hernando donned the new, and sprang into the saddle of the horse from the royal stall.

Now the bold black charger was grieved to be thus set aside, so he snorted and turned his head and rode back to Doña Teresa. When Doña Teresa saw him ride back with the empty armour, she thought that her son was dead, and rejoiced as a Christian mother, that the Moors had sent him to glory. So she laid up the ancient armour, and caressed the bold black charger, and led him to his fresh-littered stall.

Young Hernando meantime feared, as he sat on his fiery new steed, for in his far-off hillside home he had but that black charger tried. Nor had he learnt to handle the weapons they gave him to bear.

But the king, who had seen him come in bearing along such goodly spoils, took him for a practised warrior, and gave him a work to do which needed a valiant heart. "Now keep this pass," he said, "for the rocks are narrow and high, and one at a time, as the enemy comes, with your sword you will strike them down."

Young Hernando dare not say 'Nay;' for his spirit within him was bold, though his young tender flesh was weak. And as he watched there alone, with only the moon for guide, "Oh, had I my old black charger, and my father's armour!" he cried. And the bold black charger felt, as he stood in his far-off stall, that his master's son was in danger, and he snorted to get away. And Doña Teresa knew when she heard him snort and snort there was work to do far away. So she bound the armour on him, and away he fled like the wind, nor stopped till he reached Hernando.

"To me! my bold black charger! To me! 'Tis yet in time! To me!" And he mounted the charger bold, clad in his father's armour.

Then stealthily came the Moors, all creeping through the pass, and Hernando's lance and Hernando's sword laid them low on the ground that night. And when the king came up, Hernando sat at his post, with his prostrate foes around him.

When the king saw he had done so bravely, he would have given him a new suit of armour, and a new bright-coated steed. But Hernando said, "Good king! pray leave me my father's armour and my father's charger bold, for I am but a stripling, and my hand and my arm are weak, but my father's arms and my father's steed alone put the foe to flight."

So the king let him have his will; and as he found him so brave and successful against the Moors, he sent him to carry a message of encouragement to Don Diaz, to whom the Moors had laid siege. Now, as he came back from the errand, he was crossing the lonely plain, when anon it was covered with Moorish horsemen, arrayed in their might. He knew that his trust was sacred, and he might not endanger the letter he bore by encountering so overpowering a host. But 'twas vain that he tried to turn, for the bold black charger refused; but, as if he had been spurred, with all his might he dashed right into the Pagan midst.

The lance sprang in Hernando's hand and pierced through the Moorish king. Then the host, dismayed, exclaimed, "This one rider alone in his strength, no mortal man is he: it is one of their Christian saints come down to scatter the Prophet's band." So they turned and fled apace, and on the black charger rode behind, and Hernando's lance and Hernando's sword laid low the straggling host.

And such fear had fallen on all the Prophet's children that day, that on bended knee they sent to sue a truce of the Christian king. And to purchase a term of rest, they set all their captives free, and with tribute and with hostages made peace with the Christian king.

So young Hernando rode home by the steep hillside. And Doña Teresa came out to greet her boy on his gallant steed. And with her, fair Melisenda walked, who a gentler greeting gave. She was his bride betrothed, and she knew that now peace was made, they would lovingly live together, in that far-off hillside home.

And they stroked the bold black charger, and led him to his fresh-littered stall. And 'tis said that while yet the land was blighted by one strange Moor, that bold black charger never died. Whenever the fight raged high, or the Christian host needed aid, there he bore his rider to turn the day. But where he died or when he fell, no mortal ever knew.

KING ROBIN

A Portuguese story adapted from Charles Sellers' original, taken from Tales from the Lands of Nuts and Grapes, published in 1888 by The Leadenhall Press and others.

THERE WAS ONCE A LITTLE BOY called Sigli, who, I am sorry to say, took great pleasure in catching and killing little birds. His father was a notorious robber, so it was not surprising that Sigli gave way to acts of cruelty. His mother died when he was little more than a year old, and he did not know any other relation. In the north of Portugal, bands of robbers used to frequent the roads, and some of them lived in strong castles, and had a large retinue of followers. In time of war these robber-chiefs would side with the king's party, because after the war was over they received large grants of land for the assistance they had rendered the sovereign.

Sometimes when the neighbouring kings of Spain invaded Portugal, these robbers proved of great advantage in repelling the invaders; but in following up their victories they would despoil all the churches in the enemy's country of the gold and silver idols, which the priests had caused to be made in order to get the ignorant peasantry to make offerings of money, corn, and oil, in exchange for which the priests, in the name of the idols, offered all those who gave, pardon of their sins.

Now, Sigli's father had on many occasions robbed gold and silver idols, and had murdered a few brethren of the Holy Inquisition, who, in their turn, were well known for the wicked deeds they had committed, such as burning Christian men and women who did not, and could not, profess the popish faith. But in course of time the Jesuits, for so they were called, made common cause against these robbers, and either put them to death, or obliged them to leave off robbing churches and take to cheating the peasantry.

Sigli, as I said before, was a very cruel boy, and he was the terror of all the birds and beasts. He would lay traps for them, and when he had caught them he would take pleasure in tormenting them, which clearly proved that he was not a Christian, nor possessed of any refinement. But he took more pleasure in catching Robin-redbreasts than in anything else, and for this purpose he used bird-lime. He had caught and killed so many that at last King Robin of Birdland issued invitations to all his feathered subjects and to the beasts of the field, asking them to a meeting at which they might discuss the best means of putting Sigli to death, or punishing him in some other way, for the cruelty of which he was guilty towards them.

Among the many who accepted the invitation was an old fox, the first of the Reynards, and when it came to his turn to speak, he said that as Sigli was so fond of catching redbreasts with bird-lime, he (Mr. Reynard) would propose catching Sigli in the same manner; and when caught they might discuss how they should punish him, either by pecking and biting him, or by getting the wolves to eat him. In order to carry out this idea, he suggested that the monkeys should be asked to prepare the bird-lime, which they might use with safety by oiling their hands, and then gradually make a man of bird-lime close to the robber chief's castle. Sigli would probably take it for some poor man, and hit it, and then he would not be able to get away.

This idea was accepted by all in general, and by Mrs. Queen Bee in particular, who owed Sigli and his father a grudge for destroying her hive; and the monkeys cheerfully set to work, while King Robin watched the putting together of the figure, and was very useful in giving it most of the artistic merit it possessed when finished. The making took one whole night, and next morning, almost opposite the castle, stood the bird-lime figure about the size of a man.

Sigli, seeing it from his dressing-room window, and taking it for a beggar, was so enraged that he ran out without his shoes and stockings, and, without waiting to look at the man, he struck at him with his right hand so that it stuck firmly to the figure.

"Let go," he cried, "or I will kick you!" And as the figure did not let go he kicked it, so that his foot was glued. "Let go my foot," he cried out, "or I will kick you with the other;" and, doing so, both his legs were glued to it. Then he knocked up against the figure, and the more he did so the more firmly he was glued.

Then his father, hearing his cries, rushed out, and said, "Oh, you bad man! I will squeeze you to death for hurting my dear Sigli!"

No sooner said than done, and the robber chief was glued on to the bird-lime figure.

The screams of the two attracted the attention of the servants, who, seeing their robber master, as they thought, murdering his little boy, ran away and never came back again.

King Robin was now master of the situation, and he directed ten thousand bees under General Bumble, and another ten thousand wasps under Colonel Hornet, to fall on the robber and cruel Sigli and sting them to death. But this was hardly necessary, as the wriggling of their bodies so fixed them to the figure that they died of suffocation.

Then King Robin ordered the wolves to dig a large grave, into which the monkeys rolled Sigli, his father, and the bird-lime figure; and after covering it up, they all took charge of the castle, and lived there for many years undisturbed, acknowledging King Robin as their king, and if the Jesuits did not turn them out, I am certain they are still there.

THE WHITE DOE

Adapted from Romantic Legends of Spain. and taken from the original story written by Gustavo Adolfo Bécquer, translated by Cornelia Francis Bates and Katherine Lee Bates, 1909.

Chapter I

IN A SMALL TOWN OF ARAGON, about the end of the thirteenth century or a little later, there lived retired in his seigniorial castle a renowned knight named Don Dionís, who, having served his king in the war against the infidels, was then taking his ease, giving himself up to the merry exercise of hunting, after the wearisome hardships of war.

It chanced once to this cavalier, engaged in his favorite diversion, accompanied by his daughter whose singular beauty, of the blond type extraordinary in Spain, had won her the name of White Lily, that as the increasing heat of the day began to tell upon them, absorbed in pursuing a quarry in the mountainous part of his estate, he took for his resting-place during the hours of the siesta a glen through which ran a rivulet leaping from rock to rock with a soft and pleasant sound.

It might have been a matter of some two hours that Don Dionís had lingered in that delectable retreat, reclining on the delicate grass in the shade of a black-poplar grove, talking affably with his huntsmen about the incidents of the day, while they related one to another more or less curious adventures that had befallen them in their hunting experiences, when along the top of the highest ridge and between alternating murmurs of the wind which stirred the leaves on the trees, he began to perceive, each time more near, the sound of a little bell like that of the leader of a flock.

In truth, it was really that, for very soon after the first hearing of the bell, there came leaping over the thick undergrowth of lavender and thyme, descending to the opposite bank of the rivulet, nearly a hundred lambs white as snow, and behind them appeared their shepherd with his pointed hood drawn over his brows to protect him from the vertical rays of the sun and with his shoulder-bag swung from the end of a stick.

"Speaking of remarkable adventures," exclaimed on seeing him one of the huntsmen of Don Dionís, addressing his lord, "here is Esteban, the shepherd-lad, who has been now for some time more of a fool than God made him, which was fool enough. He can give us an amusing half-hour by relating the cause of his continual frights."

"But what is it that happens to this poor devil?" exclaimed Don Dionís with an air of piqued curiosity.

"A mere trifle," continued the huntsman in a jesting tone. "The case is this - that without having been born on Good Friday, or bearing a birthmark of the cross, or, so far as one can infer from his regular Christian habits, binding himself to the Devil, he finds himself, not knowing why or how he is endowed with the most marvellous faculty that any man ever possessed, unless it be Solomon, who, they say, understood even the language of birds."

"And with what does this remarkable faculty have to do?"

"It has to do," pursued the huntsman, "as he affirms, and he swears and forswears it by all that is most sacred, with a conspiracy among the deer which course through these mountains not to leave him in peace, the drollest thing about it being that on more than one occasion he has surprised them in the act of contriving the pranks they were going to play on him and after those tricks had been carried through he has overheard the noisy bursts of laughter with which they applaud them."

While the huntsman was thus speaking, Constanza, as the beautiful daughter of Don Dionís was named, had drawn near the group of sportsmen and, as she appeared curious to hear the strange experience of Esteban, one of them ran on to the place where the young shepherd was watering his flock and brought him into the presence of his lord, who, to dispel the perturbation and evident embarrassment of the poor peasant, hastened to greet him by name, accompanying the salutation with a benevolent smile.

Esteban was a boy of nineteen or twenty years, robust in build, with a small head sunken between his shoulders, little blue eyes, a wavering, stupid glance like that of albinos, a flat nose, thick, half open lips, low forehead, complexion fair but tanned by the sun, and hair which fell partly over his eyes and partly around his face, in rough red locks like the mane of a sorrel nag.

Such, more or less exactly, was Esteban in point of physique. In respect to his character, it could be asserted without fear of denial on his own part or on that of any one who knew him, that he was an entirely honest, simple-hearted lad, though, like a true peasant, a little suspicious and malicious.

As soon as the shepherd had recovered from his confusion, Don Dionís again addressed him and, in the most serious tone in the world, feigning an extraordinary interest in learning the details of the event to which his huntsman had referred, put to him a multitude of questions to which Esteban began to reply evasively, as if desirous of escaping any discussion of the subject.

Constrained, nevertheless, by the demands of his lord and the entreaties of Constanza, who seemed most curious and eager that the shepherd should relate his astounding adventures, he decided to talk freely, but not without casting a distrustful glance about him as though fearing to be overheard by others than those present, and scratching his head three or four times in the effort to connect his recollections or find the thread of his narrative, before at last he thus began.

"The fact is, my lord, that as a priest of Tarazona to whom, not long ago, I went for help in my troubles, told me, wits don't serve against the Devil, but mum! Finger on lip, many good prayers to Saint Bartholomew, who, none better, knows his knaveries, and let him have his sport, for God, who is just, and sits up thereon high, will see that all comes right in the end.

"Resolved on this course I had decided never again to say a word to anyone about it. Not for anything, but I will do it today to satisfy your curiosity, and in good sooth, if, after all, the Devil calls me to account and goes to troubling me in punishment for my indiscretion, I carry the Holy Gospels sewed inside my sheepskin coat, and with their help, I think that, as at other times, I may make telling use of a cudgel."

"But, come!" exclaimed Don Dionís, out of patience with the digressions of the shepherd, which it seemed would never end, "let the whys and wherefores go, and come directly to the subject."

"I am coming to it," calmly replied Esteban, and after calling together, by dint of a shout and a whistle, the lambs of which he had not lost sight and which were now beginning to scatter over the mountain-side, he scratched his head again and proceeded thus, "On the one hand, your own continual hunting trips, and on the other, the persistency of those trespassers who, what with snare and what with crossbow, hardly leave a deer alive in twenty days' journey round about, had, a little time ago, so thinned out the game in these mountains that you could not find a stag in them, not though you would give one of your eyes.

"I was speaking of this in the town, seated in the porch of the church, where after mass on Sunday I was in the habit of joining some laborers who till the soil in Veratón, when some of them said to me:

"Well, man, I don't know why it is you fail to run across them, since, as for us, we can give you our word that we don't once go down to the ploughed land without coming upon their tracks, and it is only three or four days since, without going further back, a herd, which, to judge by their hoof-prints, must have numbered more than twenty, cut down before its time a crop of wheat belonging to the care-taker of the Virgen del Romeral.'

"And in what direction did the track lead?' I asked the laborers, with a mind to see if I could fall in with the herd.

"Toward the Lavender Glen," they replied.

"This information did not enter one ear to go out at the other. That very night I posted myself among the poplars. During all its hours I kept hearing here and there, far off as well as nearby, the trumpeting of the deer as they called one to another, and from time to time I felt the boughs stirring behind me, but however sharply I looked, the truth is, I could distinguish nothing.

"Nevertheless, at break of day, when I took the lambs to water, at the bank of the stream, about two throws of the sling from the place where we now are, and in so dense a shade of poplars that not even at mid-day is it pierced by a ray of sunshine, I found fresh deer-tracks, broken branches, the stream a little roiled and, what is more peculiar, among the deer-tracks the short prints of tiny feet no larger than the half of the palm of my hand, without any exaggeration."

On saying this, the boy, instinctively seeming to seek a point of comparison, directed his glance to the foot of Constanza, which peeped from beneath her petticoat shod in a dainty sandal of yellow morocco, but as the eyes of Don Dionís and of some of the huntsmen who were about him followed Esteban's, the beautiful girl hastened to conceal it, exclaiming in the most natural voice in the world, "Oh, no! Unluckily mine are not so tiny, for feet of this size are found only among the fairies of whom the troubadours sing."

"But I did not give up with this," continued the shepherd, when Constanza had finished. "Another time, having concealed myself in another hiding-place by which, undoubtedly, the deer would have to pass in going to the glen, at just about midnight sleep overcame me for a little, although not so much but that I opened my eyes at the very moment when I perceived the branches were stirring around me. I opened my eyes, as I have said. I rose with the utmost caution and, listening intently to the confused murmur, which every moment sounded nearer, I heard in the gusts of wind something like cries and strange songs, bursts of laughter, and three or four distinct voices which talked together with a chatter and gay confusion like that of the young girls at the village when, laughing and jesting on the way, they return in groups from the fountain with their water-jars on their heads.

"As I gathered from the nearness of the voices and close-by crackle of twigs which broke noisily in giving way to that throng of merry maids, they were just about to come out of the thicket on to a little platform formed by a jut of the mountain there where I was hid when, right at my back, as near or nearer than I am to you, I heard a new voice, fresh, fine and vibrant, which said - believe it, Señores, it is as true as that I have to die - it said, clearly and distinctly, these very words, "Hither, here, comrades dear! That dolt of an Esteban is here!'"

On reaching this point in the shepherd's story, the bystanders could no longer repress the merriment which for many minutes had been dancing in their eyes and, giving free rein to their mirth, they broke into clamorous laughter. Among the first to begin to laugh, and the last to leave off, were Don Dionís, who, notwithstanding his air of dignity, could not but take part in the general hilarity, and his daughter Constanza, who, every time she looked at Esteban, all in suspense and embarrassment as he was, fell to laughing again like mad till the tears sprang from her eyes.

The shepherd-lad, for his part, although without heeding the effect his story had produced, seemed disturbed and restless, and while the great folk laughed to their hearts' content at his simple tale, he turned his face from one side to the other with visible signs of fear and as if trying to descry something beyond the intertwined trunks of the trees.

"What is it, Esteban, what is the matter?" asked one of the huntsmen, noting the growing disquietude of the poor boy, who now was fixing his frightened eyes on the laughing daughter of Don Dionís, and again gazing all around him with an expression of astonishment and dull dismay:

"A very strange thing is happening to me," exclaimed Esteban. "When, after hearing the words which I have just repeated, I quickly sat upright to surprise the person who had spoken them, a doe white as snow leaped from the very copse in which I was hidden and, taking a few prodigious bounds over the tops of the evergreen oaks and mastic trees, sped away, followed by a herd of deer of the natural colour; and these, like the white one who was guiding them, did not utter the cries of deer in flight, but laughed with great peals of laughter, whose echo, I could swear, is sounding in my ears at this moment."

"Bah, bah, Esteban!" exclaimed Don Dionís, with a jesting air, "follow the counsels of the priest of Tarazona; do not talk of your adventures with the joke-loving deer, lest the Devil bring it to pass that in the end you lose the little sense you have, and since now you are provided with the gospels and know the prayer of Saint Bartholomew, return to your lambs which are beginning to scatter through the glen. If the evil spirits tease you again, you know the remedy - Pater Noster and a big stick."

The shepherd, after putting away in his pouch a half loaf of white bread and a piece of boar's meat, and in his stomach a mighty draught of wine, which, by order of his lord, one of the grooms gave him, took leave of Don Dionís and his daughter and had scarcely gone four steps when he began whirling his sling, casting stones from it to gather the lambs together.

As, by this time, Don Dionís observed that, what with one diversion and another, the hours of heat were now passed and the light afternoon breeze was beginning to stir the leaves of the poplars and to freshen the fields, he gave orders to his retinue to make ready the horses which were grazing loose in the grove hard by; and when everything was prepared, he signalled to some to slip the leashes, and to others to blow the horns and, sallying forth in a troop from the poplar-grove, took up the interrupted chase.

Chapter II

Among the huntsmen of Don Dionís was one named Garcés, the son of an old servitor of the house and therefore held in high regard by the family.

Garcés was of about the age of Constanza, and from early boyhood had been accustomed to anticipate the least of her wishes and to divine and gratify the lightest of her whims.

He amused himself in his moments of leisure in sharpening with his own hand the pointed arrows of her ivory crossbow; he broke in the colts for her mounts; he trained her favorite hounds in the arts of the chase and tamed her falcons for which he bought at the fairs of Castile red hoods embroidered with gold.

But as for the other huntsmen, the pages and the common folk in the service of Don Dionís, the delicate attentions of Garcés and the marks of esteem with which his superiors distinguished him had caused them to hold him in a sort of general dislike, even to the point of saying, in their envy, that all his assiduous efforts to anticipate the caprices of his mistress revealed the character of a flatterer and a sycophant. Yet there were not wanting those who, more keen-sighted or malicious than the rest, believed that they detected in the young retainer's devotion signs of an ill-dissembled passion.

If this were really so, the secret love of Garcés had more than abundant excuse in the incomparable charms of Constanza. He must needs have had a breast of stone, and a heart of ice, who could remain unmoved day after day at the side of that woman, peerless in her beauty and her bewitching graces.

The Lily of the Moncayo they called her for twenty leagues around, and well she merited this soubriquet, for she was so exquisite, so white and so delicately flushed that it would seem that God had made her, like the lilies, of snow and gold.

Nevertheless, among the neighbouring gentry it was whispered that the beautiful Lady of Veratón was not so pure of blood as she was fair, and that despite her bright tresses and her alabaster complexion, she had a gipsy mother. How much truth there was in these rumours no one could say, for, in fact, Don Dionís had in his youth led an adventurous life, and after fighting long under the banner of the King of Aragon, from whom he received among other rewards the fief of the Moncayo, had gone to Palestine, where he wandered for some years, finally returning to establish himself in his castle of Veratón with a little daughter born, doubtless, on foreign soil. The only person who could have told anything about the mysterious origin of Constanza, having attended Don Dionís in his travels abroad, was the father of Garcés, and he had died some time since without saying a single word on the subject, not even to his own son who, at various times and with manifestations of great interest, had questioned him.

The temperament of Constanza, with its swift alternations from reserve and melancholy to mirth and glee; the singular vividness of her imagination; her wild moods; her extraordinary ways, even the peculiarity of having eyes and eyebrows black as night while her complexion was white and rosy and her hair as bright as gold, had contributed to furnish food for the gossip of the countryside. Even Garcés himself, who knew her so intimately, had come to the conclusion that his liege lady was something apart and did not resemble the rest of womankind.

Present, as the other huntsmen were, at the narration of Esteban, Garcés was perhaps the only one who listened with genuine curiosity to the details of the shepherd's incredible adventure, and though he could not help smiling when the lad repeated the words of the white doe, no sooner had he left the grove in which they had taken their siesta, than he began to revolve in his mind the most ridiculous fancies.

"Without doubt this tale of talking deer is a sheer delusion of Esteban's, who is a perfect simpleton," the young huntsman said to himself as, mounted on a powerful sorrel, he followed step by step the palfrey of Constanza, who seemed also somewhat preoccupied and was so silent and so withdrawn from the group of hunters as scarcely to take any part in the sport. "Yet who can say that in the story which this poor fool tells there may not be a grain of truth?" thought the young retainer. "We have seen stranger things in the world, and a white doe may indeed exist, since if we can credit the folk-songs, Saint Hubert, the patron of huntsmen, had one. Oh, if I could take a white doe alive for an offering to my lady!"

Thus thinking and dreaming, Garcés passed the afternoon; and when the sun began to descend behind the neighbouring hills, and Don Dionís gave the order to his retinue for the return to the castle, he slipped away from the company unnoticed and went in search of the shepherd through the densest and most entangled coverts of the mountain.

Night had almost completely closed in when Don Dionís arrived at the gates of his castle. Immediately there was placed before him a frugal collation and he sat down with his daughter at the table.

"And Garcés, where is he?" asked Constanza, noticing that her huntsman was not there to serve her as usual.

"We do not know," the other attendants hastened to reply. "He disappeared from among us near the glen and we have not seen him since."

At that instant Garcés arrived, all breathless, his forehead still covered with perspiration, but with the most happy and satisfied expression imaginable.

"Pardon me, my lady," he exclaimed, addressing Constanza, "pardon me if I have been wanting a moment in my duty, but there whence I came at my horse's best speed, there, as here, I was busied only in your service."

"In my service?" repeated Constanza. "I do not understand what you mean."

"Yes, my lady, in your service," repeated the youth, "for I have ascertained that the white doe really does exist. Besides Esteban, it is vouched for by various other shepherds, who swear they have seen it more than once; and with their aid I hope in God and in my patron Saint Hubert to bring it, living or dead, within three days to you at the castle."

"Bah! Bah!" exclaimed Constanza with a jesting air, while the derisive laughter, more or less dissimulated, of the bystanders chorused her words. "Have done with midnight hunts and with white does. Bear in mind that the Devil loves to tempt the simple; and if you persist in following at his heels, he will make you a laughing-stock like poor Esteban."

"My lady," interrupted Garcés with a broken voice, concealing as far as possible the anger which the merry scoffs of his companions stirred in him, "I have never yet had to do with the Devil and consequently I am not acquainted with his practices; but, for myself, I swear to you that, do all he can, he will not make me an object of laughter, for that is a privilege I know how to tolerate in yourself alone."

Constanza saw the effect which her mocking had produced on the enamoured youth, but desiring to test his patience to the uttermost, she continued in the same tone:

"And what if, on aiming at the doe, she salutes you with another laugh like that which Esteban heard, or flings it into your very face, and you, hearing those supernatural peals of merriment, let fall your bow from your hands, and before you recover from the fright, the white doe has vanished swifter than lightning? What then?"

"Oh, as for that!" exclaimed Garcés, "be sure that if I can speed a shaft before she is out of bowshot, although she play me more tricks than a juggler; although she speak to me, not in the language of the country, but in Latin like the Abbot of Munilla, she will not get off without an arrow-head in her body."

At this stage in the conversation, Don Dionís joined in with a forced gravity through which might be detected the entire irony of his words, and began to give the now persecuted boy the most original counsels in the world, in case he should suddenly meet with the demon changed into a white doe.

At each new suggestion of her father, Constanza fixed her eyes on the distressed Garcés, and broke into extravagant laughter, while his fellow-servitors encouraged the jesting with glances of intelligence and ill-disguised delight.

Only with the close of the supper ceased this scene, in which the credulity of the young hunter was, so to speak, the theme on which the general mirth played variations, so that when the cloth was removed and Don Dionís and Constanza had withdrawn to their apartments, and all the inmates of the castle had gone to rest, Garcés remained for a long time irresolute, debating whether, notwithstanding the jeers of his liege lord and lady, he would stand firm to his purpose, or absolutely abandon the enterprise.

"What the devil," he exclaimed, rousing himself from the state of uncertainty into which he had fallen. "Greater harm than that which has overtaken me cannot come to pass and if, on the other hand, what Esteban has told us is true, oh, then, how sweet will be the taste of my triumph!"

Thus speaking, he fitted a shaft to his crossbow - not without having made the sign of the cross on the point of the arrow - and swinging it over his shoulder, he directed his steps toward the postern gate of the castle to take the mountain path.

When Garcés reached the glen and the point where, according to the instructions of Esteban, he was to lie in wait for the appearance of the deer, the moon was slowly rising behind the neighbouring mountains.

Like a good hunter, well-practised in his craft, he spent a considerable time, before selecting a suitable place for an ambush, in going to and fro, scanning the byways and paths thereabouts, the grouping of the trees, the irregularities of the ground, the curves of the river and the depth of its waters.

At last, after completing this minute examination of the locality, he hid himself upon a sloping bank near some black poplars whose high and interlacing tops cast a dark shadow, and at whose feet grew a clump of mastic shrubs high enough to conceal a man lying prone on the ground.

The river, which, from the mossy rocks where it rose, came following the windings of the rugged fief of the Moncayo to enter the glen by a cascade, thence went gliding on, bathing the roots of the willows that shaded its bank, or playing with a murmurous ripple among the stones rolled down from the mountain, until it fell into a pool very near the point which served the hunter for a hiding-place.

The poplars, whose silvered leaves the wind stirred with the sweetest rustle, the willows which, leaning over the limpid current, bedewed in it the tips of their pale branches, and the crowded groups of evergreen oaks about whose trunks honeysuckles and blue morning-glories clambered and twined, formed a thick wall of foliage around this quiet river-pool.

The wind, stirring the leafy curtains of living green which spread round about their floating shadow, let penetrate at intervals a steal your ray of light that gleamed like a flash of silver over the surface of the motionless, deep waters.

Hidden among the bushes, his ear attuned to the slightest sound, and his gaze fixed upon the spot where, according to his calculations, the deer should come, Garcés waited a long time in vain.

Everything about him remained buried in a deep calm.

It might well be that the lateness of the hour, for it was past midnight, began to weigh upon his lids. It might well be that far-off murmurs of the water, the penetrating scent of the wild flowers and the caresses of the wind affected his senses with the soft drowsiness in which all nature seemed to be steeped. Little by little the enamoured boy, who until now had been occupied in revolving in his mind the most alluring fancies, began to find that his ideas took shape more slowly and his thoughts drifted into vague and indecisive forms.

After lingering a little in this dim border-land between waking and sleeping, at last he closed his eyes, let his crossbow slip from his hands, and sank into a profound slumber.

*

It must have been for two or three hours now that the young hunter had been snoring at his ease, enjoying to the full one of the serenest dreams of his life, when suddenly he opened his eyes, with a stare, and half raised himself to a sitting posture, full yet of that stupor with which one wakes suddenly from profound sleep.

In the breathings of the wind and blended with the light noises of the night, he thought he detected a strange hum of delicate voices, sweet and mysterious, which were talking with one another, laughing or singing, each in its own individual strain, making a twitter as clamorous and confused as that of the birds awakening at the first ray of the sun amid the leaves of a poplar grove.

This extraordinary sound was heard for an instant only, and then all was still again.

"Without doubt, I was dreaming of the absurdities of which the shepherd told us," exclaimed Garcés, rubbing his eyes in all tranquillity, and firmly persuaded that what he had thought he

238

heard was no more than that vague impression of slumber which, on awaking, lingers in the imagination, as the closing cadence of a melody dwells in the ear after the last trembling note has ceased. And overcome by the unconquerable languor weighing down his limbs, he was about to lay his head again upon the turf, when he heard anew the distant echo of those mystic voices, which to the accompaniment of the soft stir of the air, the water and the leaves were singing thus:

"The archer who watched on the top of the tower has laid his heavy head down on the wall.

The steal your hunter who was expecting to surprise the deer has been surprised by sleep.

The shepherd who awaited the day, consulting the stars, sleeps now, and will sleep till dawn

Queen of the water-sprites, follow our steps.

Come to swing in the branches of the willows over the surface of the water.

Come to intoxicate yourself with the perfume of the violets which open at dusk.

Come to enjoy the night, which is the day of the spirits."

While the sweet notes of that delicious music floated on the air, Garcés remained motionless. After it had melted away, with much caution he slightly parted the branches and, not without experiencing a certain shock, saw come into sight the deer, which, moving in a confused group and sometimes bounding over the bushes with incredible lightness, stopping as though listening for others, frolicking together, now hiding in the thicket, now sallying out again into the path, were descending the mountain in the direction of the river-pool.

In advance of her companions, more agile, more graceful, more sportive, more joyous than all of them, leaping, running, pausing and running again so lightly that she seemed not to touch the ground with her feet, went the white doe, whose wonderful colour stood out like a fantastic light against the dark background of the trees.

Although the young man was inclined to see in his surroundings something of the supernatural and miraculous, the fact of the case was that, apart from the momentary hallucination which disturbed his senses for an instant, suggesting to him music, murmurs and words, there was nothing either in the form of the deer, nor in their movements, nor in their short cries with which they seemed to call one to another, that ought not to be entirely familiar to a huntsman experienced in this sort of night expeditions.

In proportion as he put away the first impression, Garcés began to take the practical view of the situation and, smiling inwardly at his credulity and fright, from that instant was intent only on determining, in view of the route they were following, the point where the deer would take the water.

Having made his calculation, he gripped his crossbow between his teeth and, twisting along like a snake behind the mastic shrubs, located himself about forty paces from his former situation. Once ensconced in his new ambush, he waited long enough for the deer to be within the river, that his aim might be the surer. Scarcely had he begun to hear that peculiar sound which is produced by the violent disturbance of water, when Garcés commenced to lift himself little by little, with the greatest precaution, resting first on the tips of his fingers, and afterwards on one knee.

Erect at last, and assuring himself by touch that his weapon was ready, he took a step forward, craned his neck above the shrubs to command a view of the pool and aimed the shaft, but at the very moment when he strained his eyes, together with the cord, in search of the victim whom he must wound, there escaped from his lips a faint, involuntary cry of amazement.

The moon, which had been slowly climbing up the broad horizon, was motionless, and hung as if suspended in the height of heaven. Her clear radiance flooded the forest, shimmered on the unquiet surface of the river, and caused objects to be seen as through an azure gauze.

The deer had disappeared.

In their place, Garcés, filled with consternation and almost with terror, saw a throng of most beautiful women, some of whom were sportively entering the water, while others were just freeing themselves from the light garments which as yet concealed from the covetous view the treasure of their forms.

In those thin, brief dreams of dawn, rich in joyous and luxurious images, dreams as diaphanous and celestial as the light which then begins to shine through the white bed-curtains, never had the imagination of twenty years sketched with fanciful colouring a scene equal to that which now presented itself to the eyes of the astonished Garcés.

Having now cast off their robes and their veils of a thousand colours which, suspended from the trees or thrown carelessly down on the carpet of turf, stood out against the dim background, the maidens ran here and there through the grove, forming picturesque groups, going in and out of the water and splashing it in glistening sparks over the flowers of the margin, like a little shower of dewdrops.

Here, one of them, white as the fleece of a lamb, lifted her fair head among the green floating leaves of an aquatic plant of which she seemed the half-opened blossom whose flexible stem, one might imagine, could be seen to tremble beneath the endless gleaming circles of the waves.

Another, with her hair loose on her shoulders, swung from the branch of a willow over the river, and her little rose-coloured feet made a ray of silvery light as they grazed the smooth surface. While some remained couched on the bank, with their blue eyes drowsy, breathing voluptuously the perfume of the flowers and shivering slightly at the touch of the fresh breeze, others were dancing in a giddy round, interlacing their hands capriciously, letting their heads droop back with delicious abandon, and striking the ground with their feet in harmonious cadence.

It was impossible to follow them in their agile movements, impossible to take in with a glance the infinite details of the picture they formed, some running, some gambolling and chasing one another with merry laughter in and out the labyrinth of trees. Others were skimming the water, swanlike, and cutting the current with uplifted breast. Others still were diving into the depths where they remained long before rising to the surface, bringing one of those wonderful flowers that spring unseen in the bed of the deep waters.

The gaze of the astonished hunter wandered spellbound from one side to another, without knowing where to fix itself, until he

Tales From The Land Of Rabbits

believed he saw, seated under swaying boughs which seemed to serve her as a canopy and surrounded by a group of women, each more beautiful than the rest, who were aiding her in freeing herself from her delicate vestments, the object of his secret worship, the daughter of the noble Don Dionís, the incomparable Constanza.

Passing from one surprise to another, the enamoured youth dared not credit the testimony of his senses, and thought he was under the influence of a fascinating, delusive dream.

Still, he struggled in vain to convince himself that all he had seen was the effect of disordered imagination, for the longer and more attentively he looked, the more convinced he became that this woman was Constanza.

He could not doubt. Hers were those dusky eyes shaded by the long lashes that scarcely sufficed to soften the brilliancy of their glance; hers that wealth of shining hair, which, after crowning her brow, fell over her white bosom and soft shoulders like a cascade of gold. Hers, too, that graceful neck which supported her languid head, lightly drooping like a flower weary with its weight of dewdrops, and that fair figure of which, perchance, he had dreamed, and those hands like clusters of jasmine, and those tiny feet, comparable only to two morsels of snow which the sun has not been able to melt and which in the morning lie white on the greensward.

At the moment when Constanza emerged from the little thicket, all her beauty unveiled to her lover's eyes, her companions, beginning anew to sing, carolled these words to the sweetest of melodies:

"Genii of the air, dwelling in the luminous ether, enveloped in raiment of silver mist - come!

243

Invisible sylphs, leave the cups of the half-opened lilies and come in your mother-of-pearl chariots drawn through the air by harnessed butterflies.

Nymphs of the fountains, forsake your mossy beds and fall upon us in little, diamond showers

Emerald beetles, fiery glow-worms, sable butterflies, come!

And come, all ye spirits of night, come humming like a swarm of lustrous, golden insects.

Come, for now the moon, protector of mysteries, sparkles in the fulness of splendour

Come, for the moment of marvellous transformation is at hand

Come, for those who love you, await you with impatience."

Garcés, who remained motionless, felt on hearing those mysterious songs the asp of jealousy stinging his heart, and yielding to an impulse stronger than his will, bent on breaking once for all the spell that was fascinating his senses, thrust apart with a tremulous, convulsive hand the boughs which concealed him, and with a single bound gained the river-bank. The charm was broken, everything vanished like a vapor and, looking about him, he neither saw nor heard more than the noisy confusion with which the timid deer, surprised at the height of their nocturnal gambols, were fleeing in fright from his presence, here and there, one clearing the thickets with a bound, another gaining at full speed the mountain path.

"Oh, well did I say that all these things were only delusions of the Devil," exclaimed the hunter, "but this time, by good luck, he blundered, leaving the chief prize in my hands."

And so, in fact, it was. The white doe, trying to escape through the grove, had rushed into the labyrinth of its trees and, entangled in a network of honeysuckles, was striving in vain to free herself. Garcés aimed his shaft, but at the very instant in which he was going to wound her, the doe turned toward the hunter and arrested his action with a cry, saying in a voice clear and sharp: "Garcés, what would you do?" The young man hesitated and, after a moment's doubt, let his bow fall to the ground, aghast at the mere idea of having been in danger of harming his beloved. A loud, mocking laugh roused him finally from his stupor. The white doe had taken advantage of those brief instants to extricate herself and to flee swift as a flash of lightning, laughing at the trick played on the hunter.

"Ah, damned offspring of Satan!" he shouted in a terrible voice, catching up his bow with unspeakable swiftness, "too soon have you sung your victory song, too soon have you thought yourself beyond my reach." And so saying, he sped the arrow, that went hissing on its way and was lost in the darkness of the wood, from whose depths there simultaneously came a shriek followed by choking groans.

"My God!" exclaimed Garcés on hearing those sobs of anguish. "My God! if it should be true!" And beside himself, hardly aware of what he did, he ran like a madman in the direction in which he had shot the arrow, the same direction from which sounded the groans. He reached the place at last, but on arriving there, his hair stood erect with horror, the words throbbed vainly in his throat and he had to clutch the trunk of a tree to save himself from falling to the ground.

Constanza, wounded by his hand, was dying there before his eyes, writhing in her own blood, among the sharp brambles of the mountain.

THE HERMIT AND THE FIG-TREE

Adapted from Patranas; or Spanish Stories by Rachel Harriette Busk, published by Newbery and Harris, 1870.

THERE WAS AN OLD MAN OF Toledo who had one son, whom he brought up in the fear of God. Now it happened that this old man had to go to a distant town of Estremadura, to receive some money from a creditor, and with the creditor dying, his heirs disputed the debt, and drove the old man to a lawsuit which kept him absent many years. When at last the suit was just decided in his favour, the old man fell ill and also died. Meantime the son, growing uneasy at his father's prolonged absence, arranged his affairs as well as he could, and prepared to take the journey to see after him. Calling in his three clerks, Jacinto, Gonzalo, and Diego, who were all men whom his father trusted, and whom he therefore respected, he divided his property in three parts, and to each he gave charge of one part, leaving it to each to do the best he could for him, saying, "The wisdom of your grey hairs will do better for me than any instructions my inexperience could give you."

"If the Lord bless it, it shall increase, and if He curse it, it shall not prosper," answered Jacinto, the eldest. "Behold I am nothing in the matter;" and he shook his venerable head, and raised his eyes to heaven.

"Whatever I have done for your father I will continue to do for you," said Gonzalo, the second in order, and hurried back to his papers as if it was wrong to waste a moment in talking.

"I will endeavour that you shall have nothing to complain of," quietly replied Diego, the third.

The young man was pleased with what they said, and without further loss of time set out on his journey.

The weather was fair, and his father's friends by the way received him hospitably, but crossing the Sierra, a violent storm came on, and he would soon have been drenched with rain. Right glad he was to see, perched on the mountain-ledge, a hermit's cell, where he readily found shelter. In the morning, when the sky was serene again, he rose to take his leave, and as he stood on the threshold thanking the hermit for his care of him, he could not forbear pausing to admire the beauties around him. Far away stretched the plains below, studded with smiling cities and watered by the mazy windings of the rivers, and shaded by dark groves of ancient cork-trees. Behind him were rocky heights reaching to the sky, presenting every degree of rich vegetation and solemn barrenness. But what attracted his sight most of all was a luxuriant plantation of fig-trees, which made a complete bower of the hermit's cell.

"How successful you are with your fig-trees!" said the traveller. "I never saw so fine a show. You have three, one as fine as the other, and it is impossible to say which of them is most flourishing. To judge by the fruit you gave me, which doubtless is their produce, they are the finest trees in Spain, and that is saying a great deal. I must add too, after your liberality with them, that you put to shame the proverb:

"In the season of figs no one remembers his friends."

"For what you say of the proverb, son," replied the hermit, "I have no merit, for it is the very essence of my rule of life to call nothing my own, according to our Lord's counsel. These figs are the gift of God, to me, or to you, or to whomsoever is here to need them. But for the rest, you judge according to the measure of the inconsiderateness of your years. Nevertheless, you seem to me a good youth, and I will therefore show you something which may be of use to you in your dealings with the world. Know then that but one of these fig-trees is really what it seems. The other two are worthless. That is, worthless," he added, "as bearers of fruit, for there is nothing that God makes but has its worth, and even these trees which bear no fruit are useful to give shade, and for other purposes besides."

"You surprise me," said the young man. "I never saw trees of more equal promise!"

"Nevertheless, it is as I say, and if the season of figs were not just over, according to our Lord's saying, by their fruit you should know them, or, as you say in the world, 'the proof is in eating the pudding.' Meantime, learn, my son, not to judge of men and things by their appearance, but wait and see what their fruit is like."

The sun was now beginning to make way above the horizon, and, fearing to be overtaken by the heat, the young man was obliged to set out on his journey without further parley than promising to visit the hermit on his return.

Great was his grief, when he arrived at the end of his journey, to find his good father had been so suddenly called away, and instead of being clasped to his bosom, to find the last earthly communication he could ever receive from him was a scrap of paper, on which, at intervals of his death agony, he had convulsively written down a few directions to guide him in entering into possession of his worldly goods, mingled with counsels to him to continue to direct all his dealings according to the fear of God.

This sudden death had thrown matters into some confusion, and it took a considerable time to set all straight again. It was some ten or eleven months before the young merchant had to re-cross the Sierra in a homeward direction.

It was a brilliant summer evening when he came upon the hermit's cell again. The old man was sitting making his meditation before the door. Occupied with grief and care, as he had been during his absence, the bereaved son had forgotten all about the fig-trees, but, on looking around, he saw that something was changed, and soon had a clear demonstration of what the hermit had told him. One noble tree was laden with the ripe green and purple fruit. The soft, downy skins seemed ready to burst with the rich and luscious burden within, while the broad leaves spread out their hands and shaded them from the too great heat, and fanned them gently when the day was sultry.

The second tree was covered with luxuriant leaves as before, but not a single ripe fig was on it, There were a few young green beginnings, but too small and sickly to have a chance of ripening that season.

The third tree was in lamentable plight. Its attenuated climbers clung by habit to the rock, but the sap and life and energy were gone, and it seemed only fit to be cut down.

"Well, father, I see you were right as to the figs," said the young man, candidly. "There is only one of them that is a good tree after all, but it is wonderful how well favoured they looked last year!"

"Learn, my son, the counsel of the aged and the words of the wise," replied the hermit, "for as it is with trees, even so it is with men. There are many who seem to you alike honest and worthy to be esteemed, while their inner life is as different as was the fruit-bearing principle of these trees."

"But, father, will not the good be known by their good deeds and maxims, and the bad by their evil lives and counsels?"

"Even so, my son, but the difficulty is to discern which are good and which evil. This is not so easy as you seem to think. For instance, you see two men both apparently pious and charitable, while the one who appears most so, very possibly only gives his money to the poor that he may stand well with the world, and so that the poor may look up to him, and say, 'There goes one who is like a king among us'. The other, whose liberality you noticed less, drops his hardly-spared coin noiselessly into the alms-box, and sallies forth perhaps in dead of night to carry his alms to those who would blush to receive such assistance by day. One man appears to you calm and placid because he is of a phlegmatic nature, and has no effort to make in order to appear equable and ever patient, while another, whom you judge to be hasty and passionate, may be all the while struggling to conquer a hot and violent temperament which requires the courage of a hero to keep it within bounds."

"I see your moral, father," replied the young man; "and I have no doubt I often judge of men as I judged your fig-trees."

"That one," continued the hermit, pointing to the one whose fruit was even then affording a delicious meal to the birds, for the hermit called nothing his own, and the birds of heaven were welcome to share his stock, "that one was always a good and fruitful tree, and its praise is among its people, for you will find many a village about here which boasts a graft from the hermit's fig. The second one, which presented so fair a show, has something amiss which it hereto has passed my skill to find out, although I have one remedy more to try, which may recover it. And the third had a worm at the root which destroyed its vital power."

The young man passed on his way next day, and, as he journeyed, the figs of which the good hermit had given him ample provision put him in mind of his parable, and set him musing on its application. These musings weaving themselves in with his anticipations of the condition of his affairs at home, he began to consider whether the three clerks, to whom he had entrusted his property, were in any way like the fig-trees, and whether Providence had not sent him this lesson to be his guide in his future conduct.

Possessed with this idea, he resolved to put them to the test. The sun and air of the mountains had dyed his skin in a darker hue, while sorrow had marked his face with lines of care and tinged his hair with grey. By means of a false beard and a travelling merchant's dress he reckoned he could be safe from recognition, and as a stranger learn their respective worth from their own lips.

Equipped in his disguise, he presented himself at his own house, and found all three in their place, with every evidence of diligent application. So he opened the terms of his pretended business to them, and found them all ready to negotiate with him, each in his degree. Each man conducted his matter with every token of due shrewdness and integrity.

It had been part of his plan to tell them the news of their master's death, and try them by watching the effect of this intelligence upon them, but when he saw all so well-ordered he judged there was no need for further trial, and so contented himself with resuming his own attire and returning in his own person to the house.

The clerks greeted him with a joyful welcome, and received the news of his father's death with becoming expressions of sorrow, and the young man congratulated himself on having such trusty stewards of his goods.

After he had been back a day or two, he requested them to prepare for him the account of what they had done since he left, so that he might know how his affairs stood, and once more assume the direction of them. The proposal received a ready assent, and a day was fixed for going into the matter. But when the appointed day came, what was his astonishment to find only Diego in his place? His accounts were ready and all in good order; he had administered faithfully the portion of property entrusted to him, and handed it back increased by the efforts of his prudence and skill.

From Gonzalo he found a letter informing him that he had had the misfortune to be unlucky in his speculations with his property, and had lost the whole of it, consequently he had no account to render. Losing patience at this attempt at deceit, the young man had him brought before him, and asked him how he dared tell him so, when he knew that only so many days before he had been negotiating with a merchant he knew, and he named the name he had assumed in his disguise. Gonzalo was not at all disconcerted: "Oh, that business was done with my own money, though I was unlucky with yours, fate would have it that I should be very successful with my own, and out of my own earnings I have created a capital which I have multiplied an hundredfold."

When the young man heard this unblushing statement, he was filled with indignation, and insisted on taking him before the judge. But it was all to no purpose, Gonzalo had managed his fraud so cleverly that it could not be proved against him, and he had to be let go scot-free.

As for Jacinto, he never showed himself at all, nor left any explanation. He had remained up to the hour, trading with the benefit of his master's name and capital, but the moment there had been talk of giving up accounts he had gathered up all that was in his charge, and fled with it out of the country.

More grieved by the faithlessness of those he had trusted than by the loss of his gold, the young man shut himself into his chamber, to muse upon what had befallen him, and upon the uncertainty both of friendship and riches. When he reflected on the temptations which money had offered to Gonzalo and Jacinto, he was appalled at the thought of those which might be in store for him, if he continued in the pursuit of business. He thought of the peaceful hermit, whose warning parable had just received such a striking illustration. He thought of his placid content with the weather, such as God sends it, to warm him, and the fruits of the earth, such as God gives them, to nourish him. He thought of him far removed from contentions and greed of gain, and sharing his frugal meal with the stranger, the wayfarer, and the birds of heaven.

When he came down from his chamber, he called Diego to him, and commended him for his faithfulness and diligence. "And," said he, "I now give you full possession of all that you have so justly administered. For me, I have chosen a life free from care, where I shall have no use for money."

But when Diego heard it, he said, "Nay, but I will go with you. To save my master's goods for his son was my work on earth. Now that is fulfilled, no desire have I to continue amid its weariness and perils."

So they left the money to found a hospital where poor orphan children might be taken in and taught the way that is right. And they went into the Sierra, and built huts and planted fig-trees, and passed their time in holy meditation and in praising God.

THE JUDGMENT OF THE FLOWERS

Adapted from Fairy Tales from Spain by José Muñoz Escámez, published by J. M. Dent & Sons Ltd, 1913.

"IS IT TRUE THAT THE ROSE is the queen of the flowers?" asked Richard of his papa.

And the latter said to him jokingly, "Ask them themselves, they ought to be better informed."

Richard took what his father told him literally, and going down into the garden, approached a plum-tree which gallantly waved to and fro in the wind, and taking off his hat with great respect, asked it, "Mr. Plum-tree, will you be good enough to tell me if the rose is the queen of the flowers?"

But the plum-tree continued to move to and fro in the wind without answering him.

And drawing near to an almond tree, whose white blossoms had just opened, he repeated his question.

"Mr. Almond-tree, is it true that the rose is the queen of the flowers?"

The almond-tree remained silent, but its blossoms went red with envy.

"The almond-tree is also unprincipled," thought Richard. "All these trees have a discourteous tone. Let us ask the plants."

A splendid double pink, which raised its splendid corolla with a gallantry worthy of its nobility, as soon as he heard the question, graciously bowed upon his stalk and answered, "Quite so, the rose is our beloved queen, on account of being so beautiful and because her delicate aroma has no rival. But if you wish to know more, come back tonight at twelve o'clock and notice what happens in your garden."

"Thank you, kind pink. I will not miss tonight."

Richard went to bed at the usual time, but he could not sleep. At half-past eleven he dressed himself again, and slipping secretly down stairs arrived in the garden and awaited events. On the last stroke of midnight a bright light appeared from the sky and that ray of light condensed on the earth, taking the figure of a beautiful woman crowned with flowers, who carried in her hand a little golden wand which gave off brilliant reflections.

The fairy extended her hand and immediately an unusual movement was produced among the plants. The pinks turned into elegant gentlemen in bright costumes of ruby, pink, and green. The hyacinths and jasmines transformed into gallant little pages with fair hair, and the white lilies were pale ladies of singular beauty, dressed in white. The dahlias wore long trains and at the neck a ruffle of delicate lace of colours which recalled the flowers which had preceded. The violet modestly tried to hide her beautiful countenance of velvety skin and her eyes of gentle aspect among a group of poppies, who passed arm-in-arm, attracting attention by their blood red costumes. Finally from amongst a group of mournful evergreens, who were chatting with some beautiful pansies, appeared the queen of the fête, the rose. Her presence produced a murmur of admiration, never had she been so lovely. Her face held the freshness of the flower, and her pink dress with a long train was of very fine silk which rustled as the sovereign walked. An olive-tree turned into a throne and dais, and the rose, without any other ceremony than a general greeting, took her seat on the throne. She raised her arm, imposing silence, and everybody became silent.

"Gentlemen," said the queen, "once again the good magician Spring has re-animated our hearts. We have not met since last year and there are several grave matters to resolve, but the most important is the manner of defending ourselves from the bees, wasps, and butterflies who continually sip our honey, accelerating our end. On this point I have already begged Spring to have the accused appear before me, so that this gathering is really an oral judgment."

At a signal from the magician the accused appeared in costumes of etiquette, the butterfly wearing its finest clothes.

It appeared before the queen with its head modestly bent and its face lighted up by a blush.

"What does your majesty wish?" it asked.

"To inquire the motive why you presume to take away our nectar," said the rose.

"Ah, madam!" replied the butterfly, touched, "little harm I do you, because I never take more than is necessary to feed myself, and I have never abused your hospitality."

"That is well. We will take that into account as an extenuating circumstance for you. Let the wasp approach."

The wasp entered in a black dress-coat and a yellow necktie striped with black.

"I," it said, "gather nectar from you because I have proposed to work like the bee, although I have not yet succeeded in doing so since the beginning of the world, but still not much time has passed and I hope to learn."

"How can you hope to learn," interrupted the queen, "if all that you do is to eat it all without having any to make honeycombs? Your case is a very bad one. As you have not a good lawyer you are lost. Fetch the bee."

The latter appeared, her presence awakening a general murmur. It wore neither a dress-coat nor a frock-coat, nor even a lounge-coat. It was wearing a blouse covered with stains of honey and wax. All drew away from the bee for fear of getting soiled.

"Now I know what I am coming to," it said without keeping quiet. "It is always the same song - that we do take away, and that we do not take away the nectar from the flowers. Good, what about it? We do not do so for ourselves, but for our master. All the sweet syrup of your corollas we enclose in the hive, and from there every year it comes out so that Man, our master, rejoices his palate with it and embalms his breath with your aroma. After dying in summer and losing your green leaves in autumn, you still live in us, that we may make your remembrance lasting. And still you complain! You, it is true, give your blood, but it would be worth nothing if we did not gather it in order to store it. The work is ours, and the work is worth as much as your nectar. If you have to condemn me, do so quickly, I beg of you, as I am losing a great deal of work time, and we are somewhat behindhand with the work."

The rose called the pink and the violet, discussed the case with them, and after some minutes' reflection, spoke in this manner, "The wasp is an unconscientious glutton who, under the pretext of making honeycombs, which she never succeeds in doing, robs us. Give her five hundred hard lashes."

On hearing this a deadly nightshade seized the wasp and carried her away to bestow the correction.

"The butterfly's innocence and moderation favour her," said the queen, "therefore I declare her absolved with all favourable pronouncements."

The butterfly bowed respectfully and kissed the sovereign's hand. Her golden feelers glistened, she shook her wings, filling the ambient air with diamond dust, and took to flight showering cascades of light.

"With regard to the bee," continued the rose, "not only do I find her without any guilt, but wish that henceforth you do not close your petals to her, but leave her at liberty to carry away the honey that she requires. As a reward for her laboriousness, and as a symbol of perpetual friendship between us, I am going to give her a kiss."

The bee, much moved, advanced, and placing her blushing forehead within reach of the queen's lips, received a kiss of peace, which made tears of gratitude gather in her eyes.

A delicious perfume invaded the garden, the fairy raised her wand, and each flower returned to its post, recovering its original form.

The magician flew into space, wrapped in a moonbeam, and Richard remained alone, pensive in the recollection of what he had seen.

"What a beautiful lesson!" he said. "Even in the kingdom of flowers work gains the most precious reward."

THE SEVEN PIGEONS

Adapted from Charles Sellers' original, taken from Tales from the Lands of Nuts and Grapes, published in 1888 by The Leadenhall Press and others.

ON A DESERTED PART OF THE rock-bound Cantabrian coast, a poor fisherman, named Pedro, discovered a lovely maiden, magnificently dressed, combing her long jet-black hair with a golden comb studded with diamonds.

It was still early morning, and the sun had not attained its greatest power; and as the tide was at its lowest, an innumerable number of ponds were formed by the rocks which, for a distance of half a mile, were left bare by the receding sea.

Seated near to one of these ponds, and cooling her feet in the water, sat this lovely maiden; and she was so intent on performing her toilet that she did not perceive Pedro, who, thinking she was a mermaid, and might therefore cast a spell over him, hid behind a ledge of rocks, and was able to see and hear her without being seen.   Pedro heard her singing the following words:

"I am daughter of a king

Who rules in Aragon,

My messengers they bring

Me food to live upon.

My father thinks me dead,

My death he did ordain,

For that I would not wed

A wicked knight of Spain.

But those whom he did send

To kill me in this place,

My youth they did befriend,

But cruel is my case."

"Is it even so," said Pedro to himself, "that this lovely maiden is the daughter of a king? If I render her assistance I may incur great danger, and if I leave her to die it will be a crying shame; what, then, am I to do?"

As he was thus pondering in his mind, he heard a flapping of wings, and, looking in the direction whence the noise came, he saw a pair of perfectly white pigeons bearing a small basket between them, strung on a thin golden bar, which they held at each end between their beaks.

Descending, they deposited the basket by the side of the princess, who caressed them most tenderly, and then took from the basket some articles of food which she greedily ate (for she had not eaten since the previous morning), and after having finished the contents she again sang:

"I am daughter of a king,

Who thinks that I am dead;

Here on this beach I sing,

By pigeons I am fed.

Thank you, my pretty birds,

Who are so kind to me.

But what avail my words?

Oh, I a bird would be!"

This wish was no sooner uttered than Pedro, much to his astonishment, saw that the lovely princess had been turned into a white swan, with a small gold crown on the top of its head.

Expanding her wings, she gradually rose high above him, attended by the pigeons, and all three flew out to sea. Then suddenly Pedro observed a magnificent ship not far from the coast, whose deck was of burnished gold, and her sides of ivory fastened with golden nails. The ropes were of thread of silver, and the sails of white silk, while the masts and yards were made of the finest sandal-wood.

To the ship the three birds flew, and no sooner did they alight on the deck than Pedro observed that they were three beautiful maidens.

The princess sat on a richly ornamented chair, and the other two maidens on velvet cushions embroidered in gold at her feet.

Over them was spread a superb awning to shelter them from the rays of the sun, and the vessel glided about over the vast expanse of water, now in one direction, now in another, as if the breeze blew to suit the sails.

Pedro was so astonished at what he saw that eventually he got frightened, and, being young and nimble, he soon lost sight of the ship, but at every pace he seemed to hear a voice saying, "Run not away, future king of Aragon!"

Pedro continued running till he left the beach far behind, and was now in the pine-forest; nor did he stop till he was in the densest part, when, for very fatigue, he threw himself on the ground, and then he distinctly heard a voice say, "Pedro, you are destined to be King of Aragon; but tell no one."

Not till then had he discovered that he was no longer dressed in fisherman's attire, but that his clothes were of the finest cloth fringed with gold lace.

Pedro, on seeing this, said, "I am enchanted. That princess is indeed a mermaid, and has cast a spell over me. I am undone, my eyes deceive me, and what I take for so much grandeur is but a deception." Saying which, he jumped to his feet, and hurried towards his village as fast as his legs would carry him.

Arrived at the fishing hamlet, all his old companions paid him such deference that he tried to get out of their way, thinking they did but laugh at him, and, arriving at the door of his widowed mother's cottage, he ran into the kitchen. His mother happened to be frying some fish, and when she saw a grand gentleman enter the apartment she took the pan off the fire, and, bowing low, said, "My noble sir, this house is too humble for such as you. Allow me to conduct you to his reverence's house, for there you will find accommodation more suited to your high estate."

Pedro would have replied to his mother, and sought to kiss her hand and ask her blessing, after the custom of the country, but, on attempting to speak, his tongue hung out of his mouth, and he made so strange a noise and so gesticulated that his mother was glad to get out of the house, followed, however, by her son and a large crowd of villagers who had congregated to see the grand stranger.

As soon as it was known throughout the village of the arrival of the grand stranger the church bells pealed, and the parish priest mingled with the crowd desirous of seeing the new arrival; but as soon as Pedro commenced gesticulating as before, the priest and all the rest of the people were much frightened, for they thought that he was dangerously mad.

Pedro, noticing this, sorrowfully turned away from his native village and took the high-road to the next town.

As he was going along, thinking of his present trouble, he observed a wide gate made of gold, opening into a beautiful garden, into which he entered immediately, for he recollected what the wise woman of the village had once told him that "grand clothes beget respect."

"Open wide those gates, O worker midst the flowers," exclaimed Pedro to an old gardener (for he had now recovered his speech). "I come in cloth of gold to speak unto my love."

"Sir," replied the old man, "you may always enter here, for you are Don Pedro of Aragon, I well can see."

"What very high balconies, a hundred feet in height!" exclaimed Pedro. "Tell me, good old man, does the princess ever come there?"

"To those balconies so high, to feel the cooling breeze," replied the gardener, "the princess comes there every evening alone."

"Should she ask you," continued Pedro, "who I am, tell her that I am your son come from a distant land, and I will help you to water the pinks."

At her usual time the princess came to her favourite balcony, and seeing Pedro watering the flowers, she beckoned to him, saying, "Oh waterer of the pinks, come a little nearer and speak to me."

"Is it true that you desire to speak to me?" inquired Pedro of the princess.

"No mirror bright ever reflected the truth more correctly than the words I uttered to convey my desire," answered the princess.

"Here, then, you have me," said Pedro. "Order me as your slave, but give me, for I am thirsty, a small ewer of water."

The princess poured some water into a silver goblet, and having handed it to Pedro, he exclaimed, "And in this mirror bright of crystal water pure, which does reflect your form, I quench my heart's deep thirst."

"You see yonder palace at the end of the garden," said the princess to Pedro. "Well, in that palace you will be lodged for the night; but should you ever tell anyone what you see there, you will put yourself in danger and cause me great trouble."

Pedro promised to keep secret whatever he might see that night, and bidding "good night" to the princess, he hastened to the palace which the princess had pointed out to him, and, having entered it, he walked through the marble passage, which seemed to be interminable. On each side of him were rows of majestic columns, surmounted by gold capitals, and now and again he thought he saw the forms of lovely young maidens flitting among the columns.

Just as he was approaching a richly carved fountain surrounded by sacred palms, a maiden of surprising beauty seemed to be addressing a Moor in most impassioned tones, as if claiming his indulgence, but when Pedro got up to them he discovered that both were the work of the statuary.

At every step the surroundings became more magnificent, and the carved ceiling was of such exquisite workmanship that it seemed rather the work of the loom, being so like the finest lace, than of the sculptor.

At last he arrived at the end of this avenue of columns, and noticing a door in front of him, he opened it, and found himself standing on a marble quay, against which the sea waves were washing.

Scanning the vast expanse of water before him, he observed approaching him the same beautiful ship he had seen in the morning.

When the ship came alongside the quay, a sailor sprung on shore, and made her fast by a golden cable. Then, addressing Pedro, he said, "I am glad you have not kept us waiting, for our royal mistress is very wishful to consult you, as one of her favourite doves has broken its right wing, and if you cannot cure it, the princess will die of starvation."

Pedro made no reply, but stepped on board the ship, which soon got under way, and within a short time they were approaching the coast he knew so well.

Having landed, Pedro saw the princess seated on the sand, nursing one of her white pigeons.

"Pedro of Aragon," the princess exclaimed, "a stranger dared to enter my royal father's garden, and in assisting to water the pinks he trod on the wing of my favourite pigeon, and he has broken it."

"Señora," replied Pedro, "the intruder did probably seek you, and had no idea of hurting the lovely bird."

"That matters not," continued the princess, "for my principal supporter is wounded, and you must cure her. Cut out my heart, and steep this bird in my warm blood, and when I am dead throw my body into the sea."

"How can I kill one so lovely?" asked Pedro. "I would rather die myself than hurt you!"

"Then you do not care for me, or else you would do as I bid you," answered the princess.

"Princess, I cannot and will not kill you; but I will do anything else you bid me," said Pedro.

"Well, then, since you will not kill me, I order you to take this pigeon back with you; for I know it was you who walked in my father's garden today," continued the princess. "And tomorrow evening, when you see that princess whom you saw today, you must kill her, and let her blood fall over this pretty bird."

Pedro was now in great trouble, for he had promised the princess to do anything she told him to do, except killing her, and he could not break his word; so taking hold of the pigeon very gently, and bidding good-bye to the princess, he again stepped on board the ship, and so depressed was he that he had arrived at the marble quay without being aware of it.

On landing, he retraced his steps through the avenue of pillars, and found himself once more in the garden, where the old gardener was again watering the pinks.

"What very high balconies!" exclaimed Pedro. "Tell me, old gardener of the ancient times, if the princess comes here today."

"The princess loves the fresh sea-breeze," answered the old man, "and tonight she will come to the balcony, for her noble lover will be waiting for her."

"And who is the princess's lover?" inquired Pedro.

"If you will help me to water the pinks, I will tell you," said the old man.

Pedro readily acquiesced, and putting down the pigeon where he thought no harm would happen to it, he commenced assisting the gardener to water the pinks.

After a silence of a few minutes the gardener said, "There were once seven pigeons who said, 'Seven pigeons are we, and with other seven pigeons we might all be mated; but, as it is, we must remain seven pigeons.'"

"Yes," put in Pedro; "but I want to know who the princess's lover is."

The old man took no heed of the interruption, and continued, "There were once seven pigeons who said, 'Seven pigeons are we...'"

"Stop!" cried Pedro; "I will have no such idle talk. Tell me who this noble lover is, or I will do you an injury."

"Sir," cried the gardener, with a very serious countenance, "there were once seven pigeons who said, 'Seven pigeons are we, and...'"

"Take your watering-can," shouted Pedro in disgust; "I will not listen to your nonsense!"

"And yet there were once seven pigeons who said, 'Seven pigeons are we;' and now the last of them is gone, for the noble lover has been false to his trust," exclaimed the old man, looking very cunningly at Pedro.

At these words Pedro looked towards the place where he had placed the pigeon, and it was no longer there.

Seized with a fit of fury, he was about to lay hands on the gardener, when, to his astonishment, he found that he was also gone.

"I am undone," cried the unhappy Pedro, "and now I shall not see the princess again." Saying which he fainted away, and might probably have remained there some time, but then he heard a voice saying, in a jocular manner, "There were once seven pigeons who said, 'Seven pigeons are we, and…'"

Pedro started to his feet, and close to him was standing the princess whom he had previously seen in the balcony.

"Why do you thus tease me, princess?" said Pedro. "I want to hear no more about the seven horrid pigeons."

"Don Pedro de Aragon," answered the princess, "I must tell you that the old gardener to whom you spoke is a magician, and he has possessed himself of the last means I had of regaining my liberty, for I am under his power. Is it not true that you came here with the purpose of killing me?"

"I was under a vow to do so," replied Pedro; "but I cannot kill you, although I would rather slay you, fair princess, than do you a more grievous injury."

"Go back, then, to the unhappy lady whom you left on the sea-shore, and tell her that you have been false to your promises," said the princess.

"How sorry I am," exclaimed Pedro, "that I was ever destined to be King of Aragon! When I was a poor fisherman, I was far happier than I am now!"

"Pedro of Aragon, the moon will be at the full tonight, and you may then rescue me," said the princess, "if you have the courage to meet the wicked magician in this garden at midnight, for then is his power weakest."

"I am prepared for the worst," replied Pedro, "and I fear not your gaoler."

"Well, then," continued the princess, "when the magician sees you he will again tell you about the seven pigeons; but when he has finished, you must tell him that there were once seven wives who had only one husband, and that they are waiting outside to see him. Do as I tell you, and if you are not afraid of his anger, you may be able to free me."

Pedro promised to do as he was told, and the princess having retired into the palace, Pedro amused himself by walking under the lofty balconies, watching the fire-flies grow brighter as night came on.

Just about midnight the magician was seen watering the pinks, and as soon as he perceived Pedro he said, "There were once seven pigeons who said, 'Seven pigeons are we, and with other seven pigeons we might all be mated; but, as it is, we must remain seven pigeons.'"

"Quite so," put in Pedro. "And once upon a time there were seven wives who had only one husband, and they are waiting outside to see him."

The magician, at these words, lost all control over his temper, but Pedro heeded him not, rather did he endeavour to increase his rage by repeating all about the seven wives.

"I am undone!" cried the magician; "but if you will induce the spirits of my seven wives to again seek the grave, I will give you what you want, and that is the princess."

"Give me the princess first," answered Pedro, "and then I will free you of your wives."

"Take her, then," said the magician; "here she is. And forget not what you have promised me, for I may tell you in confidence that a man with seven wives cannot play the magician."

Pedro hurried away with the princess; and after they had been married and crowned, the princess, who was now queen, one day said to him, "Pedro, the magician who held me captive from you was Rank, and therefore were the balconies so high. When you saw me on the beach fed by pigeons, it was done so that you should know my power. On the shore I was attended by winged messengers, and on the sea I sailed about at pleasure."

"But what about the wounded pigeon?" asked Pedro.

"Recollect, Pedro, what you said to me in the garden," answered the princess, "that you would rather slay me than do me a more grievous injury. That poor pigeon with its broken wing could no more hope to soar aloft than an injured woman to mix with her former associates."

"And what about the seven wives who were waiting outside, and who so frightened the old magician, Rank?" continued Pedro.

"They are the seven deadly sins, who would each have a tongue for itself, and yet without tongues are enough to frighten Rank," answered the princess.

"And who am I, then," asked Pedro, "to be so exalted now?"

"You are the wise man who strove to do his best, yet tried not to exalt himself above his position," sweetly answered the princess.

"So that the magician Rank has unwillingly raised the poor fisherman to be king," whispered Pedro.

"Not Rank alone, but much more so by your own worth as a man."

Tales From The Land Of Rabbits

THE RAY OF MOONSHINE

Adapted from Romantic Legends of Spain. and taken from the original story written by Gustavo Adolfo Bécquer, translated by Cornelia Francis Bates and Katherine Lee Bates, 1909.

Chapter I

HE WAS NOBLE, HE HAD BEEN born amid the clash of arms, and yet the sudden blare of a war trumpet would not have caused him to lift his head an instant or turn his eyes an inch away from the dim parchment in which he was reading the last song of a troubadour.

Those who desired to see him had no need to look for him in the spacious court of his castle, where the grooms were breaking in the colts, the pages teaching the falcons to fly, and the soldiers employing their leisure days in sharpening on stones the iron points of their lances.

"Where is Manrico? Where is your lord?" his mother would sometimes ask.

"We do not know," the servants would reply. "Perchance he is in the cloister of the monastery of the Peña, seated on the edge of a tomb, listening to see if he may surprise some word of the conversation of the dead. Perhaps he is on the bridge watching the river-waves chasing one another under its arches, or curled up in the fissure of some rock counting the stars in the sky, following with his eyes a cloud, or contemplating the will-o'-the-wisps that flit like exhalations over the surface of the marshes. Wherever he is, it is where he has least company."

In truth, Manrico was a lover of solitude, and so extreme a lover that sometimes he would have wished to be a body without a shadow, because then his shadow would not follow him everywhere he went.

He loved solitude, because in its bosom he would invent, giving free rein to his imagination, a phantasmal world, inhabited by wonderful beings, daughters of his weird fancies and his poetic dreams. Manrico was a poet, so true a poet that never had he found adequate forms in which to utter his thoughts nor had he ever imprisoned them in words.

He believed that among the red coals of the hearth there dwelt fire-spirits of a thousand hues which ran like golden insects along the enkindled logs or danced in a luminous whirl of sparks on the pointed flames, and he passed long hours of inaction seated on a low stool by the high Gothic chimney-place, motionless, his eyes fixed on the fire.

He believed that in the depths of the waves of the river, among the mosses of the fountain and above the mists of the lake there lived mysterious women, sibyls, nymphs, undines, who breathed forth laments and sighs, or sang and laughed in the monotonous murmur of the water, a murmur to which he listened in silence, striving to translate it.

In the clouds, in the air, in the depths of the groves, in the clefts of the rocks, he imagined that he perceived forms, or heard mysterious sounds, forms of supernatural beings, indistinct words which he could not comprehend.

Love! He had been born to dream love, not to feel it. He loved all women in every instant, this one because she was golden-haired, that one because she had red lips, another because in walking she swayed as a river-reed.

Sometimes his delirium reached the point of his spending an entire night gazing at the moon, which floated in heaven in a silvery mist, or at the stars, which twinkled afar off like the changing lights of precious stones. In those long nights of poetic wakefulness, he would exclaim: "If it is true, as the Prior of the Peña has told me, that it is possible those points of light may be worlds, if it is true that people live on that pearly orb which rides above the clouds, how beautiful must the women of those luminous regions be! And I shall not be able to see them, and I shall not be able to love them! What must their beauty be! And what their love!"

Manrico was not yet so demented that the boys would run after him, but he was sufficiently so to talk and gesticulate to himself, which is where madness begins.

Chapter II

Over the Douro, which ran lapping the weatherworn and darkened stones of the walls of Soria, there is a bridge leading from the city to the old convent of the Templars, whose estates extended along the opposite bank of the river.

At the time to which we refer, the knights of the Order had already abandoned their historic fortresses, but there still remained standing the ruins of the large round towers of their walls, and there still might be seen, as in part may be seen today, covered with ivy and white morning-glories, the massive arches of their cloister and the long ogive galleries of their courts of arms through which the wind would breathe soft sighs, stirring the deep foliage.

In the orchards and in the gardens, whose paths the feet of the monks had not trodden for many years, vegetation, left to itself, made holiday, without fear that the hand of man should mutilate it in the effort to embellish. Climbing plants crept upward twining about the aged trunks of the trees. The shady paths through aisles of poplars, whose leafy tops met and mingled, were overgrown with turf. Spear-plumed thistles and nettles had shot up in the sandy roads, and in the parts of the building which were bulging out, ready to fall; the yellow crucifera, floating in the wind like the crested feathers of a helmet, and bell-flowers, white and blue, balancing themselves, as in a swing, on their long and flexible stems, proclaimed the conquest of decay and ruin.

It was night, a summer night, mild, full of perfumes and peaceful sounds, and with a moon, white and serene, high in the blue, luminous, transparent heavens.

Manrico, his imagination seized by a poetic frenzy, after crossing the bridge, from which he contemplated for a moment the dark silhouette of the city outlined against the background of some pale, soft clouds massed on the horizon, plunged into the deserted ruins of the Templars.

It was midnight. The moon, which had been slowly rising, was now at the zenith, when, on entering a dusky avenue that led from the demolished cloister to the bank of the Douro, Manrico uttered a low, stifled cry, strangely compounded of surprise, fear and joy.

In the depths of the dusky avenue he had seen moving something white, which shimmered a moment and then vanished in the darkness, the trailing robe of a woman, of a woman who had crossed the path and disappeared amid the foliage at the very instant when the mad dreamer of absurd, impossible dreams penetrated into the gardens.

An unknown woman! In this place! At this hour! "This, this is the woman of my quest," exclaimed Manrico, and he darted forward in pursuit, swift as an arrow.

Chapter III

He reached the spot where he had seen the mysterious woman disappear in the thick tangle of the branches. She had gone. Where? Afar, very far, he thought he descried, among the crowding trunks of the trees, something like a shining, or a white, moving form. "It is she, it is she, who has wings on her feet and flees like a shadow!" he said, and rushed on in his search, parting with his hands the network of ivy which was spread like a tapestry from poplar to poplar. By breaking through brambles and parasitical growths, he made his way to a sort of platform on which the moonlight dazzled.

Nobody! "Ah, but by this path, but by this she slips away!" he then exclaimed. "I hear her footsteps on the dry leaves, and the rustle of her dress as it sweeps over the ground and brushes against the shrubs."

And he ran like a madman, here and there, and did not find her. "But still comes the sound of her footfalls," he murmured again. "I think she spoke. Beyond a doubt, she spoke. The wind which sighs among the branches, the leaves which seem to be praying in low voices, prevented my hearing what she said, but beyond a doubt she fleets by yonder path. She spoke, she spoke. In what language? I know not, but it is a foreign speech."

And again he ran onward in pursuit, sometimes thinking he saw her, sometimes that he heard her; now noticing that the branches, among which she had disappeared, were still in motion; now imagining that he distinguished in the sand the prints of her little feet; again firmly persuaded that a special fragrance which crossed the air from time to time was an aroma belonging to that woman who was making sport of him, taking pleasure in eluding him among these intricate growths of briers and brambles. Vain attempt!

He wandered some hours from one spot to another, beside himself, now pausing to listen, now gliding with the utmost precaution over the herbage, now in frantic and desperate race.

Pushing on, pushing on through the immense gardens which bordered the river, he came at last to the foot of the cliff on which rises the hermitage of San Saturio. "Perhaps from this height I can get my bearings for pursuing my search across this confused labyrinth," he exclaimed, climbing from rock to rock with the aid of his dagger.

He reached the summit from where may be seen the city in the distance and, curving at his feet, a great part of the Douro, compelling its dark, impetuous stream onward through the winding banks that imprison it.

Manrico, once on the top of the cliff, turned his gaze in every direction, till, bending and fixing it at last on a certain point, he could not restrain an oath.

The sparkling moonlight glistened on the wake left behind by a boat, which, rowed at full speed, was making for the opposite shore.

In that boat he thought he had distinguished a white and slender figure, a woman without doubt, the woman whom he had seen in the grounds of the Templars, the woman of his dreams, the realization of his wildest hopes. He sped down the cliff with the agility of a deer, threw his cap, whose tall, full plume might hinder him in running, to the ground, and freeing himself from his heavy velvet cloak, shot like a meteor toward the bridge.

He believed he could cross it and reach the city before the boat would touch the further bank. Folly! When Manrico, panting and covered with sweat, reached the city gate, already they who had crossed the Douro over against San Saturio were entering Soria by one of the posterns in the wall, which, at that time, extended to the bank of the river whose waters mirrored its grey battlements.

Chapter IV

Although his hope of overtaking those who had entered by the postern gate of San Saturio was dissipated, that of tracing out the house which sheltered them in the city was not therefore abandoned by our hero. With his mind fixed upon this idea, he entered the town and, taking his way toward the ward of San Juan, began roaming its streets at hazard.

The streets of Soria were then, and they are today, narrow, dark and crooked. A profound silence reigned in them, a silence broken only by the distant barking of a dog, the barring of a gate or the neighing of a charger, whose pawing made the chain which fastened him to the manger rattle in the subterranean stables.

Manrico, with ear cocked to listen for these vague noises of the night, which at times seemed to be the footsteps of some person who had just turned the last corner of a deserted street, at others, the confused voices of people who were talking behind him and whom every moment he expected to see at his side, spent several hours running at random from one place to another.

At last he stopped beneath a great stone mansion, dark and very old, and, standing there, his eyes shone with an indescribable expression of joy. In one of the high ogive windows of what we might call a palace, he saw a ray of soft and mellow light which, passing through some thin draperies of rose-coloured silk, was reflected on the time-blackened, weather-cracked wall of the house across the way.

"There is no doubt about it. Here dwells my unknown lady," murmured the youth in a low voice, without removing his eyes for a second from the Gothic window. "Here she dwells! She entered by the postern gate of San Saturio, and by the postern gate of San Saturio is the way to this ward. In this ward there is a house where, after midnight, there is someone awake? Who can it be at this hour if not she, just returned from her nocturnal excursions? There is no more room for doubt; this is her home."

In this firm persuasion and revolving in his head the maddest and most capricious fantasies, he awaited dawn opposite the Gothic window where there was a light all night and from which he did not withdraw his gaze a moment.

When daybreak came, the massive gates of the arched entrance to the mansion, on whose keystone was sculptured the owner's coat of arms, turned ponderously on their hinges with a sharp and prolonged creaking. A servitor appeared on the threshold with a bunch of keys in his hand, rubbing his eyes, and showing as he yawned a set of great teeth which might well rouse envy in a crocodile.

For Manrico to see him and to rush to the gate was the work of an instant.

"Who lives in this house? What is her name? Her country? Why has she come to Soria? Has she a husband? Answer, answer, animal!" This was the salutation which, shaking him violently by the shoulder, Manrico hurled at the poor servitor, who, after staring at him a long while with frightened, stupefied eyes, replied in a voice broken with amazement, "In this house lives the right honourable Señor Don Alonso de Valdecuellos, Master of the Horse to our lord, the King. He has been wounded in the war with the Moors and is now in this city recovering from his injuries."

"Well! well! His daughter?" broke in the impatient youth. "His daughter, or his sister, or his wife, or whoever she may be?"

"He has no woman in his family."

"No woman! Then who sleeps in that chamber there, where all night long I have seen a light burning?"

"There? There sleeps my lord Don Alonso, who, as he is ill, keeps his lamp burning till dawn."

A thunderbolt, suddenly falling at his feet, would not have given Manrico a greater shock than these words.

Chapter V

"I must find her, I must find her; and if I find her, I am almost certain I shall recognize her. How? I cannot tell, but recognize her I must. The echo of her footstep, or a single word of hers which I may hear again, the hem of her robe, only the hem which I may see again would be enough to make me sure of her. Night and day I see floating before my eyes those folds of a fabric diaphanous and whiter than snow, night and day there is sounding here within, within my head, the soft rustle of her raiment, the vague murmur of her unintelligible words.

"What said she? What said she? Ah, if I might only know what she said, perchance, but yet without knowing it, I shall find her. My heart tells me so, and my heart deceives me never. It is true that I have unavailingly traversed all the streets of Soria, that I have passed nights upon nights in the open air, a corner-post; that I have spent more than twenty golden coins in persuading duennas and servants to gossip. I gave holy water in St. Nicholas to an old crone muffled up so artfully in her woollen mantle that she seemed to me a goddess, and on coming out, after matins, from the collegiate church, in the dusk before the dawn, I followed like a fool the litter of the archdeacon, believing that the hem of his vestment was that of the robe of my unknown lady. But it matters not. I must find her, and the rapture of possessing her will assuredly surpass the labours of the quest.

"What will her eyes be? They should be azure, azure and liquid as the sky of night. How I delight in eyes of that colour! They are so expressive, so dreamy, so, yes, there is no doubt of it, azure her eyes should be, azure they are, assuredly. Her tresses are black, jet black and so long that they wave upon the air. It seems to me I saw them waving that night, like her robe, and they were black. I do not deceive myself, no, they were black.

"And how well azure eyes, very large and slumberous, and loose tresses, waving and dark, become a tall woman—for—she is tall, tall and slender, like those angels above the portals of our basilicas, angels whose oval faces the shadows of their granite canopies veil in mystic twilight.

"Her voice! Her voice I have heard. Her voice is soft as the breathing of the wind in the leaves of the poplars, and her walk measured and stately like the cadences of a musical instrument.

"And this woman, who is lovely as the loveliest of my youthful dreams, who thinks as I think, who enjoys what I enjoy, who hates what I hate, who is a twin spirit of my spirit, who is the complement of my being, must she not feel moved on meeting me? Must she not love me as I shall love her, as I love her already, with all the strength of my life, with every faculty of my soul?

"Back, back to the place where I saw her for the first and only time that I have seen her. Who knows but that, capricious as myself, a lover of solitude and mystery like all dreamy souls, she may take pleasure in wandering among the ruins in the silence of the night?"

Two months had passed since the servitor of Don Alonso de Valdecuellos had disillusioned the infatuated Manrico, two months in every hour of which he had built a castle in the air only for reality to shatter with a breath. Two months during which he had sought in vain that unknown woman for whom an absurd love had been growing in his soul, thanks to his still more absurd imaginations. Two months had flown since his first adventure when now, after crossing, absorbed in these ideas, the bridge which leads to the convent of the Templars, the enamoured youth plunged again into the intricate pathways of the gardens.

Chapter VI

The night was calm and beautiful, the full moon shone high in the heavens, and the wind sighed with the sweetest of murmurs among the leaves of the trees.

Manrico arrived at the cloister, swept his glance over the enclosed green and peered through the massive arches of the arcades. It was deserted.

He went forth, turned his steps toward the dim avenue that leads to the Douro, and had not yet entered it when there escaped from his lips a cry of joy.

He had seen floating for an instant, and then disappearing, the hem of the white robe, of the white robe of the woman of his dreams, of the woman whom now he loved like a madman.

He ran in his pursuit. He reached the spot where he had seen her vanish; but there he stopped, fixed his terrified eyes upon the ground, and remained a moment motionless. A slight nervous tremor agitated his limbs, a tremor which increased, and showed symptoms of an actual convulsion, and he broke out at last into a peal of laughter, laughter loud, strident, and horrible.

That white object, light, floating, had again shone before his eyes, it had even glittered at his feet for an instant, only for an instant.

It was a moonbeam, a moonbeam which pierced from time to time the green vaulted roof of trees when the wind moved their boughs.

Several years had passed. Manrico, crouched on a settle by the deep Gothic chimney of his castle, almost motionless and with a vague, uneasy gaze like that of an idiot, would scarcely take notice either of the endearments of his mother or of the attentions of his servants.

"You are young, you are comely," she would say to him, "why do you languish in solitude? Why do you not seek a woman whom you may love, and whose love may make you happy?"

"Love! Love is a ray of moonshine," murmured the youth.

"Why do you not throw off this lethargy?" one of his squires would ask. "Arm yourself in iron from head to foot, bid us unfurl to the winds your illustrious banner, and let us march to the war. In war is glory."

"Glory! Glory is a ray of moonshine."

"Would you like to have me recite you a ballad, the latest that Sir Arnaldo, the Provençal troubadour, has composed?"

"No! No!" exclaimed the youth, straightening himself angrily on his seat, "I want nothing. That is, yes, I want, I want that you should leave me alone. Ballads, women, glory, happiness, they are all lies, vain fantasies which we shape in our imagination and clothe according to our whim, and we love them and run after them, but for what? For what? To find a ray of moonshine."

Manrico was mad; at least, all the world thought so. For myself, on the contrary, I think what he had done was to regain his senses.

Tales From The Land Of Rabbits

ELVIRA, THE SAINTED PRINCESS

Adapted from Charles Sellers' original, taken from Tales from the Lands of Nuts and Grapes, published in 1888 by The Leadenhall Press and others.

WAMBA WAS KING OF THE GOTHS, who inhabited the northern part of Lusitania. He was one of the bravest kings that ever reigned, and the walls of his palace still stand as evidence of the skill with which he studied to improve his capital. But although he was wise, he was not a good man, and his bravery in war was not tempered by mercy. Like all his predecessors, he was cruel to his victims, and was more feared than loved.

Wamba had but one daughter, Elvira, whose mother was a princess of the Moorish family reigning in Andalusia. She was so beautiful and so good, that she contributed in no small degree in rendering her father's reign famous. Her long hair was of a lovely glossy black; her eyes, of the same dark hue, had all the softness of her race, and it was this very tenderness of look that gave majesty to her appearance.

In those days there were but very few Christians in Europe. The Crescent of the Prophet had overcome for a time the Cross of the Saviour. To the teachings of an old man, who in secret worshipped the true God, Elvira owed the first lessons she got of Christianity; and once the good seed was sown, it multiplied.

Wamba did not know that his daughter was a Christian; but he knew that she was very good, and that for her goodness she was very much beloved by all his subjects.

Now, it so happened that in the dungeon of his palace there were many prisoners condemned to death by starvation, and it perplexed the king to know how it was that they continued to live. Every morning he would ask of the gaoler if the prisoners had died, and the answer was that they seemed quite well.

So one day he hid in a nook of the staircase, hoping to find out who fed his prisoners. He had not long to wait, for he soon saw Elvira descending, followed by a young courtier, Alaric, and carrying something in her apron.

Elvira, unknown to her father, had been in the custom of carrying bread to the poor prisoners, and she was assisted in her work of mercy by her lover Alaric.

When she got close to the king, he started out of his hiding-place, and seizing her by the arm, she, in her fright, let fall her apron, out of which fell beautiful roses, into which the bread had been transformed.

Great was the surprise of the king, for he thought she was carrying victuals. Then, in his rage, he said, "Elvira, you are in league with the evil one, and you and your lover shall die!"

Elvira and Alaric were themselves so astonished at what had taken place, that they could not speak, and allowed themselves to be led away to separate gaols without offering an explanation.

Wamba had it proclaimed that next day that his daughter Elvira and her lover Alaric would be burnt in the public square for having dealings with the evil one. Many of his oldest courtiers tried to persuade him that he was too precipitate; but he was not to be moved, and all that night Elvira and Alaric were preparing to meet death.

At the first ray of light Wamba was up, and with his soldiers and executioners hurried to the public square. Elvira and Alaric were led among a strong body of men, and everything was being prepared for burning the lovers, when Elvira's old tutor presented himself before Wamba, and said, "Know, Oh king, that your daughter fears not death, for her comfort is on her faith. If anyone be to blame, I am he, for I instructed her. Let me, then, be burned in her stead."

Wamba gazed fiercely at the old man, and, raising his massive olive staff surmounted by a gold crown, exclaimed, "You shall also die, but not before you have witnessed her sufferings. Your God is a false God, but if He has true power to save all of you, then He shall cause this ancient olive staff to grow and throw out green leaves by tomorrow morning, or else you shall all die;" and saying this, he stuck his royal staff into the ground.

Elvira was to be allowed to remain close to the staff, but with no one with her; and, so that she might not escape, guards were posted all around the square.

Kneeling at the side of that emblem of authority, which for generations had been wielded by her ancestors, she gave vent to her prayers and tears, and the latter fell so quickly that they moistened the ground; and when morning came, Wamba, on arriving, saw his royal staff growing, a sapling then, but shortly to grow into a tree, even as the Christian faith in its sapling stage was to throw out its spreading branches over the kingdom, till they all became one people, loving but one God.

Wamba caused a church to be built near the spot, which church still exists; and the olive-tree grows by its side, giving the name of Olive-tree to the Square.

Alaric was married to Elvira; and Wamba having been called to the grave of his forefathers, these two reigned conjointly, and appointed the old tutor their counsellor.

THE EMERALD EYES

Adapted from Romantic Legends of Spain. and taken from the original story written by Gustavo Adolfo Bécquer, translated by Cornelia Francis Bates and Katherine Lee Bates, 1909.

Chapter I

"THE STAG IS WOUNDED - HE IS wounded, no doubt of it. There are traces of his blood on the mountain shrubs, and in trying to leap one of those mastic trees his legs failed him. Our young lord begins where others end. In my forty years as huntsman I have not seen a better shot. But by Saint Saturio, patron of Soria, cut him off at these hollies, urge on the dogs, blow the horns till your lungs are empty, and bury your spurs in the flanks of the horses. Do you not see that he is going toward the fountain of the Poplars, and if he lives to reach it we must give him up for lost?"

The glens of the Moncayo resounded from echo to echo with the braying of the horns and barking of the unleashed pack of hounds. The shouts of the pages resounded with new vigour, while the confused throng of men, dogs and horses rushed toward the point which Iñigo, the head huntsman of the Marquises of Almenar, indicated as the one most favourable for intercepting the quarry.

But all was of no avail. When the fleetest of the greyhounds reached the hollies, panting, its jaws covered with foam, already the deer, swift as an arrow, had cleared them at a single bound, disappearing among the thickets of a narrow path which led to the fountain.

"Draw rein! draw rein, every man!" then cried Iñigo. "It was the will of God that he should escape."

And the troop halted, the horns fell silent and the hounds, at the call of the hunters, abandoned, snarling, the trail.

At that moment, the lord of the festival, Fernando de Argensola, the heir of Almenar, came up with the company.

"What are you doing?" he exclaimed, addressing his huntsman, astonishment depicted on his features, anger burning in his eyes. "What are you doing, idiot? Do you see that the creature is wounded, that it is the first to fall by my hand, and yet you abandon the pursuit and let it give you the slip to die in the depths of the forest? Do you think perchance that I have come to kill deer for the banquets of wolves?"

"Señor," murmured Iñigo between his teeth, "it is impossible to pass this point."

"Impossible! And why?"

"Because this path," continued the huntsman, "leads to the fountain of the Poplars, the fountain of the Poplars in whose waters dwells an evil spirit. He who dares trouble its flow pays dear for his rashness. Already the deer will have reached its borders. How will you take the animal without drawing on your head some fearful calamity? We hunters are kings of the Moncayo, but kings that pay a tribute. A quarry which takes refuge at this mysterious fountain is a quarry lost."

"Lost! Sooner will I lose the seigniory of my fathers, sooner will I lose my soul into the hands of Satan than permit this stag to escape me, the only one my spear has wounded, the first fruits of my hunting. Do you see him? Do you see him? He can still at intervals be made out from here. His legs falter, his speed slackens. Let me go, let me go! Drop this bridle or I roll you in the dust! Who knows if I will not run him down before he reaches the fountain? And if he should reach it, to the devil with it, its untroubled waters and its inhabitants! On, Lightning! On, my steed! If you overtake him, I will have the diamonds of my coronet set in a headstall all of gold for you."

Horse and rider departed like a hurricane.

Iñigo followed them with his eyes till they disappeared in the brush. Then he looked about him. Everyone else remained motionless, in consternation.

The huntsman exclaimed at last, "Señores, you are my witnesses. I exposed myself to death under his horse's hoofs to hold him back. I have fulfilled my duty. Against the devil heroism does not avail. To this point comes the huntsman with his crossbow. Beyond this, it is for the chaplain with his holy water to attempt to pass."

Chapter II

"You are pale. You go about sad and gloomy. What afflicts you? From the day, which I shall ever hold in hate, on which you went to the fountain of the Poplars in chase of the wounded deer, I should say an evil sorceress had bewitched you with her enchantments.

297

"You do not go to the mountains now preceded by the clamorous pack of hounds, nor does the blare of your horns awake the echoes. Alone with these brooding fancies which beset you, every morning you take your crossbow only to plunge into the thickets and remain there until the sun goes down. And when night darkens and you return to the castle, white and weary, in vain I seek in the game-bag the spoils of the chase. What detains you so long far from those who love you most?"

While Iñigo was speaking, Fernando, absorbed in his thoughts, mechanically cut splinters from the ebony bench with his hunting knife.

After a long silence, which was interrupted only by the click of the blade as it slipped over the polished wood, the young man, addressing his servant as if he had not heard a single word, exclaimed:

"Iñigo, you who are an old man, you who know all the haunts of the Moncayo, who have lived on its slopes pursuing wild beasts and in your wandering hunting trips have more than once stood on its summit, tell me, have you ever by chance met a woman who dwells among its rocks?"

"A woman!" exclaimed the huntsman with astonishment, looking closely at him.

"Yes," said the youth. "It is a strange thing that has happened to me, very strange. I thought I could keep this secret always, but it is no longer possible. It overflows my heart and begins to reveal itself in my face. Therefore I am going to tell it to you. You will help me solve the mystery which enfolds this being who seems to exist only for me, since no one knows her or has seen her, or can give me any account of her."

The huntsman, without opening his lips, drew forward his stool to place it near the ebony bench of his lord from whom he did not once remove his affrighted eyes. The youth, after arranging his thoughts, continued. "From the day on which, notwithstanding your gloomy predictions, I went to the fountain of the Poplars, and crossing its waters recovered the stag which your superstition would have let escape, my soul has been filled with a desire for solitude.

"You do not know that place. See, the fountain springs from a hidden source in the cavity of a rock, and falls in trickling drops through the green, floating leaves of the plants that grow on the border of its cradle. These drops, which on falling glisten like points of gold and sound like the notes of a musical instrument, unite on the turf and murmuring, murmuring with a sound like that of bees humming about the flowers, glide on through the gravel, and form a rill and contend with the obstacles in their way, and gather volume and leap and flee and run, sometimes with a laugh, sometimes with sighs, until they fall into a lake. Into the lake they fall with an indescribable sound. Laments, words, names, songs, I know not what I have heard in that sound when I have sat, alone and fevered, upon the huge rock at whose feet the waters of that mysterious fountain leap to bury themselves in a deep pool whose still surface is scarcely rippled by the evening wind.

"Everything there is grand. Solitude with its thousand vague murmurs dwells in those places and transports the mind with a profound melancholy. In the silvered leaves of the poplars, in the hollows of the rocks, in the waves of the water it seems that the invisible spirits of nature talk with us, that they recognize a brother in the immortal soul of man.

"When at break of dawn you would see me take my crossbow and go toward the mountain, it was never to lose myself among the thickets in pursuit of game. No, I went to sit on the rim of the fountain, to seek in its waves - I know not what - an absurdity! The day I leaped over it on my Lightning, I believed I saw glittering in its depths a marvel, truly a marvel, the eyes of a woman!

"Perhaps it may have been a fugitive ray of sunshine that wound, serpent like, through the foam; perhaps one of those flowers which float among the weeds of its bosom, flowers whose calyxes seem to be emeralds. Oh, I do not know. I thought I saw a gaze which fixed itself on mine, a look which kindled in my breast a desire absurd, impossible of realization, that of meeting a person with eyes like those.

"In my search, I went to that place day after day.

"At last, one afternoon I thought myself merely the plaything of a dream, but no, it is the truth; I have spoken with her many times as I am now speaking with you. One afternoon I found, sitting where I had sat, clothed in a robe which reached to the waters and floated on their surface, a woman beautiful beyond all exaggeration. Her hair was like gold; her eyelashes shone like threads of light, and between the lashes flashed the restless eyes that I had seen. Yes! The eyes of that woman were the eyes which I bore stamped upon my mind, eyes of an impossible colour, the colour..."

"Green!" exclaimed Iñigo, in accents of profound terror, starting with a bound from his seat.

Fernando, in turn, looked at him as if astonished that Iñigo should supply what he was about to say, and asked him with mingled anxiety and joy, "Do you know her?"

300

"Oh, no!" said the huntsman. "God save me from knowing her! But my parents, on forbidding me to go toward those places, told me a thousand times that the spirit, goblin, demon or woman, who dwells in those waters, has eyes of that colour. I conjure you by that which you love most on earth not to return to the fountain of the Poplars. One day or another her vengeance will overtake you, and you will expiate in death the crime of having stained her waters."

"By what I love most!" murmured the young man with a sad smile.

"Yes," continued the elder. "By your parents, by your kindred, by the tears of her whom heaven destines for your wife, by those of a servant who watched beside your cradle."

"Do you know what I love most in this world? Do you know for what I would give the love of my father, the kisses of her who gave me life, and all the affection which all the women on earth can hold in store? For one look, for only one look of those eyes! How can I leave off seeking them?"

Fernando said these words in such a tone that the tear which trembled on the eyelids of Iñigo fell silently down his cheek, while he exclaimed with a mournful accent: "The will of Heaven be done!"

Chapter III

"Who are you? What do you come from? Where do you live? Day after day I come seeking you, and see neither the palfrey that brings you here, nor the servants who bear your litter. Tear off once and for all the veil of mystery in which you enfold yourself as in the heart of night. I love you and, highborn or lowly, I will be yours forever."

The sun had crossed the crest of the mountain. The shadows were descending its slope with giant strides. The breeze sighed amid the poplars of the fountain. The mist, rising little by little from the surface of the lake, began to envelop the rocks of its margin.

Upon one of these rocks, on one which seemed ready to topple over into the depths of the waters on whose surface was pictured its wavering image, the heir of Almenar, on his knees at the feet of his mysterious beloved, sought in vain to draw from her the secret of her existence.

She was beautiful, beautiful and pallid as an alabaster statue. One of her tresses fell over her shoulders, entangling itself in the folds of her veil like a ray of sunlight passing through clouds; and her eyes, within the circle of her amber-coloured lashes, gleamed like emeralds set in fretted gold.

When the youth ceased speaking, her lips moved as for utterance, but only exhaled a sigh, a sigh soft and sorrowful like that of the gentle wave which a dying breeze drives among the rushes.

"You answer not," exclaimed Fernando, seeing his hope mocked. "Would you have me credit what they have told me about you? Oh, no! Speak to me. I long to know if you love me; I long to know if I may love you, if you are a woman…"

"Or a demon. And if I were?", said she.

The youth hesitated a moment; a cold sweat ran through his limbs; the pupils of his eyes dilated, fixing themselves with more intensity upon those of that woman and, fascinated by their phosphoric brilliance, as though demented he exclaimed in a burst of passion:

"If you were, I should still love you. I should love you as I love you now, as it is my destiny to love you even beyond this life, if there be any life beyond."

"Fernando," said the beautiful being then, in a voice like music: "I love you even more than you love me. In that I, who am pure spirit, stoop to a mortal. I am not a woman like those that live on earth. I am a woman worthy your of you who are superior to the rest of humankind. I dwell in the depths of these waters, incorporeal like them, fugitive and transparent; I speak with their murmurs and move with their undulations. I do not punish him who dares disturb the fountain where I live. Rather, I reward him with my love, as a mortal superior to the superstitions of the common herd, as a lover capable of responding to my strange and mysterious embrace."

While she was speaking, the youth, absorbed in the contemplation of her fantastic beauty, drawn on as by an unknown force, approached nearer and nearer the edge of the rock. The woman of the emerald eyes continued, "Do you behold the limpid depths of this lake? Do you behold these plants with large, green leaves which wave in its bosom? They will give us a couch of emeralds and corals and I - I will give you a bliss unnameable, that bliss which you have dreamed of in your hours of delirium, and which no other can bestow. Come! The mists of the lake float over our brows like a pavilion of lawn, the waves call us with their incomprehensible voices, the wind sings among the poplars hymns of love. Come! Come!"

Night began to cast her shadows, the moon shimmered on the surface of the pool, the mist was driven before the rising breeze, the green eyes glittered in the dusk like the will-o'-the-wisps that run over the surface of impure waters. "Come, come!" these words were murmuring in the ears of Fernando like an incantation.

"Come!" And the mysterious woman called him to the brink of the abyss where she was poised, and seemed to offer him a kiss... a kiss...

Fernando took one step toward her, then another, and felt arms slender and flexible twining about his neck and a cold sensation on his burning lips, a kiss of snow, and he wavered, lost his footing and fell, striking the water with a dull and mournful sound.

The waves leaped in sparks of light, and closed over his body, and their silvery circles went widening, widening until they died away on the banks.

THE MAN WITH THE TWO FACES

Adapted from Fairy Tales from Spain by José Muñoz Escámez, published by J. M. Dent & Sons Ltd, 1913.

CLAUDIO WAS SCREAMING MADLY WHEN HIS grandmother said to him, "If you cry any more you will see the man with two faces."

"Oh, I say, who is he?"

"Well, he is a very strange being, who laughs with one face and cries with the other. If a child looks at his smiling face he gives it a toy. If it looks at his sad face he bites it and tears off the tip of his ear."

"Well, then, I wish he would come, because I will be very good and he will give me a toy."

"It would be much better if he did not come, because you are very bad and you would get your ear bitten."

"But I want to see him," said the boy.

"Look for him if you like," said the grandmother, "but mind he does not hurt you."

Claudio, who was eight years old and very innocent, quite believed in the man with two faces, and resolved to look for him everywhere.

That afternoon he went to the outskirts of the town and asked some woodmen, "Where is the man with two faces?"

And they said to him mockingly, "Go to the mountain over there and you will come to him."

He followed their counsel and climbed up the mountain without finding anybody. That night he had to spend on the mountain, climbing up to the top of a tree because the howling of the wolves frightened him so much that he did not dare to go back to his home. In the morning, on getting down from the tree, a squirrel saluted him with great ceremony, and said "Good morning."

"Listen, squirrel," said Claudio, "do you know where the man with two faces is?"

"I do not know, but my friend the eagle knows many things. Come with me and we will ask him."

The boy and the squirrel went together and on the top-most part of the mountain came upon the eagle's nest. The eagle turned towards the squirrel and asked what he wanted. On being told what Claudio wanted he said to him, "I have sometimes heard this man spoken of, but I have never seen him. I only know that he is very unhappy, because he can only look at himself in the glass with his sad face, and on seeing himself so afflicted the poor fellow bursts into tears."

"And where does he live?" said the boy.

"He lives so far away that you would never be able to reach the place, but if you like I will carry you there, through the air, in my claws, and we shall be there in a twinkling. I cannot do any more for you than carry you to the door of his house, and I cannot answer for what may happen to you."

"Never mind," said the boy; "take me, for I want to see him."

The eagle caught up the boy by his belt and the squirrel got into one of Claudio's pockets. The eagle began its flight and the three found themselves in the air. When Claudio saw that he was so high up he shut his eyes, full of terror.

When the squirrel appeared from the boy's pocket the trees looked like the size of pins, and he went quickly back again for fear of being seasick. After several hours' flying, the eagle descended on a little mountain and there left Claudio, startled at his own temerity.

"When you wish to come back, if they let you, blow on the whistle which I am carrying round my neck. Keep it, for I have very sharp ears and can hear the sound of it for five hundred leagues. As soon as I hear it I will come, and pop! I will take you by the belt to my nest."

When the eagle had gone the squirrel came out of Claudio's pocket and said to him, "Have we arrived already, my little friend?"

"Have you come too?" exclaimed Claudio joyfully.

"Yes, but incognito. I liked the look of you and wish to help you with my advice. You know that squirrels, modesty apart, are very sharp."

"All right, what am I going to do now?"

"Do you not want to see this man? Then let us go on, because I also would like to know him."

"And if he wants to hurt us?"

"Then we will defend ourselves. I will go first and explore the surroundings, and will come back at once."

And saying this, the squirrel started to run with the quickness usual to his race, returning after a little while very much frightened.

"Do you know," he said, "that the man with the two faces is at the present moment giving a terrible hiding to some boys that he has shut up in a cage?"

"They must be naughty boys, but I am good, and he will give me toys."

"I don't know about that, because the only thing I have seen him give is knocks, and do you know what he was saying? 'This one I like, that one, no. But I shall kill them all, Oh!'"

"Was he saying that?"

"Just what I am telling you. I have only seen his gay face which is in the back of his head, and on seeing him I closed my eyes and came away quickly, for if he sees me he will tear me to bits."

"What are we going to do?" said Claudio, startled.

"Climb up this pine tree with me and from there we will watch."

They climbed up a tree and from it saw a house, or rather a great cage, formed of big iron bars with an iron roof. In the centre was seated the man with the two faces with a whip in his hand, punishing a number of boys of all ages who filled the cage.

The temptation seized Claudio to blow the whistle and make the eagle come back to fetch him away, but his curiosity overcame his fear, and he said to himself, "After all, I can go away whenever I like."

A little later they saw the man with two faces come out of the cage and walk in the direction of the place where Claudio was. On his approach they saw such a woebegone countenance that Claudio was filled with fear. As the squirrel saw him shudder, he said to him in a very low voice, "Close your eyes or we are lost."

The boy obeyed and the man with two faces passed close to them without noticing their presence. When he felt him pass, Claudio half opened his eyes and saw his gay face. Again he had to close them, for he could hardly stop laughing, so strange was the face.

On his disappearing in the distance, both the friends descended from the tree and went up to the cage. On seeing them the boy prisoners began to shout, full of joy, "Have you come to set us free?"

"Yes," said Claudio, "but I don't know how to, because you are locked up. Well, failing the key, let us look for other means."

And, examining the doors, he came upon one without a lock. He opened it and went into the cage, but he had no sooner entered than the door closed of its own accord, leaving him a prisoner.

"Poor little boy!" shouted the others, "you are quite lost, for this is a kind of mouse-trap where you can enter but can't get out."

At this moment, the man with two faces arrived. He opened the door and, facing Claudio, looked at him with the serious face which made the boy shut his eyes to keep from crying.

"What! Have I got one pupil more?" he exclaimed. "Good, now it is your turn to laugh, as it is the first day."

And seizing his head with both hands he turned it round so that the gay face came in front of the boy. The latter looked a moment, and again shut his eyes to keep from laughing aloud.

"I see that you are strong, but tomorrow we shall see," said the monster, and he locked Claudio up with the other little ones.

Now it was night. All were sleeping, including the horrible gaoler.

Claudio was half asleep when he heard himself called softly. It was his friend the squirrel, who had got in through the iron bars and said to him, "Be sure that tomorrow I will save you."

And without saying anything more he turned and went out by the way he had entered.

The following day, at the usual time, the monster showed his sad face. The prisoners began to cry. Claudio shut his eyes, and the monster gave one of his ears a bite and showed him his teeth.

"That's for today; tomorrow there will be more," he said.

And after throwing a few pieces of bread to the boys he went away.

No sooner had he gone than millions of squirrels gathered round, and with the quickness of lightning made an enormous gap in the cage. Through this the boys escaped, and the squirrels entered in their place. The boys hid themselves in a distant grotto, and there waited to see what would happen.

The man with the two faces arrived at the cage and, on seeing the squirrels there, became extremely angry, and seized a whip with which to give them the daily beating, when all those little animals came out through the iron bars.

The monster, putting on some very high stilts, started to run in search of the boys, blowing a whistle. They, terror-stricken, were hiding in the grotto without daring to breathe for fear of being discovered. After eight or ten hours of giddy running, the man with the two faces fell down exhausted and went to sleep on the ground near the grotto. Then the squirrel asked Claudio for the whistle that the eagle had given him, and without making any noise hung it round the monster's neck.

Then the latter, awakened by the cold of the night, again caught hold of the whistle and started to blow it madly. The eagle hastened to the sound of his whistle, and thinking that it was Claudio, seized the man with the two faces in his claws and rose up to a great height.

The eagle soon noticed that his voice was unknown, and without more ado let go of his load and the monster was dashed to pieces on the rocks below.

He flew again towards the place where he had left Claudio.

"Don't be afraid," said the eagle, "because of the two faces neither remains. They have just been smashed up against the stones, and he will never torment anybody anymore."

The children returned to their homes, where their coming was celebrated with great feasts, and Claudio's grandmother, when she heard what had happened, after welcoming him on his return, only said to him, "Do you want to see the man with two faces again?"

THE ENCHANTED MULE

Adapted from Charles Sellers' original, taken from Tales from the Lands of Nuts and Grapes, published in 1888 by The Leadenhall Press and others.

THERE WAS ONCE A VERY MERRY, but very poor hostler in Salamanca. He was so poor that he had to go about his business in rags. One day when he was attending on the richly caparisoned mule belonging to the Archbishop of Toledo, he gave vent to his feelings in words.

"Ah," said he, "my father was always called a donkey from the day of his marriage; but would to goodness I were the archbishop's mule! Look at the rich livery he bears. Look at his stout sides, See how he drinks up his wine and eats his maize bread! Oh, it would be a merry life, indeed! My father was, they say, an ass, so I would be a mule!"

And then he leant against the manger, and laughed so heartily that the archbishop's mule stopped eating to look at him.

"What ho!" said the mule. "Remember that my reverend master, being a corpulent man, is somewhat heavy, but if you will change places with me, you need but take hold of both my ears, and, caramba, a mule you shall be, and in the service of the Archbishop of Toledo!"

"And that will I," answered Pablo the hostler; "for better be a well-fed mule than a starving hostler." So saying, he seized the mule by the ears, and, looking at him in the face, he was immediately transformed, but, to his surprise, he saw that the quondam mule was changed into a monk.

"How now!" cried Pablo. "Wily you not bring me some more wine and maize bread, sir monk? Will you not be my hostler?"

But the monk turned away and left the stable, and Pablo then saw that he had made a mistake. But he resolved that as soon as he was led out into the street he would run off to his old mother, and implore her to intercede on his behalf with the patron St. James of Compostela.

When the archbishop had rested, he called for his mule, which was brought out; and, in the absence of the hostler, whom they could not find, one of the attendants was about tightening the girths, when the mule Pablo, seizing the opportunity, bolted away as hard as he could down the road in the direction of his mother's house.

The archbishop thought his mule had gone mad, and as the servants followed it, running, and crying out, "Stop the beast - stop it!" the rabble joined in the chase, but Pablo never stopped till he got to his mother's house.

The old woman was at the door, spinning at her distaff, and as she was very deaf she had not heard the clamour. Pablo, bending over her, tried to kiss her hand, to ask her for her blessing, but his tongue now failed him. So frightened was she at the approach of the animal that she hit him over the head with her distaff, and cried out, "Abernuncio!"

By this time the servants had surrounded him, and were trying to lead him back, but he would not go. He stood on his hind-legs, and then lay down on his side, and rolled in the dust till the scarlet saddle-cloth was spoilt, and then, suddenly rising, rushed into the cottage, and tried to sit on his accustomed chair.

His mother fled the house, and the rabble entered, and so cudgelled Pablo that he was fain to return to the inn; and, after being groomed, he allowed the archbishop to mount him. However, the archbishop had not gone far before he exclaimed, "By St. Iago, this mule has the pace of a camel!"

Pablo, not being accustomed to four legs, did not know how to use them, so that he would move his right fore and hind legs together. This caused the archbishop great inconvenience, for, being a corpulent man, it made him roll about on the saddle like the gold ball on the cathedral of Sevilla, when the west wind loosened it, and the east wind blew it down.

Seizing the pommel with both his hands, and raising himself in his shoe stirrups, he looked as if he intended to vault over the head of the mule; and as they were at this moment going through a village, the inhabitants, who had come out to see the archbishop, thought he was about to deliver a sermon. So, surrounding the mule, they uncovered their heads, and knelt awaiting the blessing.

Pablo, forgetting he was a mule, thought the people were doing homage to him, and being of a merry disposition, he gave way to such inward laughter that it brought on a violent fit of coughing, which the faithful, not seeing the face of the archbishop, for they devoutly bent their heads towards the ground, took to be the natural clearing of the throat before speaking. But the archbishop, who was now becoming seriously frightened, and thinking that the evil one had entered the body of his mule, exclaimed, "Exorciso te abernuncio!"

Then Pablo sat down on his hind-quarters, so that the archbishop slid off the saddle and rolled on the ground, and another "Abernuncio!" in a deeper tone, brought the devout people to their feet. Pablo at this moment got up, and by so doing completely capsized the venerable archbishop, causing him to turn over on to his head.

Full of dust and anger, the prelate jumped to his feet, and carefully examined his mule to see if he could account for this peculiar behaviour. Sorely grieved did Pablo feel at having caused the good archbishop so much annoyance, and, so as to show his contrition, he went down on his fore-legs, thinking to kneel, which so frightened all the people that they instinctively took shelter behind the archbishop. But he was as much afraid as the rest, and had it not been that they held him by his robes, he would have run away.

"This beats the mule of Merida," cried one, "who ran away with the miller's wife and then regretted the bargain. See, he is craving for pardon."

Pablo the mule rose after kneeling for some time, and, after the fashion of trained animals of this breed, he extended his fore and hind-legs, so as to facilitate the archbishop mounting him, which he soon did, feeling convinced that the mule had intended no harm. Pablo, regretting his mistake and the loss of time it had caused, set off at a quick amble, which so disconcerted his rider that he had to hold on by the pommel and the crupper; and thus he was hurried out of the village, and the people were done out of the blessing.

The attendants, who were on foot, tried to keep up with Pablo, but this they could not do, owing to his long strides, and not until they were within sight of Toledo did they get up to their master, who, by this time, was out of breath and countenance. They, fearing that the mule might start off again, placed a man on each side holding the reins, and thus did they approach the eastern gate of the city, at which many priests were waiting with the cross and the sword of the archbishop, in order to give him a fitting welcome, according to the rules of the Church.

Pablo, seeing the large silver cross, the emblem of Christianity, slackened his pace, and when within a few yards of it, in obedience to what his mother had taught him as a child, dropped down on his knees, bending his head to the ground; but this he did so suddenly, that the archbishop fell off the saddle on to his neck, and, to break his fall, caught hold of his servants by their ears, nearly tearing them off, and causing them also to tumble. Thinking that the evil one had seized them, they struck out right and left, and nearly stunned their master with the blows and kicks.

Pablo, hoping to retrieve his fortune, jumped to his legs with the archbishop clinging round his neck, and galloped after the two servants with his mouth open, so that, should he catch them, he might bite them. But they, surmising what he meant, sought refuge among the priests, and these in their turn made haste to get into a small chapel close by.

"Our archbishop must have changed mules with Beelzebub," said a fat priest, "for no earthly animal would thus treat a prince of the Church!"

"Ay," continued one of the runaway servants; "and if his neck had been a foot longer I should have been dangling in mid-air like the coffin of the false prophet."

"I never thought to have run so fast again," ejaculated a very short and stout priest. "Faith, my legs seemed to grow under me, as our sacristan said after he had been tossed by the abbot's bull."

"But what has become of the archbishop?" said another. "We must not leave him in his sorry plight." Saying this, he carefully opened the door of the chapel, and there they saw their prelate swooning on the pavement, and Pablo dashing full tilt among the crowd, trying to wreak his vengeance on as many as he could possibly get hold of.

Having torn the leather breeches of some half-dozen sightseers, and knocked down and trampled on some score of men and women, he rushed out of the city by the same gate, and never stopped till he arrived at the inn where he had been hostler. The master of the inn, thinking that some mishap had befallen the archbishop, made haste to secure the mule, but as it was already night, he postponed sending off one of his servants till next morning.

Once again at the manger, Pablo had time to consider over the mistake he had made, and he would gladly have undergone any punishment, could he but have regained his former shape.

While he was thus musing, he saw the monk approaching, looking very sorrowful indeed.

"Pablo," said he, "how do you like being a mule?"

Now, Pablo was cunning, and, not wishing to let the monk know what had happened, he answered, "As for liking it, I enjoyed carrying the archbishop as much as he liked being carried, but I am not accustomed to such gay trappings and good living, so that I am afraid of injuring my health."

"If that be the case," continued the monk, "hold down your head, and I will relieve you of the danger; for, to tell you the truth, I find out that my wife is still living, and she recognized me although I was disguised as a monk. By my faith, I would rather bear my master's harness to the grave than my wife's tongue from morning till night! Caramba, I hear her knocking at the door! Dear Pablo, let us again exchange conditions."

And Pablo, when he awoke next morning, was tightly grasping a beam, thinking he was the Archbishop of Toledo clinging on to the mule's neck.

Tales From The Land Of Rabbits

THE DEVIL'S TOURNAMENT

Adapted from Fairy Tales from Spain by José Muñoz Escámez, published by J. M. Dent & Sons Ltd, 1913.

GREAT ANGER FILLED THE BREAST OF the very ugly Don Teobaldo de Miguelturra as he rode his horse at full gallop after a cunning hare. Lance at rest he pursued it, blind with fury, for the wicked animal from time to time stopped, sat down on its hind paws, and made amusing grimaces at its pursuer.

The latter, filled with wrath, did not leave off using his spurs, and followed after the animal, loudly calling it a coward, rogue, and thief.

"Wait, wait!" he shouted; "you will have to pay for all this! What a fine stew I shall make with you this evening!"

And he rode on like a madman, leaping streams, rocks, and pits. But it seemed as if wings had grown on the hare's feet, such were its leaps, while fleeing from the proposed stew. And at each instant it turned round and jocularly made signs with its ears and forepaws, and smiled in that amusing way which disturbed the knight so much.

"Even if you hide yourself in the very middle of the earth, I shall reach you," he roared.

And he again spurred on his horse, which was nearly frantic, excited by pain and the shouting of its rider.

A moment arrived in which the knight almost had it within lance thrust, but once more it commenced to gain ground.

"One effort more, my horse," shouted Don Teobaldo, but in vain. In going up a very steep slope the poor animal fell dead from fatigue, and the rider also was quite dazed.

As soon as he could he disengaged himself from the stirrups, and throwing down his useless lance beside the dead horse, Don Teobaldo unsheathed his sword, victorious in a hundred fights, in order to pursue to the very end that hare which had stopped very tranquilly on a rock from which it made fun of the knight at its ease.

This raised the hunter's indignation to its highest, and in a moment of anger he exclaimed, "I would give a year of my life to run my sword through you."

The hare, on hearing this, gave a jump and fell at Don Teobaldo's feet, who cut it into two pieces. The spitted hare said to him before dying: "It will cost you a year of your life; don't forget it."

The man shuddered and would have liked to undo the mischief, but now it was too late.

"And to think that such a little beast should make me lose three hundred and sixty-five days of my life!" he cried. And, full of rage, he trampled on the hare until he was quite tired.

But on raising his eyes once more he saw another exactly the same as the one that he had killed, and which made the same gestures as the first.

Then he could not any longer contain himself, and started to run after the second hare, entangling his spurs in the under-growth and stumbling and falling at every step.

Like one who took no interest the hare went slowly to its lair, and after it our enraged Don Teobaldo, resolved to make a terrible hash of the jesting animal.

"This seems to be a thing of the devil," he said. "All the hares have agreed to make fun of me."

At length, after a good while, Don Teobaldo, with his tongue hanging out, arrived at a kind of cave, in the black depths of which he lost sight of the hare.

"Well, now, I have to find you even if you are the devil himself in person."

"Your servant," said a voice of rare quality, and a man with a strange face and eyes of fire presented himself before Don Teobaldo, saluting him with burlesque courtesy.

"Caramba!" exclaimed Don Teobaldo, without being frightened, because he was a very valorous man. "If I must tell the truth, I wished to know you personally."

"And do you not feel afraid?"

"Not at all. And since you are so familiar with me, I shall treat you in the same way. I want to make an arrangement with you."

"Speak."

"First answer me. Are you the hare that I pursued?"

"The same. I knew that you were engaged in an affair and wished to speak to me, and brought you to my house so that we could talk comfortably."

And the devil started laughing, flames shooting out of his mouth. It was a sign that he was happy.

"Well, you shall see. You must know that tomorrow the tournament in which the hand of the king's daughter is to be disputed will take place. The victor will become hereditary prince, and I, frankly, wish to occupy the post. It is therefore necessary that you make me conquer in the fray."

"And what will you give me in exchange?"

"Whatever you ask me."

"That you make the princess forget her faith in God. I already have you, and I want the princess."

"Agreed."

"Agreed."

And the devil and Don Teobaldo shook hands. The latter drew his back, saying, "How you burn."

The devil said to him, "Tomorrow, at the hour of the fight, a squire in black armour will come and see you. I will give you a cuirass made in such a way that it cannot be pierced through, a shield which will dazzle and stupefy your adversaries if only looked at, a charmed sword, a touch with which will produce death; and a horse as black as ebony which has the advantage of requiring neither curb nor spurs: you will only wear them as ornaments.... In a word, the horse will be me."

"Oh, thanks, but I am sorry to trouble you."

"Don't let us say a word about this affair. I have resolved to carry away the soul of this princess, who wearies me with her prayers and psalms, and I have not been able to make her sin, even in thought."

And the devil caught up Don Teobaldo with his cape and left him at the door of his house, after passing through the air at a prodigious speed. On disappearing, he said in his ear, Good-bye till tomorrow."

On the following day the city was decorated with pennons and banners. The entire population flocked to the place where the hand of the beautiful princess, whose virtues everybody praised highly, was to be won in open contest.

Thirty knights took part in the struggle, and as they were the bravest in the kingdom the spectacle promised to be interesting, though barbarous; but such were the customs of those times.

The king and the court occupied the grand stand, the princess being in the front row. The public took the rest of the seats, and the heralds announced that the jousts were about to commence.

Don Teobaldo appeared in the foreground upon a beautiful black horse, large black plumes waved over the crest of his helmet, and the armour which he wore was also black.

On seeing his proud countenance one could not doubt his certainty of obtaining the victory.

The signal was given, and another valiant knight came into the arena and rushed upon horrible Don Teobaldo at his horse's full gallop.

When he was near, the devil's friend oscillated his shield, and his adversary, without being able to prevail, fell to the ground unconscious.

Another and another and another, and twenty more, went forth to fight and suffered the same fate. Whoever resisted the mysterious action of the shield, fell dead from a blow of the sword, even when only touched with the flat of it.

The people gave shouts of despair on account of the horror which that man inspired in them. The princess was on the point of losing consciousness from terror on seeing that terrible spouse who was offering her his disgrace.

"Heaven!" she exclaimed, "death before being the wife of that wicked man."

And now, the last champion having suffered the same defeat as the others, they were about to proclaim Don Teobaldo conqueror, and therefore the husband of the princess, when the trumpet sounded, announcing that a noble knight asked permission to take part in the struggle.

The king looked at his daughter and, on seeing her so sorrow-stricken, gave the desired permission, with the remote hope that the new-comer, whoever he might be, would vanquish the terrible champion.

They requested him to tell his name and surname, but the knight said, "My name is Miguel. My surname I reserve until after the fight, if I emerge victorious, but rest assured that there is no one more noble on earth."

And he rode into the lists, arousing a murmur of admiration. His armour was all white as ermine, and the plumes of his helmet were also white.

White, of a dazzling white, was the beautiful horse he rode.

Don Teobaldo was greatly impressed by the sight, and more so the devil, who with a neigh said, "I am glad you have come to fight, Miguel. We have an old account to settle."

And turning his head to Don Teobaldo, he added, "Pull out one of the hairs of my mane and keep it in your pocket, with this you will have as much power as I. Try to defend yourself to the last, for our adversary is terrible."

No sooner said than done. Don Teobaldo pulled out one of the hairs of the devil's mane and kept it, and immediately felt strong and powerful. Blinded by all the pride of the Infernal One, he assailed the knight of the white armour, trying to fascinate him with his shield. Useless task!

The knight raised the visor of his helmet and showed the handsomest countenance that ever was seen. That lovely face sent out celestial rays.

"Ah, Luzbel!" cried he. "Do you rebel against me?"

And, throwing aside his spear, he drew his sword, whose brilliance eclipsed that of the sun itself, and threw himself upon Don Teobaldo. The black horse snorted, roared, bounded, evading the blows with superhuman skill. Don Teobaldo's sword fell upon Miguel's white shield two hundred times, but in vain, until dazed and vanquished horse and rider fell at the feet of the handsome knight.

327

"Get you hence!" he said in a voice of infinite pity. "Know that you are my slave until the completion of the centuries, and that you have no power against God our Lord."

"Princess," he added, "you are saved. Your prayer reached the Most High, and I, who am the Archangel Miguel, came to set you free from the snares of the demon. Continue virtuous and you will receive your reward."

And so saying he disappeared.

Meanwhile the devil wished to vanish, but Don Teobaldo remembered his deceit, and as he had power over the demon, thanks to the hair that he had pulled out, began to belabour him with spurs and sword, making him bounce as high as the highest houses. Don Teobaldo did not move from the saddle and finished by giving the devil such a superb thrashing as nearly finished him.

"Let me be, and I will not trouble you again," cried Luzbel.

"Will you ask for my soul?"

"Neither your soul nor your body, but let me alone now."

Then Don Teobaldo, whose heart had been touched by the glance of the angel and moved to repentance, dismounted from the horse and left it free to disappear.

And so ended those famous jousts, which were never eradicated from the memory of the public.

The princess, the following year, married a prince as virtuous as herself, and Don Teobaldo did penance and became a good Christian who had a just satisfaction in having administered a sound thrashing to the devil.

TROMPETILLA AND TROMPETIN

Adapted from Fairy Tales from Spain by José Muñoz Escámez, published by J. M. Dent & Sons Ltd, 1913.

"WHAT ARE YOU DOING HERE, BOY?" asked a venerable friar of Rupert, who was sitting near his accordion in the neighbourhood of a wood as if he were preparing himself to give a solemn performance to the oaks.

"I was resting after a long walk," answered the boy, "and as they say that sleep is food, I wished to forget in slumber that not a mouthful has passed my lips for many hours."

"Poor little boy," exclaimed the father. "If you want a sumptuous meal go near the third cork-tree on the right-hand side. Go round three times, playing the accordion, and a door will open. Pass through it and you shall eat splendidly."

Rupert went to the spot indicated and, playing a "Habanera" dance, made the three turns prescribed; a piece of bark came away and disclosed a little iron door, artistically ornamented. He pushed it gently and it opened noiselessly, and there was Rupert inside a beautiful palace, whose magnificent rooms were illuminated with hidden fires, which, while giving light, sent out sweet fragrance. "These smells are not bad," said Rupert, "but I would rather they came from a nicely cooked chop."

At that moment a hundred succulent chops which were saying "Eat me!" began to balance themselves in space. Being neither stupid nor lazy, Rupert tried to get hold of the nearest, but they all began a frantic career round the room. In the centre of the latter appeared a table covered with appetising eatables, but as soon as Rupert went near they once more took to flight as if on invisible wings. A magnificent stuffed turkey hit him on the nose. The breast of a chicken nearly knocked him over, and all this while the boy was running, like a mad thing, after those exquisite dainties, hungrier than a bear after a fortnight's fast.

"This is only an invitation to see!" exclaimed the lad. "It is enough to make one's teeth grow longer!"

He had hardly uttered these words than his teeth began to grow in such a disordered fashion, and so quickly, that the shortest was not less than three yards long. The viands were caught on them as if on lances, a further difficulty for Rupert, who could not succeed in seizing the coveted prey which was fixed on his own teeth.

Then a monkey appeared, and climbing on to the boy's teeth, began very impudently to eat those exquisite viands, making signs of satisfaction which threw Rupert into a rage.

"You great thief!" he cried. "What do you mean by laughing at me?" And catching up his accordion he threw it at the animal with such accuracy that, hitting him on the head, it knocked him senseless. A great noise was heard and the monkey disappeared, Rupert's teeth grew shorter and, while the accordion played, of its own accord, the celebrated air "No me matas," a woman appeared in the middle of the room who, for size, looked like a whale, and who would have been beautiful if she had not had a turned-up nose and fixed eyes, one weeping oil and the other vinegar, and who would certainly have had a fine head of hair if she had not been bald, and a fine set of teeth if a single tooth had remained in her head.

"Who are you?" asked Rupert, a trifle startled.

"I am the witch Trompetilla, the daughter of the celebrated Trompeton and grand-daughter of Trompetazo, and am looking for my son Trompetin everywhere, without being able to find him."

"Why do you speak to me about Trompetilla and Trompetin when I never played a trumpet in my life?"

"Ah, unhappy me!" sobbed the witch. "In vain I have offered a pennyworth of toasted chick peas and a measure of tiger nuts to the mortal who discovers the whereabouts of my son. I have wept so much oil and vinegar that I have spoilt all the furniture in my house."

"What a fine salad you could make if you bought some lettuces!"

"You will get a salad made of blows if you don't help me to look for my Trompetin, and if we find him I will invite you to supper, and moreover will give you a penny so that you need never do any more work in your life."

Roused by such a magnificent promise, Rupert offered to look for Trompetin, even if he were under a cruet.

"What is he like?" he asked.

"The size of a pea, a head like pin, and legs like needles."

"Well, then, he must be sticking in a pin cushion or in a needle-case."

"A needle-case would not hold him, for he has a beard two yards long."

"It must trail on the ground!" said Rupert, full of astonishment.

"Well, now," said the witch, "while I go and mend some clothes, begin to look for my pet."

This said, she disappeared.

The boy was confused by so many comings and goings, and appearances and disappearances, but as hunger afflicted him, he proposed to find Trompetin, and taking a turn round the room, began to shout, "Trompetin, where are you?"

"Here!" groaned a tiny voice.

"Where? I can't see you."

"In this crack," replied the voice.

Rupert searched, and at last found the witch's son in a crack between two bricks. The enormous beard was a hair two yards long, which grew out of his nose.

Rupert took him up carefully, and placing him on his hand, asked him, "Are you Trompetin, the son of Trompetilla?"

"The same."

"Why have you been lost so long?"

"Because my mother is deaf and cannot see well, so that, although I shouted a lot, she did not hear me."

"Well, now, tell me who the monkey is that climbed up on to my teeth?"

"It is a wizard, nastier than medicine, who is angry with us because his grandfather died from a trumpet-blast that my great-great-grandfather sounded in his ear. It was he who made your teeth grow, and didn't allow you to eat. Knock on this wall and he will reappear, then pull out my hair and thrash him with it."

"A fine thrashing to be given with a hair!"

"Try, and you will see!"

Rupert struck the wall, and the monkey appeared, sparks flying from his eyes. He was about to throw himself on Rupert, but the boy pulled out Trompetin's hair, which turned into a fine cudgel, with which he dealt the monkey a vigorous hiding. The animal leapt high into the air several times, but that was useless, as the stick lengthened as if it were elastic and reached him wherever he was. When the monkey could resist no longer, he took human shape, and on his knees begged Rupert not to grind his ribs, and in return he offered to give him as much wealth as he might desire.

"Call Trompetilla," shouted the lad, "and let us have a talk."

The witch appeared, this time crying with joy at seeing her son, and after kissing him, stuck him in her dress so that he should not be lost again. The wizard gave Rupert a lot of money and the witch gave him a splendid supper of stew and hemp-seed.

When supper was over they affectionately took leave of one another, and the wizard took Rupert out into the fresh air, carrying him carefully to the same spot in which he was when he met the priest. There he left the boy sleeping soundly, dreaming of a sweet awakening, the dream of the person who sees his future assured by reason of not having done anything wrong.

Tales From The Land Of Rabbits

THE DRAWING SCHOOL

Adapted from Fairy Tales from Spain by José Muñoz Escámez, published by J. M. Dent & Sons Ltd, 1913.

ONCE THERE WAS A BOY SO fond of spoiling walls, doors, and windows with grotesque drawings that there was no way of stopping him from practising his silly cleverness wherever he was. And I say silly, because from his hand came forth some primitive dolls, with heads as round as a billiard ball, eyes and nose forming a sort of cork, and arms and legs like thin thread, terminating in hands and feet which required an inscription in order not to be taken for scourges.

One afternoon he approached the very wall of the school, and there, with the greatest coolness, commenced to draw with a piece of charcoal some of his strange figures. Perico, for so the boy was called, traced the figure of the head of a puppet, made the eyes and the mouth, and, oh, how strange! the doll began to wink and open its mouth and put its tongue out like anything.

Perico was not timid, and therefore the moving of the eyes and mouth did not startle him, and so without paying attention continued with sketching the arms and the rest of the body. But he had hardly finished when the doll's hand came out and gave him such a tremendous knock that it made him lose his balance, and he would even have fallen to the ground if another blow with the other hand and on the opposite cheek had not kept him on his feet. And as if this was not enough, the legs sprang out of the wall, and two vigorous kicks that Perico received in the pit of the stomach quite convinced him that there was one too many creatures here, and that he was the one. Thus convinced he was about to run away when the whole doll came away from the stone, and at a bound leapt on his shoulders and began to bite him in the back of the head.

Perico ran towards his house like a greyhound, feeling on his neck the weight of that unexpected load, when the latter grew heavy, as if, instead of a charcoal picture, he had to deal with a bronze statue.

The poor little boy sank to the ground, and on getting up saw at his side, in the middle of the square, the doll in question, as tall as a giant and changed into a motionless iron statue.

He tried to fly, but the statue caught him with its great hands by the neck and, raising him up, placed him on its shoulders, and this being done commenced to run in the direction of the country. Its footsteps produced a very disagreeable noise of ironmongery, something like a sack of nails being shaken up.

It was night-time and our giant, with Perico on its shoulders, ran as fast as anything to a neighbouring mountain, until he came to a dark grotto into which he penetrated without any need of matches, because intense lights shone from his eyes.

During all this Perico, needless to mention, was more afraid than ashamed, and did not know, nor could even imagine how, it was going to end.

At length, after some minutes' walk in the grotto, the iron man straightened himself, and turning the light of his eyes towards a corner, lighted up by a glance the lamp which hung down from the rocky ceiling, and this being done, took Perico down from his shoulders and sat down.

"You do not know who I am," said the doll, opening his mouth with a horrible smile, "but when you do know, it will make your hair stand on end from fright."

"I am sure it won't," said the lad, "because it is already doing so, and as I cannot be any more afraid than I am now, on account of being so much afraid, the fear which I felt is passing away."

"Well, then, I am the magician Adefesio, and I am tired of your drawing me so ugly and so similar to all the boys. The thing which puts me out most is that you draw my eyes without pupils and my nose without nostrils. Moreover, the ears which you sketch look like jug handles, and I am sick of my portrait going about the world so disfigured and so badly done. Could you not have learnt to draw a little before commencing these pictures? Well, the punishment that I reserve for you is to draw your portrait every day."

"What a punishment!" exclaimed Perico.

"The fact is that I do not know how to draw either," answered the man of iron, "and the worst of it all is that while I am drawing you, you will grow like my sketch, so that in a twinkling you will be disfigured. There, does not that seem a severe punishment to you? Well, you will see!"

And seizing Perico by one arm he pulled the lamp which hung down. Then a hole opened in the ceiling and the lamp went up, dragging the doll and Perico through the air.

The light continued to rise through a sort of well which was lighted up, and whose walls were lined with books full of badly-made drawings, spoilt plans, pieces of forms with engravings made with penknives, and table-covers destroyed through having been drawn on. That was the museum of the man of iron, and each time he saw it he was filled with anger towards the young draughtsmen who spoilt everything.

Soon they found themselves in a spacious room decorated in Arabian style and furnished most luxuriously. In the background there was an easel of great size, and on it a blackboard on which were drawn a lot of dolls of the same sort that Perico drew.

"Dear me, how fine!" said the boy looking at the sketches. "It seems that I did them."

"Well, now you will see the consequences," and snapping his fingers he produced a metallic sound, and immediately a multitude of boys of different ages came through a door. But what funny boys! All had round heads, eyes like fishes, flat noses, and mouths like letter boxes, wide open and showing teeth like saws. Their arms were thin as wire, ending in long fingers without joints. Perico was not startled when they came in.

"Well, that is how you will look in a little while," said the iron man.

"He always exaggerates!" exclaimed Perico aside, "but seeing is believing."

The man of iron seized a piece of chalk, and going near to the board began to draw Perico's head, but the latter called the doll's attention, and when he looked the other way rubbed out what he had drawn.

# Tales From The Land Of Rabbits

The man could not have seen very well because he went on drawing very tranquilly, and Perico continued rubbing out what the other drew, and when he thought that he had finished he caught up the boy, brought him to the light, and imagine his surprise on seeing him the same as before. He went back, full of rage, to the blackboard; but Perico tripped him up, and did it so well that he fell down. Then he threw the board and easel on him, and climbing on top, began to jump on the doll, and calling to his companions, shouted, "Come here so that he will not be able to run away!"

The boys drew near and, climbing on the blackboard, by their weight prevented the iron doll from moving.

But things did not rest thus, because Perico was a very daring boy, and taking up a rope, which was close at hand, hung the iron man by the neck to the lamp, and pulling on the other end of the rope, hauled him up with the help of his companions.

As he was made of iron he was not choked, but hanging up he could do nothing except make grimaces like a jack-in-the-box, which was just what he looked like hanging in the air.

"Let me down!" shouted the unhappy man, "and you may draw whatever you like."

"That won't do, my friend," answered Perico, laughing at the doll's movements. "I should not be so stupid as to let you escape. As the song says, 'Here, sirs, came to an end the life of Don Crispin.' Do you think I have forgotten the punch you gave me?"

The other boys tied the rope to a sofa so as not to get tired, and led by Perico began to explore the rooms of the cave. They were all beautiful save that the ornaments on the walls were of dolls as grotesque as the master.

339

The way out of the grotto could not be seen anywhere. And the reason was simple, as the means of exit was by the lamp to which the doll was hanging; but the boys did not like the idea of going down one by one, with a great risk of breaking their heads.

Perico, now uneasy, recommenced to run about the rooms, and troubled by seeing on the walls what recalled his unfortunate adventure, pulled out his handkerchief and rubbed out all the drawings, seeing, with extraordinary surprise, that the boys recovered their original shapes.

On rubbing out the last drawing a formidable noise was heard. The iron man vanished as if he were smoke, the palace disappeared, and they found themselves at the entrance to the cave. From there they marched to the town, where their parents were anxiously waiting for them, and there they related what had occurred.

All returned thanks to God and promised not to draw dolls again anywhere.

Perico became a very honourable man, devoted himself to drawing, and became a great artist, but he never forgot those dolls, which might have cost him so dear.

HISTORICAL NOTES

This section contains some brief biographical notes about the original collectors and their books featured in this collection. These notes have been adapted from those primarily on Wikipedia along with other supporting sources and notes.

Andrew Lang

Andrew Lang FBA was a Scottish poet, novelist, literary critic, and contributor to the field of anthropology. He is best known as a collector of folk and fairy tales. The Andrew Lang lectures at the University of St Andrews are named after him.

Lang was born on 31st March 1844 in Selkirk. He was the eldest of the eight children born to John Lang, the town clerk, and his wife Jane Plenderleath Sellar, who was the daughter of Patrick Sellar, factor to the first duke of Sutherland. On 17th April 1875, he married Leonora Blanche Alleyne, youngest daughter of C. T. Alleyne of Clifton and Barbados. She was (or should have been) variously credited as author, collaborator, or translator of Lang's Colour / Rainbow Fairy Books, which he edited.

He was educated at Selkirk Grammar School, Loretto School, and the Edinburgh Academy, as well as the University of St Andrews and Balliol College, Oxford, where he took a first class in the final classical schools in 1868, becoming a fellow and subsequently honorary fellow of Merton College. He soon made a reputation as one of the most able and versatile writers of the day as a journalist, poet, critic, and historian. In 1906, he was elected FBA.

He died of angina pectoris on 20th July 1912 at the Tor-na-Coille Hotel in Banchory, survived by his wife. He was buried in the cathedral precincts at St Andrews, where a monument can be visited in the south-east corner of the 19th century section.

Lang is now chiefly known for his publications on folklore, mythology, and religion. The earliest of his publications is *Custom and Myth* (1884). In *Myth, Ritual and Religion* (1887) he explained the "irrational" elements of mythology as survivals from more primitive forms. Lang's *Making of Religion* was heavily influenced by the 18th century idea of the "noble savage", in it, he maintained the existence of high spiritual ideas among so-called "savage" races, drawing parallels with the contemporary interest in occult phenomena in England.

His *Blue Fairy Book* (1889) was a beautifully produced and illustrated edition of fairy tales that has become a classic. This was followed by many other collections of fairy tales, collectively known as *Andrew Lang's Fairy Books*. In the preface of the *Lilac Fairy Book* he credits his wife with translating and transcribing most of the stories in the collections.

Lang was one of the founders of "psychical research" and his other writings on anthropology include *The Book of Dreams and Ghosts* (1897), *Magic and Religion* (1901) and *The Secret of the Totem* (1905). He served as President of the Society for Psychical Research in 1911.

He collaborated with S. H. Butcher in a prose translation (1879) of Homer's *Odyssey*, and with E. Myers and Walter Leaf in a prose version (1883) of the *Iliad*, both still noted for their archaic but attractive style.

Lang's writings on Scottish history are characterised by a scholarly care for detail, a piquant literary style, and a gift for disentangling complicated questions. *The Mystery of Mary Stuart* (1901) was a consideration of the fresh light thrown on Mary, Queen of Scots, by the Lennox manuscripts in the University Library, Cambridge, approving of her and criticising her accusers.

Lang was active as a journalist in various ways, ranging from sparkling "leaders" for the Daily News to miscellaneous articles for the Morning Post, and for many years he was literary editor of Longman's Magazine.

Rachel Harriette Busk

Rachel Harriette Busk,1831—1907, was a British traveller and folklorist. She was born in 1831, in London, the youngest of five daughters of Hans Busk the elder and his wife Maria. She was the sister-in-law of Sir Robert Loder, 1st Baronet through her sister Maria Georgiana.

She collected tales from Italy, Spain, Mongolia and elsewhere. Her collection included folklore, supernatural events, legends of saints, and humorous anecdotal material. Her work on Italian folklore was strongly influenced by the work of Giuseppe Pitrè

She converted to Catholicism in 1858 and lived in Rome after 1862.

She died at Members' Mansions, Westminster, on 1 March 1907, and was buried in the family vault at Frant, near Tunbridge Wells.

Tales From The Land Of Rabbits

José Muñoz Escámez

Yet to turn anything up about José Muñoz Escámez.

Charles Sellers

Charles Sellers is the author of the folklore collection, *Tales from the Land of Nuts and Grapes: Spanish and Portuguese Folklor*e. Upon its publication in 1888, Sellers was the first author put these classic folk tales on paper. The author thought that the poetry, songs, and stories of the Portuguese and Spanish people had been ignored for too long and sought to correct this literary oversight by publishing his folklore collection. Sellers said that in other parts of the world, such as England, tales are told and transcribed for generations, but even the elders of Spain and Portugal don't have records to preserve the tales. He had spent his youth living between these two lands, born and bred in the north of Portugal, according to the book's preface. *Tales from the Land of Nuts and Grapes: Spanish and Portuguese Folklore* is Sellers' only book, but it's a rich work of folklore.

Source: Fairytalez.com

Gustavo Adolfo Bécquer

Gustavo Adolfo Claudio Domínguez Bastida, better known as Gustavo Adolfo Bécquer, 1836 – 1870, was a Spanish Romanticist poet and writer. He was also a playwright, literary columnist, and was a talented draughtsman and illustrator. Today he is considered one of the most important figures in Spanish literature, and is considered by some as the most read writer after Cervantes.

He adopted the alias of Bécquer as his brother Valeriano Bécquer, a painter, had done earlier. He was associated with the romanticism and post-romanticism movements and wrote while realism was enjoying success in Spain. He was moderately well known during his life, but it was after his death that most of his works were published. His best known works are the *Rhymes and the Legends*, usually published together as *Rimas y leyendas*. These poems and tales are essential to the study of Spanish literature and common reading for high-school students in Spanish-speaking countries.

His work approached the traditional poetry and themes in a modern way, and he is considered the founder of modern Spanish lyricism. Bécquer's influence on 20th-century poets of the Spanish language can be seen in the works of Luis Cernuda, Octavio Paz, and Giannina Braschi.

Katherine Lee Bates

Katharine Lee Bates, 1859 – 1929, was a prolific American writer, college professor, scholar, and social activist. Although she published volumes of poetry, travel books, essays, children's books, books for young adults, and editions of many earlier writers' works, today Bates is primarily remembered as the author of *America the Beautiful*.

While on the Wellesley College faculty, Bates mentored many young poets (including some, like Robert Frost, not enrolled at Wellesley) and helped establish American literature as a field for college study by creating an early course on the genre and writing a textbook for the field.

Bates was born in Falmouth, Massachusetts to the town's Congregational minister William Bates and Cornelia Frances Lee. Her father died a few weeks after she was born, and she was primarily raised by her mother and a literary aunt, both of whom had graduated from the all-women's Mount Holyoke Seminary. She attended Wellesley High School (then called Needham High

School) in 1872 and then Newton High School until 1876. Bates entered Wellesley College, a women's college, as part of its second class in 1876. She graduated with a B.A. in 1880. She taught at Natick High School in 1880–81 and at Dana Hall School from 1881 until 1885.

In 1889 Bates's young adult novel *Rose and Thorn* won a prize awarded by the Congregational Sunday School and Publishing Society. It incorporated poor and working class women as characters to teach readers about social reform. She popularized the concept of Mrs. Claus in her poem *Goody Santa Claus on a Sleigh Ride* from the collection *Sunshine and other Verses for Children* (1889).

Taking advantage of new educational opportunities available to women after the American Civil War, Bates used prize money from *Rose and Thorn* to travel to England and study at Oxford University between 1890 and 1891. She then returned to Wellesley as an associate professor in 1891, earned her M.A. there, and was promoted to a full professor of English literature. Near the end of the Spanish–American War, she worked as a war correspondent for The New York Times, and strove to reduce widely-circulating negative stereotypes about Spaniards. She contributed regularly to periodicals (sometimes under the pseudonym James Lincoln), including *The Atlantic Monthly, The Congregationalist, Boston Evening Transcript, Christian Century, Contemporary Verse, Lippincott's,* and *The Delineator*.

In 1906 Bates and her brother Arthur signed a mortgage for a Wellesley houselot and house to be built on it for the Bates family (Cornelia, Jeanne, and Katharine) and their tenants. While the house was being built, Bates traveled to Egypt and the Holy Land with Wellesley College president Caroline Hazard. Upon returning to Wellesley, Bates named the house "The Scarab," after the sacred Egyptian insect she admired as "always climbing."

While working at Wellesley, Bates was elected a member of the newly-formed Pi Gamma Mu honour society for the social sciences because of her interest in history and politics. She retired from Wellesley in 1925 at the age of 66. In retirement, Bates continued to write and to publish poetry, and was in great demand as a writer and speaker.

Bates was also a social activist interested in the struggles of women, workers, people of colour, tenement residents, immigrants, and poor people. She helped organize the Denison House, a college women's settlement house, with other women friends and colleagues in 1892. She wrote and spoke extensively about the need for social reform and was an avid advocate for the global peace movement that emerged after World War I. She was especially active in attempts to establish the League of Nations. Long an active Republican, Bates broke with the party to endorse Democratic presidential candidate John W. Davis in 1924 because of Republican opposition to American participation in the League of Nations. She said: "Though born and bred in the Republican camp, I cannot bear their betrayal of Mr. Wilson and their rejection of the League of Nations, our one hope of peace on earth." Thinking of herself as a "global citizen," Bates decried the American policy of isolationism.

Bates died in Wellesley, Massachusetts, on March 28, 1929, while listening to a friend read poetry to her. She is buried in Oak Grove Cemetery at Falmouth.

ABOUT THE EDITOR

I was born in 1962 into a predominantly sporting household – Dad being a good footballer, playing senior amateur and lower league professional football in England, as well as running a series of private businesses in partnership with mum, herself an accomplished and medal winning dancer.

I obtained a degree in History from Leeds University before wandering rather haphazardly into the emerging world of business computing in the late nineteen-eighties.

A little like my sporting father, I followed a succession of amateur writing paths alongside my career in technology, including working as a freelance journalist and book reviewer, my one claim to fame being a by-line in a national newspaper in the UK, The Sunday People.

I also spent 10 years treading the boards, appearing all over the south of the UK in pantos and plays, in village halls and occasionally on the stage of a professional theatre or two.

Following the sporting theme, and a while after I hung up my own boots, I worked on live TV broadcasts for the BBC, ITV, TVNZ, EuroSport and others as a rugby "Stato", covering Heineken Cups,

Six Nations, IRB World Sevens and IRB World Cups in the late '90's and early '00's.

I try to combine my love of storytelling with a passion for information technology, and am currently Vice President - Technology with a major UK FinTech company.

You can find out more about Clive's work and contact him at. www.boyonabench.com

 **SOLITUDE**

CPSIA information can be obtained
at www.ICGtesting.com
Printed in the USA
BVHW071149191219
567196BV00001B/216/P